DO NOT DIE TODAY

Do Not Die Today

KACEY CARPENTER

Copyright © 2025 by Kacey Carpenter

Cover art and design by Kate Henke

All rights reserved. No part of this publication may be reproduced, stored, or transmitted in any form or by any means, electronic, mechanical, photocopying, recording, scanning, or otherwise without written permission from the publisher. It is illegal to copy this book, post it to a website, or distribute it by any other means without permission.

This novel is entirely a work of fiction. The names, characters, and incidents portrayed in it are the work of the author's imagination. Any resemblance to actual persons, living or dead, events or localities is entirely coincidental.

Published by Carpenter Publishing
Lake Oswego, Oregon, 97035

ISBN: 979-8-9897006-4-6 (Paperback)

Library of Congress Cataloging-in-Publication Data has been applied for.

First Printing, 2025

To the original stewards of this land, the 15 tribal communities whose connection to Joshua Tree National Park inspires deep respect. I am grateful to write about this place and honor the people past, present, and emerging.

To the rangers, staff, and volunteers whose work preserves these spaces. To the advocates for wildlife and nature. To those who find peace and adventure in the outdoors. And to the readers whose love for mystery-thrillers inspires my writing.

This book is for you.

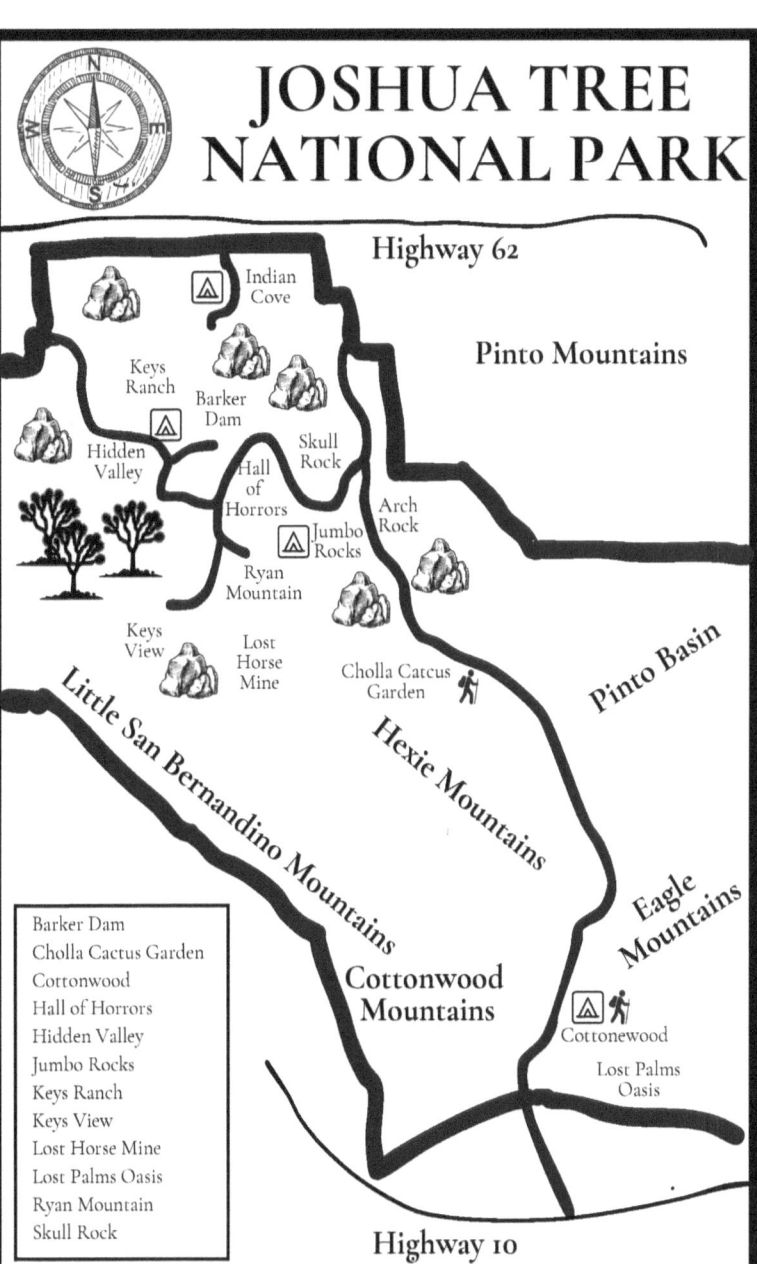

Chapter 1

Mitch

Friday, December 13—Greyhound bus in the Colorado Rocky Mountains.

I woke with a start as a flash of lightning sliced through the sky, followed by a booming explosion. Sparks flew outside the window, and I heard passengers screaming as the 747 plunged toward the cold and fierce ocean below. *Is this the day I die?*

Boom! Another loud crash. My ears were ringing and, at first, I couldn't remember where I was. I looked around and realized I wasn't on an airplane, but a Greyhound bus headed for California. The recurring nightmare that had haunted me for over twenty years had me gripping the armrests, shooting jolts of fear through my veins. I looked out the window, a chill against my forehead, and saw a small sliver of the moon over white mountain peaks. Fog darkened the weak glow, perhaps a bad omen.

Most passengers slept as we headed farther from Denver. I noticed an older woman in the aisle gathering items that had fallen from the storage rack. Her suitcase had spilled across the narrow gap between the seats on both sides of the bus. I jumped to assist her.

"Can I help?" I asked as I picked up her empty suitcase and helped her settle back into her seat in the row in front of me.

"Why, thank you, young man," she said.

I gathered her clothes, books, knitting needles, and other items from the floor, repacked her suitcase and noticed a faint floral scent. I couldn't fit everything back in the dimly lit, cramped space and attempted to cram her extra blanket in as the bus driver glared at me from his seat twenty rows ahead. The bus continued to careen dangerously around the rocky mountain roads slick with ice and snow.

"Oh, dear, you must be freezing. Here, take this blanket. It's nice and cozy," the old woman said, pulling the blanket from the suitcase and handing it to me.

"Okay, yes, would be nice," I replied, latching her suitcase and storing it safely in the rack above her seat.

I shivered and pulled the warm, soft, knitted blanket over my shoulders, snuggling my comfy hat over my ears. I imagined we were passing over the summit of the Continental Divide, which runs through Colorado and is home to some of the best scenic views. Exhausted but warm, I drifted off to sleep, remembering hiking in the Rockies as a child with my best friends.

* * *

I woke again to the beautiful view of the sun rising outside and warming the window as our bus came to a screeching halt. This trip from Colorado to California would take over twenty-four hours. Standing and stretching in the aisle, I handed the blanket to my new friend with a smile of appreciation.

"My name's Martha. Would you like to join me for breakfast?" she asked as additional passengers boarded the bus.

"Sure, I'm Mitch. Thank you," I replied. "So, have you taken this route before?"

"Oh, many times! When I was a child, my grandparents took me to Palm Springs. We always took the Greyhound Scenicruiser."

"It must have been quite an experience."

"The Scenicruiser was perfect for taking in the views. The Rockies were breathtaking. I remember sitting by those big windows, just mesmerized by the mountains. The elevated seats gave us a fantastic vantage point. We'd always stop for breakfast and have a Denver omelet. It became a little tradition for us."

"Sounds wonderful. I can imagine how those memories would stick with you."

"Absolutely. It was such a comfortable bus with its two levels. It felt like an adventure every time. And those trips with my grandparents are some of my fondest memories."

"Do we have time to get breakfast now?" I asked.

"No, this stop is only five minutes, and a lot has changed since those days," Martha replied. "But I did bring breakfast, and I have an extra sandwich in my ice cooler if you'd like one. Please join me."

"Thank you, Martha," I said, sitting next to her.

"You know, traveling by Greyhound today is quite different from when I was a child. Back then, the Scenicruiser was comfortable and stylish. Nowadays, you have to be prepared for a few challenges."

"Like what?" I asked.

"Well, for starters, the buses are often late. It's not uncommon to wait an extra thirty minutes to an hour, sometimes longer. And you never know who you'll end up sitting next to, which can be quite an adventure. That's why I always reserve two seats."

"I've noticed." I chuckled. "Anything else?"

"The Wi-Fi rarely works, and only half of the power outlets seem to function. But it's all part of the experience. You just have to be prepared and go with the flow."

"Sounds like good advice," I said, nodding.

"Despite these little hiccups, I still love the journey. The views are still breathtaking, and there's something special about meeting new people and hearing their stories," Martha said with a smile. "It's not quite the same as it used to be, but it's still an adventure worth taking."

"Glad to hear it. I'm looking forward to the rest of this trip."

"Me too, Mitch, me too," Martha said, handing me the sandwich. "Here's to new adventures and making the best of every moment."

As I unwrapped the sandwich, the aroma of ham and egg hit me first, making my mouth water. I took a bite, tasting the delicious flavors, and wished I had a cup of coffee to go with it.

"This is amazing! What is it?" I asked, the greasy feel of the paper wrapping the sandwich warming my hand as I took another bite.

"It's a Denver omelet sandwich," Martha replied with a smile. "You know, it has quite an interesting history. It started as a sandwich, can you believe it? Back in the nineteenth century, cattle drivers and Chinese railroad cooks would make a sandwich with eggs, ham, onions, and bell peppers. Eventually, it evolved into the omelet we know today."

"Really? I had no idea."

Martha nodded enthusiastically. "Yes! While some call it a Western omelet, it's the same thing. The main difference is how it's cooked. For a Denver omelet, you cook the eggs first and then add the vegetables and meat."

I smiled, appreciating the sandwich and newfound knowledge. "Thanks for sharing, Martha. I think I'll order a Denver omelet the next chance I get."

"Where are you heading?" Martha asked.

"Uh, I'm going to Joshua Tree National Park."

"Joshua Tree! It's incredible! I love it there. I'm a longtime member of the Sierra Club and have visited Joshua Tree many times over the years for hikes and outings. Be careful, though. It can be dangerous. Is this your first time? Are you going by yourself?" she asked, her eyes filled with concern.

"My first time, but I'm camping with friends. Why? Is it really that dangerous?"

"Oh, don't get me started! There are snakes, spiders, poisonous plants, flash floods, and especially now, being outdoors and exposed to the cold at night with the temperature dropping below freezing. Are you sure you're prepared? Aside from your warm hat, your windbreaker won't be adequate."

"Thank you. My friend Ben is bringing all the camping gear and supplies in his camper van and meeting me there. He's a reliable scout; we met as kids in elementary school, and he's been camping and hiking outdoors for years. I've packed everything I need in my backpack."

"Good to hear but be careful. I wouldn't leave it alone on the bus," she replied as she handed me a mug and poured a cup of steaming-hot coffee.

"Thank you," I said, feeling the warmth of the mug seep into my hands. The heat from the mug is actually quite soothing, and the aroma is complex. "This is exactly what I needed."

She pulled a wrinkled brochure out of her large purse. "Here's a Joshua Tree National Park map that might be helpful for you to read before you arrive. Where are your friends coming from? Are they also taking a bus trip?"

"Ben's driving his campervan from Oregon, and Alex is flying in from Texas. We grew up together in Colorado, but it's been over ten years since we've seen each other."

"Sounds wonderful, Mitch. I hope you all have a fantastic time," Martha said with a cheerful smile.

Suddenly, I heard a muffled bark coming from her seat. I noticed for the first time Martha was sneaking a piece of ham from her sandwich to a small dog in her bag. She had been hiding it well.

"Is that your dog?" I asked, surprised.

Martha smiled and nodded. "Yes, this is Lily, my Bichon Frise puppy. They don't allow dogs on the bus anymore, so I have to be careful to hide her from the driver. But Lily's small and does no harm."

"She's adorable," I said, watching Lily nibble on the sandwich. "I didn't even notice her until now."

"Thank you," Martha replied. "Bichons are known for their small size and friendly nature. Lily makes my travels much more enjoyable."

"Don't worry, your secret is safe with me," I said with a wink.

I finished the sandwich, noting the ham-to-egg ratio, which was surprisingly balanced. I carefully placed the wrapper in my backpack. Returning to my seat, I quickly calculated that we had approximately twelve more hours, possibly more, given the unpredictability of travel logistics. I glanced around the bus, a kind of low-grade anxiety creeping in. It was interesting to note Martha had managed to conceal a dog so well, and I have to admit that this whole trip is veering into a level of the unexpected that is, well, more interesting than anticipated ... or at least, less boring.

"Hey, kid, you're blocking the aisle," the bus driver barked, glaring at me again as I returned to my seat. I made a mental note of the driver's expression. What was I doing that prompted such a strong reaction? I'd only been standing there for a few seconds. Was there something about my backpack?

* * *

Back in my seat, I scanned the gritty Greyhound with practiced precision, taking in the dim lighting, the worn upholstery, and the passengers. Old habits die hard. *Assess the environment, identify potential threats.* It was almost automatic now, a mental checklist running in the background.

Too many people, narrow aisles, not enough exits. *A recipe for chaos in an emergency.* And those emergency exits? Rusted, probably wouldn't budge. *Not ideal.* The driver—another chokepoint. If he went down, we were all in trouble. He was more focused on the passengers than the road. *Another vulnerability.*

I noted a man in a dark hoodie and a woman clutching a bulky bag, her eyes darting nervously. Teenagers huddled, whispering, phones glowing in their hands. *Could be harmless, or ...*

I'd picked an aisle seat for a reason—best vantage point, quick access to an exit if needed. *Stay alert and observe. Be ready.* My phone was within reach, just in case.

The bus was packed, mostly with people headed for Vegas—a mix of tourists hoping to strike it rich and weary—looking folks who probably called the bus home more often than not. I was going to transfer at the Vegas stop and continue to Palm Springs.

There was a younger woman, about my age, looking out the window, wearing a rainbow-colored shirt with long, dark hair cascading down her shoulders. Her smile lit up the bus and I wondered what she saw in the window. In contrast, a group of gritty passengers filled the middle rows, their faces hardened by life on the road. Their conversations were low and guarded, a stark contrast to the cheerful smile of the woman. An older man behind me and across the aisle dozed, his head slumped against the window, a worn cowboy hat perched on his knee. The bus, a fifty-five-footer, had been modified to accommodate two wheelchair-bound passengers, reducing the seated capacity.

I noticed a guy a few rows ahead. Bulky jacket, unshaven, something hard and rectangular pressed against his side. It was likely a small book, but my mind immediately imagined images of a concealed weapon, a gun, reminding me of the villain in the murder-mystery book I had been reading. *Never let your guard down, Mitch.*

Riding the bus wasn't the first-class jet experience Alex would appreciate, but it was a nice way to get away for a few days. Flying wasn't for me. The crowded, gritty bus ride reminded me of the camping trips to the Colorado Rockies as a child, though it lacked the nostalgic charm of Martha's grandpa's stories from the 1960s. Despite that, it was still an adventure, an opportunity to see new places, and time to think. Meeting with my friends in Joshua Tree made this bus ride tolerable. I used the time to read and observe the landscape. Once I felt more secure, I examined the Joshua Tree National Park map Martha had shared and downloaded the official National Park Service app, saving the map for offline use. Then, I cross-referenced information from my phone, focusing on potential desert hazards. Safety protocols are a priority.

I looked at the map, my fingers tracing the lines of trails and canyons—*790,000 acres of desert. Two ecosystems. Rugged, beautiful, dangerous.*

Trails, from easy strolls to hardcore hikes. No water at the campsites so gotta be prepared. Permits for backpacking and no campfires, which makes sense—dry as a bone out here. Climbing's cool if you know what you're doing, but watch out for snakes. And, most importantly, drink plenty of water. Like, a gallon a day. And forget about cell service.

The guidebook was full of warnings too—rattlesnakes, flash floods, scorching sun, cliffs everywhere. *Not to mention mountain lions and those giant hairy spiders.* My brain raced with all the potential dangers, each one more ominous than the last. Typical, always thinking of the risks like a real-life game of Dungeons & Dragons.

Still, Ben was experienced. *He'll have a plan. We'll be careful.*

I pulled out my phone and texted Ben, letting him know my ETA. No response. I activated my custom weather app, accessing a sophisticated, multi-source model and pulled data from various satellite feeds and weather collection points. The data was clear: a large, uncharacteristic storm system was rapidly forming off the Pacific, heading directly towards Joshua Tree. This was inconsistent with the basic online weather reports that showed clear skies. I double-checked my backpack, including my backup battery, and tools, then adjusted the position of my hiking boots, and tucked in my clothing.

The bus rumbled on, the miles blurring into a steady rhythm. The hum of the engine and the sounds of the wheels on the road were comforting. I thought about Ben and Alex, wondering how the years had changed them. Would we still connect like we did as kids?

Ben, the responsible dad. Alex, the charming risk-taker, even postdivorce. And me? In my thirties and still the quiet kid, more at ease with code than people. No longer short at six feet tall but still more comfortable hunched over a keyboard in my aunt's spare room, coding in the thin mountain air. Mitchell Donovan, software engineer, successful recluse. Not exactly a tagline to attract a girlfriend.

* * *

The hours melted away as I scrolled through code forums, the mobile Internet optimized on my phone, the steady drone of the bus engine a lullaby as the neon glow of Vegas shimmered on the horizon of my mind. But first, a pit stop.

This stop didn't feature a restaurant, and we didn't have much time. There was a gas station with restrooms and a retail market. The rest area was a combination of smells—diesel fumes, stale coffee, and hot dogs rolling on a greasy grill. The passengers, most of them looking as road-weary as I felt, shuffled toward the gas station market. Our bus driver was having a tense exchange with a couple guys in the alley, his face tight with worry. *Maybe not the safest place to be stranded.*

I joined the line at the cash register. The fluorescent lights buzzed overhead, adding to the general sense of fatigue.

Ahead of me, a man fumbled with a handful of coins, his face a mix of desperation and shame as the cashier, a middle-aged woman with a bored expression, tapped her fingers on the counter. "Not enough," she said, her tone leaving no room for negotiation. "Step aside."

Without thinking, I pulled out my card. "I'll cover it," I said, handing my debit card to the cashier. The cashier raised an eyebrow but swiped it without a word.

The man turned, eyes filled with gratitude. "*Gracias, señor.*"

"No problem," I replied. "*¿Hablas inglés?*"

"*Un poco.*" He nodded, struggling with the words. "I go ... Las Vegas ... *trabajo* ... casino ... *restaurante* ... *dinero* ... *familia.*"

Ah. He was going to Las Vegas to find work in a casino restaurant, hoping to send money back to his family in Mexico.

"*Buena suerte,*" I said, wishing him luck.

He smiled, the tension in his face easing.

As I turned away, a flash of color caught my eye. I accidentally bumped into the woman with the rainbow shirt and an incredible smile. She had been standing right behind me.

"Are you okay?" she asked, concerned.

"Yes, oh, I'm sorry," I stammered, my cheeks flushing. My usual awkwardness had returned.

"I noticed you helped that man. It was kind of you."

I shrugged, feeling embarrassed. "It was nothing. Just trying to help."

"Well, it was something to him. I'm Jamie," she said.

"I'm Mitch," I managed, surprised by how my voice squeaked.

"Are you going to Palm Springs?" she asked. "I noticed your map sticking out of your backpack."

"Uh, yes. Well, no ..." I hesitated, then nodded, my voice barely above a whisper. "I'm meeting some friends there, and we're going on a camping trip in Joshua Tree."

"Sounds like fun! I'm heading there too but for a yoga retreat. Would you like to join me for lunch? It's not exactly a five-star restaurant, but it's better than eating alone."

I felt my cheeks flush at her invitation. "Sure, I'd like that," I replied, my voice steadier this time.

We ended up sharing a picnic table outside in the parking lot, the cool air a welcome change from the stuffy bus. Time flew by, filled with easy conversation and laughter.

"Thanks for lunch," she said as we boarded. "Maybe we'll run into each other in Joshua Tree."

Then, the man with the bulging jacket pushed me forward. I looked over my shoulder and saw the bus driver, not Jamie. "Hurry up, find your seat! It's time to go!" he yelled at me.

I'm such a dork, I thought, kicking myself for not asking for her number.

The man gripped my arm as he pushed past. I looked up, startled, as he pressed something into my hand. His face was shadowed by the brim of his hat, but I caught a glimpse of wild, desperate eyes. He clutched a worn bible, his knuckles white against the leather cover. "The end is near!" he hissed, his voice a frantic whisper. "Don't trust anyone! They'll deceive you! Only the righteous will be saved!"

He released my arm and hurried down the aisle, his frantic cries reverberating through the bus. I stared at him, then looked down at my hand. It was a page torn from his bible, the words a jumble of fire and brimstone. My heart pounded. What the hell was that?

Back by my seat, Martha winked. "She's cute."

I shoved the page into my pocket, forcing a smile. "Yeah," I mumbled, my mind distracted.

The bus lurched forward, pulling away from the station, carrying us deeper into the night. It's not the dark that scares me. It's what's hiding in it. That man, his warning ... It was like stepping into a nightmare, a premonition of danger lurking just beyond the horizon."

Chapter 2

Ben

Saturday, December 14—Drive from Ashland Oregon to Joshua Tree.

The blare of the buzzer blasted through the gym as the basketball bounced off the rim, falling to the polished wooden floor. Fans erupted in cheers. Outside, Ashland was a typical Oregon town with constant rain and a winter chill seeping into every corner.

Inside the gym, it was different. Hot and humid with the scent of sweat and the thumping of basketballs. The six-and-under championship game had gone into overtime, further delaying my departure. I glanced at my watch, feeling stressed. I was running late and balancing precious time with my family and a trip to see my childhood friends.

I needed this trip to Joshua Tree, a chance to reconnect with nature and a break from the relentless demands of daily life. But as I stood there, watching my son dribble the ball down the court, I felt guilty for leaving my family behind, even if just for a few days. The gym's oppressive heat mirrored the turmoil inside me, a contrast to the cold, wet world outside.

Darn it, I'm already running late. I was distracted from the game, looking ahead to the long drive in my camper van from Oregon to the Southern California desert. I had planned to leave last night, but both my son and daughter's teams had moved on to the finals. Now this game had gone into overtime, I'd be even later. I had committed to pick up Mitch at the bus stop in the desert later today.

Standing next to me was Jenny, my wife and the love of my life. I saw fatigue in her eyes. She would be left alone before the holidays with our children, her important work, and our family.

The buzzer's shrill ring snapped me back to reality. The game was about to resume.

"I should have left yesterday," I muttered to myself, the words slipping out before I could stop them.

"Ben, you could have left yesterday," Jenny said, her voice competing with the crowd noise. Her eyes, however, spoke volumes, a mix of frustration, annoyance, and concern. "We talked about this. They'll be fine. They're grown men, and Mitch can just meet up with Alex instead."

"I know, I know," I replied, running a hand through my hair. The weight of my delayed departure pressed on me. "But I couldn't miss the kids' games. They've worked so hard this season."

Jenny sighed, her expression softening as she watched our son pass the ball. "I know. And they love having you here. But you also committed to your friends. I just wish we'd talked about it first."

Her words felt like a Scout's oath, a reminder of my commitments. She was right. I did commit. And not just to Mitch and Alex but to her, to my family. I turned to her, our eyes meeting. "I'm sorry, Jenny. I didn't mean for things to turn out this way."

She gave me a small smile, squeezing my hand. "I know. And I appreciate you being here for the kids. But remember, you also made a promise to me and our family, as much as to your friends."

Her words mattered to me, a reminder of the delicate balance I needed to maintain between my family, friends, and my job. As I watched our son score a basket, I felt proud and grateful. Despite the delay, I wouldn't trade this moment for anything.

We cheered as the buzzer sounded again. My son ran to me with a big smile. I stepped down the bleachers and hugged him.

"Great game, son! I'm so proud of you," I said as his mom kissed him on the cheek.

"It was so awesome! Coach called a play just for me!" he shouted as he raced away to join his teammates, jumping together at the official's table with the championship trophy.

* * *

An hour after the postgame celebration, we were back at home, the echoes of the cheers from the game still ringing in my ears. I took with me some leftover game snacks, provided by the parent volunteers, to save time rather than stop for lunch. I unloaded the basketball equipment bags from the car to the garage, my mind already shifting gears.

Next, I loaded my restored camper van with all the gear and equipment I had carefully laid out for this trip. It was more than just a checklist; it was a precious responsibility, something I'd enjoyed with my family vacations and a reminder of my memories camping in the Rocky Mountains with the Scouts. This familiar routine, though tedious, gave me a sense of comfort, a reminder of the past in the chaos of the present, a grounding force, like a well-worn trail map in the wilderness of daily life.

A few minutes later, I was navigating the Oregon mountain curves of Interstate 5, my mind a jumble of thoughts. A twelve-hour drive lay ahead, the road stretching endlessly toward Southern California. It felt like I was heading into the great unknown, like those old Scout trips, except this time I was the leader, and I had to get it right. A nagging feeling kept bothering me, like a stone in my shoe, constantly reminding me I'd forgotten something, something important, probably related to the trip, but maybe it was the kids or Jenny. I just couldn't shake it. I checked the list again in my mind. Shelter? *Check*. First aid? *Check*. Everything was there, wasn't it?

I was excited about the trip, no doubt. It'd been too long since I'd seen Mitch and Alex. A decade or more. It was a gift of time to get together again, to remember old times. But I felt bad leaving Jenny to handle everything alone, especially with the holidays just around the corner.

Those simpler days, back in Denver as kids, roaming the creek with Mitch and Alex, building a fort in the trees, dreaming of adventures. We'd all gone our separate ways, of course. Alex, chasing his football dreams in Texas, becoming a high-flying businessman, always pushing the limits. Mitch, burying himself in books and computers, escaping to the quiet world of coding and algorithms at MIT. And me? Well, let's just say life had a way of throwing curveballs. Instead of chasing down bad guys like my dad, a police detective, I ended up chasing toddlers and changing diapers.

It was hard to believe I was now "Mr. Ben Foster," a dad, husband, and tree hugger in Oregon. These days I dressed for comfort—jeans, flannel shirts, hiking boots—the uniform of a man trying to juggle family life, late-night security guard shifts, and a desire for those simpler times.

Despite our different paths, we were getting together again more than a decade later for a camping trip. It was my idea. It's been too long, you know? Even with that whole mess our last summer together ... we needed this. *I* needed this. A chance to hit the reset button.

I was normally very responsible, always have been, darn it. But, those back-to-back championship games, they threw a wrench into my carefully planned departure, and now I couldn't shake the feeling I'd left something important behind. It was like losing your keys. I needed to go through my pre-trip checklist again, picturing the van with each item in its designated spot.

Shelter. Three four-season tents to withstand unexpected desert winds; winter sleeping bags rated for subfreezing temperatures; insulated pads for extra warmth—gotta keep those guys comfy, like a good night's rest at home. And those compact camping pillows—a touch of luxury for our weary heads. *Check.*

Clothing. Jackets, thermal underwear for layering, sturdy waterproof boots—those desert trails can be treacherous. Gloves, hats, scarves—desert nights can get chilly. Warm socks—essential for happy feet, can't have Mitch complaining about cold toes. *Check. Check.*

Food and water. Two cases of water, plus caching containers—hydration is a must in the desert, just like Jenny always reminds the kids to drink their water. Trail mix, canned goods, pasta, energy bars, and coffee—got to keep those energy levels up for all our planned adventures. Plus, a grocery run once we arrive to cater to Mitch and Alex's picky palates. And, of course, the lightweight camping stove, fuel, pots, and utensils—no gourmet restaurants out in the wilderness, though Alex would probably prefer it. *Triple check.*

First-aid kit essentials. Map, compass, headlamps with extra batteries—gotta see where we're going, even if it's just to find the bathroom at night. Sunscreen, sunglasses—the desert sun can be brutal, even in winter. Trash bags, toilet paper, shovel—Leave No Trace principles, always, can't leave the place worse than we found it. *Quadruple check.*

Everything seemed to be in order. So why couldn't I shake this nagging feeling? It wasn't the usual pre-trip jitters. Or was there something else I was missing, something crucial?

I continued driving, feeling more comfortable riding along the highway through California in my prized camper van. It was a classic I'd bought, used and restored with additions over the years. Driving it, I felt better, embracing freedom and adventure. My van was equipped with a standard stick shift and clutch, reminding me of a simpler time. I had upgraded it to meet the demands of my off-grid camping lifestyle. It was fully loaded with built-in camping essentials, including a folding table, various seating arrangements for sleeping, water storage and pump, a cold box, electrical hookup, storage cabinetry, and curtains on the side windows.

Over the years, I had meticulously maintained and upgraded this van, transforming it into a reliable companion, adding a sink with an electric pump and an electric fridge. I loved the blend of nostalgia and modern conveniences, planning and preparing getaway vacations with my family, and this year, for the first time in years, a reunion with my childhood friends.

As I drove down the open road, my trusty old van feeling more like a time machine than a vehicle, my head was a whirlwind of thoughts and emotions. The past few months, heck, the past few years, had been stressful, not just for me but for my entire family. Sometimes, I felt like we were holding everything together with duct tape and wishful thinking.

The good news was Jenny had recently returned to her career after staying at home to raise our kids when they were younger. It has been a transition for all of us. The demands of her new job, coupled with the needs of our increasingly active kids, had put a strain on our family. Basketball practices, playdates, school events—the modern lifestyle of children in America was a far cry from the simpler times of my childhood in Denver. Growing up, we were free to roam the creek, hike, bike, and explore with my friends. We were bound by a shared sense of adventure and a love for the outdoors.

As I navigated the open road, each mile taking me further from home, I began to feel better, though there was still guilt for leaving my family, along with excitement for the week in Joshua Tree. Despite the chaos of my thoughts, one thing was clear: I needed to reconnect with my best friends and find a way to balance my responsibilities with my family. I hoped getting back to nature would help me find a way back to myself, too.

* * *

As I continued my drive, the miles blurring beneath the wheels of my van, I thought about the fun we'd have camping, hiking, and rock climbing in Joshua Tree and imagined the breathtaking sunsets, the quality time with my friends, and the beautiful stars at night. These thoughts brought a smile to my face and a sense of anticipation for the week ahead.

I thought about Mitch and Alex, their faces forming in my mind, memories from the past. The laughter, the adventures, the stupid things we'd done ... Alex, always the first to jump, and Mitch, always a step behind with a map or a fact, like that time Alex wanted to jump the creek, and Mitch had the geological survey map that showed it was shallower than it looked.

I glanced at the passenger seats, empty but somehow filled with their presence. Maybe this trip was more than just a getaway. Maybe it was a chance to find balance, an elusive equilibrium between the man I'd become—the dad—and the boy who'd once led outings in the mountains.

I pulled into a gas station, the neon sign buzzing in the darkness. As I filled the tank, the attendant, a grizzled old-timer, leaned against the van, watching me with curious eyes. He handed me my receipt, and I noticed a newspaper headline peeking out from under a pile of papers: MULTIPLE WOMEN VANISH: BEVERLY HILLS AND PALM SPRINGS.

"Heading south, huh?" he asked, nodding toward my van.

"To the desert," I replied, my hand steady on the pump, my eyes still glancing at the headline.

"Be careful. You know there's a big storm brewing down there, right? Might wanna reconsider your plans."

"Thanks for the heads-up." Of course, I thought, it wouldn't be an adventure with Mitch and Alex without a little bit of weather.

"It's gonna be a monster," he added, his gaze locked on the horizon, like he knew something I didn't.

A monster storm? The last thing we needed, I thought, the image of the newspaper headline flashing in my mind. But I thanked him for the warning and got back into my van.

Gotta make up for lost time. I pushed the accelerator a little harder, the engine humming. I pictured the route ahead, winding through the mountains, down into the Central Valley, then the long, straight stretch of Highway 5, a river of headlights slicing through the darkness. I'd be sharing the road with those massive eighteen-wheelers, their rumbling engines a constant presence. My goal, reach Joshua Tree before midnight, and, hopefully, not encounter dangers in the desert.

I turned on the radio, hoping to learn more about this sudden weather pattern forming in the desert. The news confirmed the attendant's warning—a storm was heading from the Pacific Ocean toward California.

Hopefully, it'll blow over, I thought, tightening my grip on the steering wheel. But despite the unexpected news, I was excited. After all, every adventure has its challenges. And this trip, it seemed, was no exception.

* * *

I looked at my phone and noticed I had missed a few messages from Mitch. I called Mitch through the hands-free phone system I'd installed in my van, keeping both hands firmly on the wheel as I waited for him to pick up.

"Hey, Mitch," I said when he answered. "I'm sorry, man. I'm running late. The game went into overtime."

There was a pause on the other end of the line, and I could almost hear Mitch's frustration. "Ben, we had a plan," he said, his voice disappointed. "I'm almost at the bus stop."

"I know, I know," I replied, pulling my hair. "And I'm looking forward to the trip. You have no idea how much I've needed this."

Mitch sighed, and I could tell he was trying to keep his frustration in check. "Did you pack all the gear?" My weather app is showing that a strange storm is heading towards the desert, and I'm a little nervous about how much trouble we could be in."

"Of course," I replied, my confidence wavering, thinking about the *monster storm* and the headline about the missing women, and now, Mitch's increasing anxiety. "I've got everything we need."

Mitch replied, forcing a calmness into his voice, though I could hear the underlying tension. "Just so you know, the bus ride was ... something. A stranger gave me this weird bible page and told me not to trust anyone."

A pause, then Ben's voice, calm but concerned, the mention of the note immediately overriding any thoughts about the storm. "Maybe he's just some nut, messing with you." Ben's skepticism was understandable. "What else happened?"

"I can't talk now. It's too crowded. I'll tell you everything when I get there.

"Sounds good," I said.

There was another pause, then Mitch said, "Ben, I met this woman on the bus. I ... I hope I see her again."

His confession surprised me. Mitch rarely talked about his personal life. "Great," I said. "But listen, since I'm arriving late tonight, it might be better for you to connect with Alex."

The line went silent.

"Mitch?" I asked, my voice soft with concern, wondering if the stranger on the bus had unnerved him more than he was letting on.

"Ben, you know how Alex can be," Mitch said, his voice strained. "He's ... overwhelming." His words, though quiet, hinted at a deeper anxiety about the trip and the relationship between the three of us.

"I know," I replied, trying to reassure him, even as I felt a pang of guilt. "But we're all in this together, right? We'll make it work."

Another call came in. It was Alex, video calling us from his first-class seat on his flight from Dallas to Palm Springs. His face filled the screen on my phone mounted on the dashboard, his booming voice and energy cutting through the miles.

"Hey, guys!" Alex exclaimed, his voice filled with excitement, oblivious to the tension. "Can't wait to see you both!"

"I'm running late, Alex," I said, my voice filled with regret, the weight of my delay compounded by the weather and Mitch's concerns. "Can you meet up with Mitch at the bus stop?"

Alex laughed, a sound that was both comforting and slightly irritating. "Better than that, Ben," he said, waving a dismissive hand, "I'll get us a limo. And, Mitch, how about we take the Palm Springs Aerial Tramway for the sunset view?"

I imagined Mitch's face paling at the suggestion. "Alex, you know I'm afraid of heights," he said.

Alex just shrugged, his smile never wavering. "You'll be fine. It's all part of the adventure. Hang tight, I'll video call you back with the details."

Chapter 3

Alex

Saturday, December 14—Flight from Dallas to Palm Springs.
"Mr. Sterling, would you like another glass?" the flight attendant asked.

"Yes, and please call me Alex," I replied with my most charming smile as she filled my glass with champagne.

In the business world, it was Alexander or Mr. Sterling, but with friends, and especially girlfriends, I was just Alex.

I was feeling on top of the world, reclining in my first-class seat, flying from Dallas to the Sonny Bono Palm Springs Airport. The last drop of champagne lingered on my tongue as I savored another bite of my perfectly seared salmon. I signaled the flight attendant for a refill, my mind racing toward the adventure awaiting me in the desert.

I glanced out the window as we approached Palm Springs, the snowcapped mountain peaks contrasting the rugged desert landscape. The breathtaking vista, stretching as far as the eye could see, encompassed Joshua Tree National Park—our playground for the next week. I loved the view—golf courses, mountains, giant windmills, all bathed in the soft glow of the setting sun. I pictured a sunset tram ride up to the top of San Jacinto Peak, the desert spread out beneath us like a giant map.

My first-class seat on this flight was nothing short of luxurious. I deserved it, damn it. I'd worked my ass off to get to this point, to afford this kind of comfort and privilege.

The seat was spacious and plush, designed for ultimate relaxation. It was more than just a seat; it was a personal retreat. I could work, I could sleep, I could even watch movies on my private screen.

The service was impeccable. Those flight attendants were attentive and professional, catering to my every whim. From the moment I stepped on board, I'd been treated like royalty.

Sure, the first-class experience was expensive, but it was worth every penny. Plus, the board would approve my expense report. The meal wasn't your typical rushed airplane food; it was a leisurely feast. Gourmet dishes, fine wines, top-shelf liquor ... a reminder that success tasted damn good.

I sipped my champagne, the bubbles tickling my nose, as I watched the scenery below. I was more than just a passenger on a flight; I was a highflier, a Dallas star, heading off to an adventure.

Other people might be jealous of this comfort and privilege, but I didn't care. I'd worked hard to reach this position of success, and moments like these were my reward. I leaned back in my seat with a contented smile.

* * *

It's easy to be a confident, successful businessman in control and ensuring everything runs smoothly with my stellar support staff, ready to assist twenty-four by seven.

I texted my exec admin to arrange for the limo and reservations for the aerial tram and dinner. Then I clicked on the video conference call, and Ben and Mitch's faces appeared on the screen, their expressions a mix of anticipation and exhaustion. Ben was running late—unusual. Mitch looked worried—normal. But I knew we'd be fine. I was Alex freakin' Sterling, after all. I could handle a few logistical hiccups.

"Alex here, gentlemen," I announced, the faint hum of the first-class cabin audible in the background, just a subtle reminder of my baller status. "Mitch, I've taken the liberty of arranging a limo to pick you up from the dusty bus stop."

Mitch's voice, tinny and a bit shaky, came through. "That's ... that's kind of you, but—"

"And that's not all," I continued, excitement creeping into my voice. "I've booked us a sunset tram ride up to San Jacinto Peak and a killer dinner reservation at Peaks Restaurant. The limo will drop us off at our Airbnb after. Everything will be ready for you when you arrive."

There was a pause, and I could practically hear Ben's internal struggle—*Mr. Responsible*—battling with *Mr. Fun*. His voice, when he finally spoke, was less confident than usual. "I appreciate it, Alex, but I'm still a good six to eight hours out, depending on traffic."

Mitch, always cautious, said, "Maybe we could just grab a burger somewhere ... on solid ground?"

I laughed, shaking my head. "No, no, everything's settled. We're doing this. It's gonna be epic."

I ended the call, ready for the weekend ahead. Despite the minor logistical hiccups, I was pumped for this reunion.

As the plane started its descent, my excitement ramped up. I had some big news to share with the guys, news that was gonna blow their minds. I couldn't wait to see their faces.

The flight attendant, a cute redhead with a killer smile, came by to collect my empty champagne flute.

"Anything else I can get you, Mr. ... Alex?" she asked.

"Actually," I said, leaning in, "how about you join us for a tram ride and dinner tonight? The view is incredible, and the company wouldn't be too bad either."

She laughed, a polite but firm rejection. "I'd like to, but I've got another flight later tonight."

"Another time, then," I said, not missing a beat. Rejection? Just a minor setback in the game of life. Because I was Alexander Sterling, a successful businessman living the dream in Dallas. Season tickets to the Cowboys and the Mavs, a penthouse apartment overlooking the city, a company poised for a major merger. Life was good. Damn good.

Sure, the divorce had been a bit messy, but I was never single for long. There was always a beautiful woman on my arm, a new adventure on the horizon. Still, it felt great to get away for a week from the whirlwind of my Dallas life, to enjoy some memories of simpler times, those camping trips with Ben and Mitch back in the Rockies. It'd been years since we'd all been together. Crazy how time flies. But that last adventure was brutal.

* * *

Soon, I was striding through the Palm Springs Airport, grabbing my luggage, my Texas swagger in full force.

The California sun hit me with a blast of heat as I stepped outside. Damn, it felt good to be back in the desert. I slipped on my shades, those new Ray Bans, an early birthday gift to myself.

Despite the bright sun, there was a chill in the air, a reminder it was still winter. I pulled on my coat, appreciating the paradox of needing both sunglasses and winter wear in this desert city.

Exiting the airport, I was greeted by the sight of the majestic San Jacinto Mountains in the distance, their peaks dusted with snow. I spotted Mitch standing by the limo, looking like a lost puppy in a sea of tourists.

"Mitch, my man!" I boomed, already moving toward him.

He jumped, startled, those big blue eyes bloodshot and weary behind his glasses. His dark hair, usually neat, was a hot mess. Twenty-four hours on a Greyhound. Yeah, that'll do it.

"Hey, Alex," he mumbled, managing a weak smile. "You look ... well-rested."

"Must be the desert air," I said, pulling him into a tight hug. I could feel the tension radiating off him, all those anxieties buzzing beneath the surface. Poor bastard. Next trip, I was chipping in for his plane ticket.

"Well, look at you, Mitchell Donovan," I said. "You haven't aged a bit since you played shortstop back in the day."

"Except for the hair," Mitch said, tugging on the end of his ponytail as he adjusted his glasses."

"Yeah, well, some of us can't pull off the rockstar-scientist look, Mitchell Donovan." I ran a hand over my short buzz cut. Force of habit, keeping it trim. Dad's voice still sounded in my head sometimes: *A clean cut shows discipline, son. Project a commanding presence.* Not that I needed help in the commanding-presence department.

"So, where's Ben? Decided to walk from Oregon?" I asked, my tone light and teasing.

"He's running late. Should be here by midnight."

"*That late*? He'll miss a great meal." My stomach growled loudly. "I'm starving. How about we get a tram up the mountain first? Best views in the state, and they've got a killer restaurant at the top."

Mitch looked like he'd seen a ghost, his face drained of color, and muttered, "You know I hate heights, Alex."

I chuckled, throwing my arm around him and steering him towards the limo. "Come on, *Mitchie*, live a little! Besides, they have Texas-sized portions. You can keep your feet firmly on the ground and your stomach full of steak and potatoes." I could tell he was on edge about something, but I figured a little distraction was the best medicine.

As we piled into the limo, the cool leather seats a welcome contrast to the bright sun, the driver tipped his hat. "Where to, gentlemen?" he asked.

As Mitch was settling into the limo seat, he started to say something, his voice hesitant, "Hey, Alex, before we go, I wanted to tell you—" but I cut him off, eager to get this trip on the road, "No time for stories, *Professor*. Let's get this adventure started!". I didn't have time for whatever was bothering him, and I was ready for some action.

"All right, let's kick this adventure into high gear," I told the limo driver, settling back into the plush leather seat. "First stop, the Palm Springs Aerial Tramway. I hear those three-hundred-sixty-degree views from the top of Mount San Jacinto are something else."

Mitch, who'd been staring out the window at the passing palm trees, turned to me, his eyes wide. "Wait, seriously? You're not kidding about the tram?"

"Of course, I'm not kidding." I laughed. "What better way to start our desert adventure than soaring over those canyons in a rotating tram car? Think of it as a preview of the breathtaking scenery we'll be exploring all week. And besides, they've got a restaurant at the top. You can admire the views while indulging in some great food. No need to worry about those pesky heights, my friend."

The driver chuckled. "You got it, boss. The tramway, it is." He smoothly pulled the limo into traffic, heading toward the base of the mountain. "And after?"

"After we've had our fill of mountaintop magic," I said, "take us to our luxury Airbnb in Yucca Valley. Got a hot tub, a pool table, and a killer view of the desert. We'll chill there for a bit, tonight maybe enjoy a celebratory beer before we hit the jackpot: Joshua Tree National Park."

* * *

Before we knew it, we'd pulled up to the Palm Springs Aerial Tramway, the imposing structure rising like a concrete-and-steel spacecraft against the mountain backdrop.

"Great to see you, Mitch," I said, pulling him close for another bear hug. "But, dude, seriously? That backpack? And your hat? You're gonna scare the tourists!"

"Hey, give me a break," Mitch grumbled, adjusting his backpack straps. "It's functional. And this hat," he added, pulling it down tighter over his ears, "keeps me warm. You're gonna wish you had one when we're out in that desert."

"Yeah, yeah, whatever you say, *Professor Gadget*. But trust me, a little wardrobe upgrade wouldn't hurt your chances with the ladies."

Mitch paused at the entrance, his eyes glued to a sign listing all the rules, his brow furrowed like he was deciphering code. I, of course, was already striding towards the ticket booth, those VIP e-tickets glowing on my phone screen. No time for reading fine print, I'm a *doer*, not a *ponderer*. "All visitors are subject to a bag search," the sign declared, and I couldn't resist. "What, you think I'm packing heat?" I joked, throwing a wink at the attendant.

Mitch, still looking at the sign like it was about to explode, started reading aloud, "No weapons, no pepper spray, no tasers, no machetes, swords, hatchets, or large knives. No explosives or fireworks. No pets, only registered service animals. No scooters, skateboards, bicycles, drones, illegal substances, nor outside alcohol. No inflatable rafts, sleds, toys, or balloons. And no sleds or toboggans with metal runners."

He sounded like a robot reciting the terms of service. I laughed, shaking my head at his nerdy intensity. "Got it," I said, because obviously.

Mitch, finally catching up, mumbled, "Just so you know, all photoshoots and filming are subject to approval. So, maybe put your phone away for a few minutes, huh?"

I just laughed, waving my phone in the air. "Relax, I'm not gonna cause an international incident. Just a few harmless selfies." What's life without a little fun, right? This was going to be fun, and I was ready to capture every second of it.

* * *

As we stepped into the tram car, the doors hissed shut behind us, sealing us into a world of glass and steel. The car started to rise, the ground falling away, revealing a panorama of desert stretched out as far as the eye could see. Mitch moved away from the windows, his knuckles white as he gripped the handrail.

"Pretty awesome, huh?" I said, snapping a few photos. "I told you this was gonna be incredible."

The tram continued its smooth ascent, the desert landscape spreading out below like a giant, wrinkled map.

Mitch was in the middle of the car, eyes darting nervously between the other passengers.

"Relax, buddy," I said. "It's perfectly safe. Besides, you're missing the show."

"I'll admire the view from solid ground, thanks."

I just laughed, shaking my head. Some things never changed.

The tram car was packed with a mix of tourists—a family with screaming kids, a group of elderly folks in conversation, a tall man wearing an expensive suit with his date, and a couple college girls who kept glancing our way, their giggles ringing in the enclosed space.

"Hey, those girls are checking us out," I whispered to Mitch, nudging him.

He looked at his shoes. "Just ignore them, Alex."

"Why? They're cute." I winked at one of them, a blonde with a killer smile, and she smiled back. *Score!*

"Hey, ladies," I called. "My friend and I are celebrating. Drinks and dinner at the top? Our treat!"

The blonde giggled, but her friend, a brunette with a wary expression, shook her head. "Thanks, but we've already got plans." She turned away, tucking a strand of hair behind her ear and looking away at a couple standing across from us.

"More for us," I said.

* * *

The restaurant at the top of the Palm Springs Aerial Tramway buzzed with energy. Tourists and locals mingled, their voices a happy murmur against the backdrop of clinking glasses and soft jazz music. Panoramic windows offered a breathtaking view of the city lights and the desert stretching under the setting sun.

"Not bad, huh?" I said, pointing at the view. "Beats a greasy diner, right?"

Mitch nodded. The tram ride had clearly rattled him.

Our table, seated four, with a killer view in the corner. Nearby was the family of five with an extra highchair squeezed in for the baby—the parents were celebrating their anniversary. The place was packed! Glad I got reservations in advance!

And then, the tall man, impeccably dressed in a tailored suit, strolled over with a confident swagger, and screamed *money*. His date, a striking brunette, eyes darting around the restaurant, trailed him. I caught his eye, and he's already flashing a charming, but slightly arrogant smile, the kind I often use when schmoozing a new business contact or a potential love interest.

"Mind if we join you?" he asked, his voice smooth and confident. "Seems all the other tables are full."

I sized him up quickly—expensive suit, fancy watch, the kind of guy who's used to getting his way. I recognized the type immediately. We'd probably have some interesting conversations, and he might know some people I need to know.

I was about to say something, but Mitch, in the quiet way of his, interjected. "Naturally, Alex would be happy to host you," Mitch said, giving me a playful nudge.

"Always the gentleman, Alex. I appreciate the gesture," the man replied, shaking my hand. The man's handshake was firm, his grip strong and slightly unnerving. He clearly liked me, and I knew I could work with him. "Sure, the more the merrier," I said, flashing a smile. "Alex Sterling, at your service."

"Randall Thorne" the man replied, extending a hand. "But everyone calls me Randy. And this is ..." He hesitated, glancing at the woman, who seemed to shrink under his glare. "This is Evelyn." I noticed the hesitation, how he almost seemed to be checking himself.

"Nice to meet you," I said, giving her a nod, but Evelyn just mumbled, her eyes downcast. She excused herself to the restroom, her movements stiff, almost robotic. She seemed uncomfortable. Maybe Randy was a bit too much for her. Not my problem, though.

Randy, completely ignoring her departure, launched into a story about his latest business deal, a real estate venture in Palm Springs. The numbers he tossed around made my head spin. This guy was loaded.

She had been gone for a while, and I was wondering if she was okay. She finally returned from the restroom.

Mitch, who'd been quiet, leaned closer, his voice low against the racket of the restaurant. "Something's not right with that couple, Alex," he said. "She seems ... off. Scared, maybe. Or drugged?"

I rolled my eyes. "Relax," I said. "They're probably just having a lover's spat. Don't be such a buzzkill."

Dinner was a feast—prime rib, succulent lobster tails, and a bottle of Napa Valley Cabernet Randy insisted on ordering. I spared no expense, adding a few appetizers and a round of after-dinner cognac. Mitch surprised me by ordering the braised pork osso buco, and I, of course, went for the ribeye, medium rare, with a side of truffle fries. I picked up the tab, of course. Had to keep up appearances, especially when you're dining with a high roller like Randy.

Randy's endless anecdotes and boisterous laughter dominated the dinner conversation. Mitch remained quiet, his eyes narrowing and frequently examining the couple, an unmistakable look of concern betraying his usual analytical mood.

The father with the big family asked to get a group photo of them in front of the window view.

As I framed the shot, Randy was leaning in close, his hand resting possessively on Evelyn's arm. Her face was downcast, her expression hidden. "Say cheese!" I said, snapping a few pics.

As the plates were cleared, I snagged a copy of the receipt, tucking it into my wallet. Gotta keep those board members happy. I grabbed a photo of the dessert menu—key lime pie, chocolate lava cake, and crème brûlée—just for good measure.

"Perhaps we'll run into each other again in this vast desert playground," Randy said, his voice smooth, but the look in his eye as he flashed his expensive watch felt more like a threat than a friendly farewell.

* * *

The tram glided back down to the valley floor, the city lights blurring into a distant glow as we descended.

As we stepped off the tram, Mitch let out a sigh of relief, his grip on the handrail finally loosening.

"Still in one piece, Mitch," I said. "See? Wasn't so bad."

He just shook his head, digging through his backpack. "I'm never getting on one of those things again."

The limo was waiting for us, its sleek exterior a welcome sight.

"All right, let's head to the Airbnb," I said to the driver. "Mitch needs to unwind after the harrowing experience." I grinned at Mitch, who was already scribbling notes in his notebook, probably calculating the tram's cable tension or something.

It was almost midnight when we pulled up to the Airbnb, a sprawling ranch house nestled in the foothills of the Yucca Valley. Ben's van was already parked in the driveway.

"This place is awesome!" Mitch said his earlier anxieties were forgotten as he surveyed the spacious living room, the pool table in the corner, and the sliding glass doors led out to a patio with a hot tub and a killer view of the desert.

"Ben's out back," I said. "Looks like he's got the party started."

We found Ben on the patio, a couple beers chilling in a cooler, a contented smile on his face. He looked exhausted, his face shadowed with stubble, clothes rumpled from the long drive, but his smile was genuine.

"About time you two showed up," he said, pulling Mitch into a bear hug. "Looks like you survived the tram."

"It wasn't just the tram." Mitch laughed, accepting a beer from Ben.

"Don't worry, buddy, I'll protect you from the wild women of Palm Springs," I joked.

We sank into the steaming hot tub, the desert stars blazing above us in the dark sky, the tension melting away.

"I can't believe it's been more than ten years," Ben said, shaking his head. "It feels like just yesterday we were playing poker in the treehouse."

"Enjoy this, guys," I said, raising my beer in a toast. "Because tonight, we sleep like kings, sunk deep in soft beds with those fluffy pillows and thick blankets. Tomorrow, the real adventure begins. And trust me, those sleeping bags on the hard, cold desert ground won't feel anything like this."

Chapter 4

Mitchell, Benji, Alexander

Saturday, February 15—Ten-year-old Scouts in Estes Park, Colorado.

The big bus bumped along the twisty mountain road, its tires crunching on the new snow. We were going on a whole week of camping with the Scouts in Estes Park, and we could hardly wait!

"I can't wait to go hiking," Benji shouted. "Remember the time we climbed all the way up to the top of the giant waterfall? That was so cool!"

"Yeah, and remember those big fish we caught in the lake?" Alexander said. "I bet I can catch an even bigger one this time!"

"I'm just happy to be here with you guys," Mitchell said.

The bus twisted and turned through the huge mountains, leaning to get a closer look, and staring at all the cool stuff outside. The mountains were so tall, covered in snow, and the forests looked like a green carpet. The air smelled of pine and fresh dirt.

We'd planned their Scouts camping trip to the Colorado Rockies for weeks. The timing was perfect. Mitchell was thrilled to celebrate his tenth birthday with his best friends in Estes Park. As we looked out the bus window, the mountains looked just like the photos the Scout leaders had shown them, all jagged peaks and thick forests.

Alexander's window was open, and the icy wind slapped him in the face, but he didn't care. The roar of the river grew louder as their bus crawled higher into the Rockies.

We were ready for a weekend of adventure with Alexander and Benji like balloons about to burst, bouncing around in the seat behind Mitchell, who was glued to the window.

As the bus climbed deeper into the mountains, Alexander and Benji couldn't contain their excitement. Every time they passed a bend in the road, they yelled out something new.

"Benji, do you think we'll see a bear?" Alexander asked.

"I hope so!" Benji replied and slammed shut his book, probably about some kind of monster fish, and practically climbed over Alexander to get a better look out the window.

Mitchell was too busy staring out the window, trying to act cool but probably imagining bears.

The higher we climbed, the more it felt like we were driving into a picture book. Lakes so blue they hurt their eyes, mountaintops covered in snow glitter even though the sun was bright.

"Look at that!" Alexander exclaimed, pointing to a herd of elk grazing in a nearby meadow.

"Wow, they're so big!" Benji said.

* * *

"Hey, Ben-Ben!" Alexander boomed, giving him a playful shove. Even though it was a long bus ride, he was already hyped.

Benji rolled his eyes but grinned. "Yeah, yeah, very funny. But seriously, it's Benji. My dad's name is Benjamin Senior, and I'm Benjamin Junior, so my parents nicknamed me Benji."

Mitchell was staring out the window, probably already memorizing every rock and tree they passed.

"What about you, Mitchie?" Alexander asked, trying the nickname. He always got this funny look when they called him Mitchie.

Mitchell blinked a few times as if he forgot we were there. "Uh ... Mitchell's fine."

"Just Mitchell? Come on, man, you need a cool nickname for this trip! Like, no cool nicknames for a future astronaut?"

Mitchell ducked his head and went back to staring out the window.

"Well, that's boring," Alexander declared, striking a dramatic pose. "From now on, for this trip, I'm *Ace*. *Ace the Amazing Adventurer*! And you," he pointed at Mitchell, "are *Mitchie the Magnificent Professor*!"

Even Mitchell cracked a smile. "*The Professor*, huh?"

"Yep! *Professor of ... uh ... adventure*!" Alexander said, trying to sound cooler.

Benji chuckled. "I like it. It suits him."

Mitchell laughed. "Yeah, okay, *Professor*. Better than *Four-Eyes*."

"That's the spirit!" Alexander said. "*Ace, Professor ... and Benji*! The Three Amigos of Adventure! We're gonna rock these Rockies!"

* * *

"Dude, check it out, the mountains are huge!" Alexander shouted, practically bouncing off his seat.
We were all squished against the bus windows now. The closer we got, the bigger those mountains seemed to get.
"I bet a bear is hiding behind that one," Benji said, pointing to a peak so high it looked like it was trying to touch the clouds.
"Don't say *bear*," Mitchell said. "Remember what happened last time Benji mentioned bears on a camping trip?"
We all laughed, remembering the time a raccoon got into their snacks and Benji swore it was a baby bear.
"This time's gonna be different," Benji insisted. "I can feel it. Adventures, here we come!"
The mountains looked just as cool as they did in the pictures the Scout leaders showed them, all jagged and covered in trees. Every time we went over a bridge, Alexander felt like he was gonna puke but in a good way. Like being on a roller coaster.
Mitchell, of course, was already spouting off facts about every animal he might see. "Did you know there are bobcats here? And mountain lions? And listen to this," Mitchell said, his voice hushed even though the bus engine was rumbling. He'd pulled out a battered paperback—*Rocky Mountain Wildlife*—and was squinting at the pages. "It says bobcats are good at climbing trees. They can even jump down on their prey from above!"
Benji gasped. "From trees? Like, ninja bobcats?"
Alexander tried to play it cool, but the hair on the back of his neck stood up. "Okay, kinda creepy."

Mitchell shrugged. "And it's not even the coolest part. It says mountain lions live here too ..."

"Mountain lions?" Benji squeaked. "Dude, those things are, like, super rare, right?"

Mitchell nodded. "Super rare ... and super dangerous."

Alexander swallowed hard, picturing a mountain lion now instead of a bear.

"Dude, stop," Benji said, his eyes wide.

But they were kinda into it. Bobcats? Mountain lions? Now that would be a story to tell back home.

Even though we were still on the bus, it already felt like the adventure had begun.

* * *

The bus screeched to a stop, and we were practically climbing over each other to get off. Backpacks thumped, someone yelled "escape," and we were finally free!

The campground was like something out of a movie. Huge mountains circled around us; their peaks capped with snow glittered even in the shade. A stream gurgled nearby, so clear we could see the rocks at the bottom. It was far cooler than our boring old park back home.

We were all decked out in our Scout uniforms—blue shirts, yellow scarves, hiking boots laced up tight. Alexander's had this awesome patch he got for building a campfire all by himself last summer. He puffed out his chest a little, hoping some of the other Scouts would notice.

"This place is awesome!" Benji said, already spinning in a circle to take it all in. He was always the most prepared with his special compass that he had gotten from his dad.

Mitchell was quieter, but he kept looking around like he was trying to memorize every detail. "It's even better than the pictures," he said.

The campground buzzed with other kids, everyone yelling and laughing. We dumped our stuff in the cabin—bunk beds!—and raced out to explore.

"I'm gonna climb that giant rock!" Alexander yelled, already halfway up before Benji could even say anything.

"Be careful!" Mitchell called out. He was always worried.

Benji was checking the map. "Let's go down by the stream first. I bet we could catch some trout."

It was perfect. The sun was out, the air smelled like pine trees, and we had a whole week of adventure ahead. What could possibly go wrong?

* * *

That afternoon, we hiked with the rest of the Scouts and our leaders. The trail was steep and rocky, but we scrambled up like mountain goats, even Mitchell! When we reached the top, it was like we could see forever!

"Woo-hoo!" Alexander yelled, throwing his arms out wide. The wind whipped his face, but he didn't care. He felt he could almost fly.

Benji was busy pointing out different mountains and landmarks, using his trusty compass to get his bearings. Mitchell, though, was just standing there, taking it all in.

The next few days flew by in a blur of awesome. We went on more hikes, learned how to tie knots that could probably hold a bear, and even tried to catch some fish in the stream. We even went to the town nearby where we checked out all the shops and played games, our pockets stuffed with souvenirs and candy.

The campfire nights were the best. We'd roast marshmallows until they were gooey and melty, tell spooky stories that made us jump at every shadow, and laugh until our sides hurt. It was even Mitchell's birthday one of those nights!

"Happy birthday, buddy!" Benji and Alexander yelled, surprising Mitchell with a snack cake they'd snuck into the campground from town. It wasn't anything fancy, just a ding dong with a camp candle, but Mitchell's face lit up like it was the best cake in the world.

Everyone in our Scout group gathered around, singing "Happy Birthday" and clapping along.

* * *

After days of playing it safe under the adults' watchful eyes, we were itching for some real adventure. As we sat around the campfire that night, everyone else already snoring away in their tents, Alexander pulled out his trusty map. It was almost midnight, the fire casting flickering shadows on the trees around us.

"Guys," Alexander whispered, "I have an idea. A midnight hike to a secret spot. Way cooler."

Mitchell frowned. "But the leaders said—"

"Don't be such a scaredy-cat, Mitchell," Alexander said. "It'll be fun! We'll be back before anyone even notices." He pointed to a spot on the map he'd been studying earlier. "There's this awesome overlook I heard a leader talking about. Amazing view of the night sky."

Benji, cautious, rubbed his chin. "I don't know. It's pretty late ... and dark."

Mitchell nodded. "Yeah, and what if it rains? We don't want to get caught in a storm."

"Rain? Please, it's a clear night! Come on, guys, live a little!"

In the end, Alexander's powers of persuasion won us over (it usually wasn't hard). We snuck away from the campsite, our flashlights cutting through the darkness. The woods were silent except for the crunch of our footsteps and the occasional hoot of an owl.

"It's kinda creepy out here," Mitchell whispered.

"That's what makes it an adventure!" Alexander said, trying to sound braver than he felt.

"It's so dark," Mitchell whispered, his flashlight barely illuminating the path ahead. The moon and stars were hidden behind thick clouds, casting an eerie darkness over the forest.

Alexander, leading the way, nodded. "Yeah, but that's what makes it an adventure."

The forest was full of eerie sounds—the distant howl of a coyote, bushes rustling, and thunder rumbling in the distance.

"Did you hear that?" Benji asked, stopping. "I think something's moving over there!"

Alexander shrugged. "Probably just a raccoon or something."

We kept going, following the map Alexander had shown us. But the farther we went, the more scared we felt.

"Are we lost?" Mitchell whispered.

"No way," Alexander replied, but he didn't sound so sure. "We just gotta keep going."

We'd been walking for about half an hour when the first raindrops started to fall.

"Told ya," Mitchell muttered.

At first, it was just a drizzle, but then the sky opened up, and it was like someone was dumping buckets of water on us. Lightning flashed, thunder roared, and the wind howled through the trees. We were soaked in seconds, our clothes sticking and making us shiver.

"We need to find shelter!" Benji yelled over the wind.

They scrambled for cover, their flashlights barely cutting through the downpour. Everything was blurry, the path treacherous.

"Over there!" Benji shouted, pointing to a rocky overhang. It wasn't much, but it was better than nothing. We huddled together under the rock, shivering

"We should've listened to the leaders," Mitchell said, his teeth chattering.

"Yeah, well, we didn't," Alexander grumbled.

We were lost, soaked to the bone, and a storm raged around us. What had we gotten ourselves into?

* * *

We ran through the woods, our flashlights useless against the driving rain. We could barely see two feet ahead. The path had turned into a slippery stream, and we kept tripping and falling, our laughter replaced by gasps of fear. Each flash of lightning illuminated the panic on our faces.

"There!" Benji shouted, pointing his flashlight to a small cave hidden behind a rock.

We squeezed inside, shivering like crazy. Alexander, being the tallest, struggled to fit, but with a bit of effort, he managed to get inside.

Mitchell was small enough to squeeze into the driest corner in the back.

"We need a fire," Benji said.

Mitchell was already digging through his backpack. "I might be able to start one," he said, pulling out waterproof matches.

We scooted closer together to fit under the rocks. Benji found a few twigs and used Mitchell's trusty fire starter.

After what felt like an eternity, a tiny flame flickered to life.

"You're a lifesaver, Mitchell," Alexander said, holding his hands out to the warmth.

We huddled there for hours, the storm raging outside. The fire felt good, drying our clothes and chasing away some of the chill, but it couldn't chase away the fear.

"What are we going to do?" Mitchell asked. "We can't stay here."

"We'll figure it out," Alexander said, trying to sound confident. But the truth was, we had no idea what we were going to do after we'd snuck out and disobeyed the leaders.

Sleep was impossible. Every howl of the wind and every clap of thunder made us jump. We huddled together, whispering stories and trying to ignore the gnawing fear that this was more than a simple adventure gone wrong. This was serious.

* * *

When the first rays of sunlight peeked through the cracks in the rocks, we felt a rush of warmth and hope. After being lost in the dark, stormy forest, the sunlight made us believe everything would be okay. We had survived the night. But we were still far from camp and knew we were in big trouble.

We crawled out of their hiding spot, the rising sun doing little to warm our chilled bones. Everything sparkled with a million tiny raindrops, the air thick with the smell of wet earth and pine.

"We need to get back before anyone notices," Alexander said.

We stumbled through the muddy undergrowth, every muscle aching. The woods seemed different in the daylight—less magical, more menacing. Every shadow seemed to hold the shape of a wild animal, and every rustle of leaves made our hearts race like we were facing a pack of wolves.

"Do you think they'll send us home?" Benji asked.

Mitchell didn't answer, just kept his head down, eyes on the path.

The closer we got to camp, the more our hearts pounded. We could picture the disappointed faces of the leaders, our parents' lectures about responsibility repeating in our ears.

Finally, through a gap in the trees, we spotted the familiar clearing of the campsite. But as we stumbled out of the woods, pale and shivering, we realized our troubles were far from over. A group of adults rushed toward us, their faces a mixture of relief and anger.

"Boys!" one of the leaders boomed, his voice carrying through the camp. "Where have you been? We've been worried sick!"

Alexander started to stammer out an excuse, but the words caught in his throat. Benji just hung his head, his face flushed.

Then, one of the leaders knelt in front of Mitchell, placing a hand on his shoulder. His voice was softer now, but there was something in his eyes that made Alexander's stomachache.

"Mitchell," he said, "we need to talk. There's been ... an accident."

"An accident?"

The leader hesitated, then said the words would change Mitchell's life forever.

"Mitchell, it's your parents. There was an airplane crash. We need to transport you to your aunt's place immediately."

Chapter 5

Mitch

Sunday, December 15—Day one, Hidden Valley Campground, Joshua Tree.

I woke with a gasp, a dream still clinging to me. The scent of pine, the crisp mountain air. For a moment, I was back in the Rockies, a carefree ten-year-old with Ben and Alex at my side. Then, the dream took a dark turn. I remembered the day my world shattered; the day I lost my parents in a plane crash.

I blinked as the California sun streamed through the window, rousing me from the painful memory. More than twenty years. It felt like a lifetime ago, and yet, the memory of the leader's somber face, the phone call from Aunt May, and the news was as vivid as yesterday. I was in Joshua Tree now, a world away from the Colorado mountains where it all happened. Ben and Alex were here too, their lives as different from mine as our chosen modes of transport—campervan, jet, and bus.

"Good morning, sleepyhead," Alex said, stretching his long arms. "What's for breakfast? I'm starving."

"Hold your horses," I said, already heading for the kitchen. "Unless Ben packed an entire grocery store in his van, we're missing some essentials. Pancakes need syrup, you know."

Alex nodded. "I'll go. Ben, do you want me to drive your van while Mitch makes breakfast?"

Ben didn't even look up from the coffee maker. "Already got it, in my van" he said, tossing the keys with a flick of his wrist. "And, yes, that includes *real maple syrup*. From Vermont, of course."

Alex snagged the keys out of the air, a cocky grin on his face. I got to work on the pancakes, glad for the familiar routine. Alex was back in a flash and the whole place smelled like home.

We gathered around the table, Ben's Vermont syrup already making the pancakes taste better than anything I'd had in months. It wasn't long before we were trading stories, our laughter bouncing off the walls, taking us back to those carefree days in the Rockies.

"Hey, remember that raccoon we tried to catch for, like, *hours*?" Alex asked, shaking his head.

"And how, in the end, it stole our sandwiches?" Ben added.

* * *

As we piled into Ben's van—Alex tossing his designer luggage into the back with a dramatic flourish, me carefully stowing my backpack, and Ben making sure everything was perfectly organized, as usual—the conversation turned to the inevitable catch up.

"So, Mitch," Ben began, "how's it going living back home in Denver with Aunt May?"

"It's good," I said, picturing Aunt May's smile and the way she always had a pot of tea brewing. "Quiet, but good."

"Aunt May, huh? Sounds like you're living the high life, Mitch! Probably spending your days reading sci-fi and drinking tea, right? Meanwhile, back in the real world, I've been living the dream in Dallas. Season tickets for Cowboys and Mavs, baby! You guys should come out for a game."

Ben chuckled, shaking his head. "Sounds like you. Always a sports fan."

"And what about you, Ben?" I asked. "How's life in Oregon?"

"It's been a whirlwind. My wife is back at work, and the kids are growing up too fast. They both won their YMCA basketball tourneys this weekend."

"That's amazing," I said, trying to sound more enthusiastic than I felt. Truth be told, hearing about Ben and his family brought a pang of ... something. Longing? Envy? I wasn't sure.

As we pulled out of the driveway, Ben's van humming like a contented beast, I reached into my pocket and touched the torn page from the bible. I remembered the crazed man and Martha's warnings about the dangers in the desert. Then, with a sigh of relief and a small smile, I crumpled the page, pushing it deep into my pocket.

* * *

"All right, guys," Ben said, "Joshua Tree, here we come! But first, a quick safety briefing."

"Bring on the danger!" Alex whooped, throwing his arms up like he was wrestling a mountain lion.

I rolled my eyes, a smile tugging at my lips. Some things never changed.

"Mitch, can you pull out the binder in the back seat?"

"Sure, got it!"

Ben ignored Alex. "Okay, so I've reviewed the Sierra Club's safety guidelines for desert environments—"

"Dude, relax! It's just a camping trip, not a military operation," Alex said, grabbing a handful of trail mix.

"Safety is always important, Alex, especially in a place like Joshua Tree," Ben insisted. "We need to know what to do in case of dehydration, heat exhaustion, flash floods, rattlesnake encounters—"

"Dude, you're killing the vibe." Alex laughed.

Ben sighed. "All right, all right. But promise me you'll at least carry extra water?"

"Fine, Mom," Alex said, grinning.

"Okay, let's go over our itinerary. Hidden Valley's our first stop," Ben said, pointing to a place on Mitch's map. "Lots of easy hikes there, some cool rock formations, perfect for getting back into the camping groove."

"Rock climbing? Bring it on!" Alex said.

Ben smiled. "I knew you'd be excited."

"I've seen pictures," I said. Those rock formations looked steep. My palms were already starting to sweat.

"Don't worry, Mitch. No one's climbing Everest here. Later in the week, we'll check out Jumbo Rocks and Skull Rock, and head out to the Cholla Cactus Garden, maybe do some stargazing on the eastern side of the park," Ben said, tracing a route with his finger. "There's a campground at Cottonwood, or we could find a more secluded spot if you guys are feeling adventurous." He paused, smiling. "And, of course, no trip to Joshua Tree would be complete without a hike up Ryan Mountain. Amazing views, plus some cool history stuff—abandoned mines, old homesteads. I figured we could save it for the end of the week, give Alex a chance to get used to the elevation."

"Can't wait to conquer Ryan Mountain!" Alex said. "More hiking, more fun!"

Ben chuckled. "That's the spirit!"

"Sounds like a plan. I'm ready for anything!" Alex replied.

"Maybe we should plan a rest day too?"

"A rest day sounds good," Ben replied.

* * *

"Here we are, guys," Ben said, pulling the van into a parking spot. "Home sweet home for the next week."

We unloaded the van, each man grabbing his gear. I hefted my trusty backpack, feeling the familiar weight settle onto my shoulders. Ben, as always, was armed with a meticulously organized assortment of camping equipment. And then there was Alex.

"Seriously, dude?" I said, watching him wrestle several massive suitcases from the back of the van. They were the kind of luggage you'd expect to see at a luxury resort, not a dusty campground in Joshua Tree.

Alex laughed, unzipping his two large Hermès Taurillon Clemence RMS Gold suitcases. Alex unzipped one of the cases, revealing a stack of neatly folded cashmere blankets. "Just the essentials. You know, in case the desert gets a little chilly."

I peeked inside. Nestled among the luxurious blankets were items that seemed completely out of place in this rugged environment—a pair of Leica binoculars, a S'well water bottle crafted from teakwood, and a gleaming Stetson cowboy hat. And that was just the first suitcase.

"Don't tell me you brought your espresso machine too," I said, shaking my head.

Alex laughed. "I like to be prepared. Besides, a little bit of Dallas luxury never hurt anyone, even in the middle of the desert."

Leave it to Alex to turn a camping trip into a glamping extravaganza.

"Let's get these tents up," Ben said, eager to start exploring. Years of camping with the Scouts had instilled in him a need for order.

We fell into a familiar rhythm, our movements practiced and efficient.

"Seriously, Mitch," Alex said, watching me set up a compact, single-person tent, "is that all you brought? Just a backpack and your dorky hat?"

"I'm good." I preferred to travel light, to carry only what was essential.

Ben had struck a balance between Alex's indulgence and my minimalism. He'd outfitted his van with everything we might need, from a portable stove to a first-aid kit that could rival a small hospital.

"Check this out, guys," Ben said, swinging open the back doors of his van. Inside, a custom-built cabinet held a neatly organized collection of camping supplies. "We've got a water pump, a cooler that can keep ice for days, even a solar panel to charge our phones."

"Ben, I'd pay premium dollars to swap my tent for a night in your van," Alex said.

Ever since his days in the Scouts, Ben's meticulous planning and preparation had been as reliable as a Swiss watch, ticking away with precision.

I finished setting up my tent, not bothered by Alex's teasing. *It's not about how much you bring but about bringing what you need.* I patted my backpack. It was deceptive in its simplicity, holding more than thirty carefully selected and packed essentials. "I mean, who wouldn't want to go on a camping trip with two guys who barely survived the rope swing incident in junior high" I added with a smile.

As I began to unpack, Ben and Alex watched in surprise. From a compact tent to a survival blanket and rain cover, a first-aid kit to an instant fire starter, my backpack was a treasure trove of camping essentials. I wasn't just prepared but ready for anything.

"Wow, Mitch," Alex exclaimed, "I didn't know you could fit an entire campsite in a backpack!"

* * *

With camp set up, we decided to hit one of the popular trails. "Ready to discover Hidden Valley, guys?" Ben asked.

"Let's do it!" Alex said, lacing up his hiking boots—surprisingly sturdy ones, considering his usual preference for designer footwear. He donned his cowboy hat, grabbed his binoculars and water bottle, and opened the Yeti cooler. "I've got some Texas-style sandwiches here," he announced, revealing three hearty sandwiches packed with smoked brisket and potato chips. "These should fuel us for our hike."

"I'm in," I agreed.

Ben, looking surprised, asked, "Alex, where did you get those?"

Alex grinned. "Texted my admin to deliver them to the Airbnb earlier this morning before we left. Figured we needed a little taste of home. I stashed them in your van when I went for the syrup."

Ben shook his head. "Of course you did, Alex. You always must take things to the next level. But I must admit, those sandwiches do look amazing."

* * *

As we started our hike, the landscape unfolded before us like a scene from another planet. Joshua trees, their branches twisted and spiky, stretched toward the vast blue sky. Massive boulders, sculpted by centuries of wind and rain, rose from the sand like memories of a lost civilization. The silence was broken only by the crunch of our boots on the trail and the distant call of a desert wren.

"Do you hear that?" Ben asked, pausing to listen. "The desert has its own music."

He was right. The rustle of the wind through the dry grasses, the clatter of a lizard scrambling over rocks, even the silence itself felt like a symphony of nature.

"Remember when we used to pretend we were explorers, discovering new lands?" I asked.

Alex chuckled. "Yeah, and Ben was always the one drawing the maps."

"And they were pretty accurate maps, if I do say so myself," Ben replied.

We fell into a comfortable silence, each of us lost in thought as we hiked deeper into Hidden Valley. The trail wound through a maze of towering boulders, creating a sense of both wonder and claustrophobia. I couldn't shake the feeling we were being watched, unseen eyes followed our every move, and I was having a hard time relaxing.

But the feeling something was wrong just wouldn't go away. I reached into my pocket and unraveled the torn bible page. *Never let your guard down, Mitch.*

"Hidden Valley is amazing," Ben said, his voice enthusiastic. "It's like a natural amphitheater, ringed by these giant boulders. They were formed millions of years ago when molten rock cooled beneath the surface. Apparently, cattle rustlers used to hide out here back in the day." He pointed toward the maze of rock formations. "There are all sorts of cool spots for bouldering too." He grinned. "I figured you guys might want to give it a try."

I lost track of Ben's nature talk as I looked around the trail.

"Hey, uh, guys," I said, my voice a little shaky, "something weird ..."

Alex rolled his eyes. "Relax, Mitch. You're letting your imagination run wild."

Ben, trying to be supportive, put a hand on my shoulder. "We'll be careful, Mitch. Always be prepared, right? The motto isn't just for Scouting—it's for life."

I appreciated Ben's support. My thoughts kept looping back to the frantic man on the bus and Martha's warnings.

To distract myself, I changed the subject. "Look at this," I said, pointing to a Joshua tree. "Did you know these trees are a type of yucca and can live for hundreds of years?"

"Fascinating. I'll be sure to quiz the next yucca tree I meet about its retirement plans," Alex joked.

"Don't listen to him," Ben said. "It's cool to know stuff like that."

The trail was bustling with other hikers, and we crossed paths with several groups. Among them were a family with a young child, a couple, and a solo hiker.

A little ways ahead, the couple had stopped, pointing excitedly at something in the brush.

Alex, ever eager to be in the know, bounded over to them, binoculars raised. "Hi, I'm Alex, what are you looking at there? A roadrunner?"

"Hi, I'm Sarah, and this is John," the woman said, smiling. "Yep, it's a Greater Roadrunner, all right. They're pretty common around here."

"See how big it is? It's a large, brown cuckoo," John, clearly an enthusiast, started talking about other creatures we might see—bighorn sheep, chuckwallas, even a cactus wren nesting in a prickly pear. Sarah added facts about beavertail cacti and desert tortoises. They were a walking encyclopedia of desert knowledge, and even Alex seemed impressed.

"Will we see more animals?" a little girl asked.

"Absolutely!" Sarah said, bending down to her level. "What's your name? We can walk together and keep a lookout."

"Sofia."

The girl's parents, a friendly looking couple, smiled and introduced themselves as Marco and Isabella. Their daughter, Sofia, was already skipping ahead with Sarah, eager to spot more desert creatures.

The trail wound through a natural bowl formed by massive granite boulders. John pointed out the different rock formations, explaining how millions of years of erosion shaped them. "It's a delicate ecosystem," Sarah added. "We need to be careful not to disturb it."

I lost track of the nature talk as I looked around the trail. *Keep your eyes peeled, Mitch. Pay attention.* I noticed a man hiking alone a ways behind us. He hadn't joined any of the other groups, and his eyes seemed to linger on our little party a little too long. Okay, weird. Surely, a hiker was nothing to worry about, but I couldn't shake the feeling it was something else.

"Hey, Mitch, you coming?" Ben's voice pulled me back.

I quickly caught up to them. *Don't let them see you sweat, Mitch. Keep it together.*

* * *

Alex veered off the trail and scrambled up a steep rock face. "Hurry up, guys!" he called. "The view is awesome!"

Just looking at the massive boulders made my palms sweat. "I think I'll stay back and take some pictures," I said, trying to sound casual.

Ben pulled out his map. "This route cuts through to the main trail. Otherwise, we're looking at adding more miles to our hike. We might not get back before late."

I glanced at the setting sun, then back at the rock.

"Just do it, Mitch! Don't be a pussy!" Alex shouted from above.

Okay, I couldn't let my fears hold me back.

Taking a deep breath, I started to climb. Each step felt precarious, the boulders rough and rugged. My heart pounded, a drumbeat of fear urging me to turn back. But I kept going, one step at a time, refusing to look down. When I finally reached the top, the view was indeed breathtaking. *I did, I really did!*

Alex was already snapping pictures. "See, you made it! Told you it was worth it."

Ben slapped me on the back. "Good job, Mitch. Proud of you for facing your fear."

I felt my heart rate slow down, and a surprising surge of pride replaced my usual nerves.

As we made our way across and back down, carefully navigating the rocky path, Sofia tripped and let out a cry, her ankle twisted at an awkward angle.

Ben was at her side in an instant, his first-aid kit already open. He helped stabilize her ankle while expertly wrapping it with medical tape.

"Just a minor bump," he reassured Sofia and her worried parents. "But a good reminder. Even on easy trails, we need to watch our step." Ben looked at me and Alex, a serious expression on his face. "Always be aware of your surroundings and look out for each other. It's what Scouts do, right?"

With Sofia's ankle wrapped, we headed back to the campground.

As we emerged from the trail, a park ranger, his face weathered and his uniform crisp, approached us. He glanced at our group and then his eyes scanned Sofia's ankle and our packs. "Everything okay here?" he asked.

"Only a minor twist," Ben assured him. "She's tough."

The ranger nodded. "Just making sure there are no unauthorized campers and everything is in order."

"Our tents are registered for Hidden Valley," Ben replied.

"Great, and a heads-up, folks ... the weather can change quickly out here. We're expecting some heavy rain later this week, so be careful of flash floods." His eyes met mine. "And always stick together. It's easy to get lost among these rock formations."

As the ranger walked away, I asked, trying to sound like it wasn't a big deal, "Did anyone else notice the weirdo with shorts and knee sox who was following us earlier?" *I can't let my guard down.*

Alex, who had been scanning the area with his ridiculously oversized binoculars, lowered them and nudged Ben with his elbow. "Dude, you'd think we were in a spy movie, not a nature hike. Relax, Mitch. Maybe he was just admiring your awesome hat."

He's so dismissive, but I can't just let it go.

"Still, it's a bit strange," I persisted. He was definitely watching us, I thought. "I know I'm probably being paranoid, but something about the guy just looked ... *weird*." I needed to trust my gut, despite what Alex thought.

Ben, sensing my concern, gently placed his hand on my shoulder, his touch reassuring and supportive. "Don't worry, Mitch." His voice was calm, but I could see his eyes scanning the area, taking in everything, assessing the situation. He was always so good. Then, he turned to the group, his tone shifting to a more upbeat one. "How about dinner at the campsite in an hour? We can share some stories and watch the stars come out. It'll be a good way to unwind."

"Yeah, sounds good," I said, making an effort to sound confident.

* * *

Later that evening, the aroma of camp cooking filled the air, a comforting blend of savory spices and sizzling ingredients from our camping stoves. We gathered around the picnic table, our faces lit by the soft glow of lanterns. It felt good to be surrounded by friends, both old and new. The campground was filled with laughter and stories, creating a warm atmosphere.

After dinner, the campground transformed into a stargazing spot.

"Today was quite an adventure, wasn't it?" Ben remarked. "And we've only just begun."

Sarah shared stories of their past hikes in Joshua Tree. John chimed in with his own, entertaining our group.

I was always more comfortable observing than participating. Turning to John, I said, "As a seasoned climber, what's the most important advice you'd give to someone new to rock climbing?" The question wasn't entirely out of curiosity. The climb earlier had stirred a familiar fear.

Marco offered a reassuring smile. "What starts as an easy hike can become challenging. Always respect nature and be prepared, and " he paused, then continued, "make sure you're using the right gear—good shoes, a harness, and a helmet. Always double-check your knots and your partner's setup. And most importantly, trust your instincts. If something doesn't feel right, it's okay to back off."

His words offered little comfort. I turned to Laura, hoping to glean some wisdom about the desert flora. "Could you tell me about some of the local plants?" I asked. "I've heard some can be quite ... unforgiving."

Laura, a botanist, was happy to share her knowledge. "Oh, definitely. Take the cholla cactus, for instance. Its spines are a nightmare to remove." She paused, eyes narrowing slightly as she thought of another plant. "And then there's the datura. That one's particularly dangerous because it can cause a wide range of symptoms—delirium, hallucinations, even death in extreme cases."

Ben listened intently to Laura. "So, it's not just the wildlife we have to worry about, but also the plants. Good to know."

"This is all so overwhelming. It's like we're in a real-life survival game and one wrong move can cost us," I mumbled, adjusting my glasses, and unconsciously reaching to the pocket where I kept the crumpled page from the bus. *Trust no one, not even plants.* "I think I'm going to add a plant guide to my backpack," I said, "just to be safe. It's always better to be prepared." I decided to ask Laura more about the datura plant. "Are there any other plants we should be cautious of?"

Laura continued, "It's important to be cautious, but also remember the desert is full of wonder. These plants have adapted to survive in this harsh environment, and it's truly amazing."

As the conversation flowed, Alex, with his normal enthusiasm, began sharing his vision of a luxury camping experience in Joshua Tree.

"Imagine," he began, "waking up to this view but with all the comforts of a five-star hotel." He pointed toward the vast expanse of the desert. "Luxury tents with plush bedding, gourmet meals prepared by a private chef, guided tours of the park, and personalized spa treatments under the stars." He paused, letting the image sink in. "We could call it *Desert Oasis* or *Luxury Under the Stars*. It would be an experience unlike any other, blending the raw beauty of nature with the luxury and comfort of a high-end resort."

"Alex, this is a national park, a sacred land that needs to be protected from development," Ben said. "The beauty of camping here is to appreciate nature as it is, not to transform it into a fancy resort."

Sarah added, nodding in solidarity, "I agree with Ben. The charm of Joshua Tree lies in its raw, untouched beauty. Introducing luxury camping could disrupt the delicate balance of this ecosystem."

Sofia, who was filled with energy despite her earlier fall, exclaimed, "I can't wait to see more animals!"

Sarah reassured her, "I'm sure we will. The desert comes alive in the most unexpected ways."

The mention of animals, however, made my thoughts drift back to the unsettling image of the lone hiker I had seen earlier. "Did anyone else notice the hiker who was following us earlier?"

The group seemed to ignore my question as if they dismissed it as nothing to worry about. The stars seemed to grow brighter, creating a breathtaking display. Even Alex, who usually focused on the next adventure, was captivated by the beauty of the night sky. As I looked at my friends, I felt grateful for this moment, for their easy laughter and companionship. Marco and Isabella, Sofia's parents, shared their love for family and the outdoors, emphasizing the importance of creating memories and teaching Sofia about nature. Ben talked about his family in Oregon. It was comforting to hear them, to feel connected in this wide-open space. But even with the sounds of their voices, my mind kept drifting back to the dangers of the desert, the poisonous plants, the dangerous animals, and that stranger.

Chapter 6

Ben

*M*onday, *December 16—Day two, Hidden Valley Campground, Joshua Tree.*

The smell of freshly brewed coffee led us toward a campsite among the Joshua trees. Mitch and Alex followed close behind, drawn in by the aroma.

"Morning to ya, fellas, isn't it a grand day?" an older man greeted, putting down his newspaper, his voice as warm as the coffee he sipped. "Name's Sam, and this is my best friend, Rusty. Care to join me for a cup of joe?"

"Morning, Sam," I said, settling on a nearby rock. Rusty, a handsome golden retriever, nudged my hand with his wet nose, demanding attention. "Good boy," I said, giving him a scratch behind the ears. "Say, are dogs allowed in the park? I always thought—"

Sam chuckled. "Ah, Rusty's more than just a pet, he is," he said, giving the dog an affectionate pat, "he's my partner in crime, he is." He winked. "But we gotta play by the rules. Dogs are welcome, but only in designated areas, and always on a leash, the rangers aren't fooling around."

Alex, already restless, leaned forward, "Hey, Sam, you got the sports page? Gotta keep up with my teams, you know?"

Sam, holding his mug, gestured to the newspaper. "Help yourself, son. My ranger buddy brings one most days, a good lad, he is, always looking out for an old man."

Alex quickly flipped to the sports section. "Damn! The Cowboys lost again!"

I sipped my coffee, but then noticed something on the front page. "Hold up, Alex ... let me see." My eyes scanned the headline. ROCK CLIMBER SOUGHT IN CONNECTION WITH MISSING PERSONS CASES.

"Pretty creepy, right?" Alex looked at me. "Sounds like something out of a movie."

"This is no joke, Alex. It says here the article details a series of disappearances in a few cities nearby. Each case involved a wealthy woman who vanished without a trace."

Mitch leaned forward, peering over my shoulder. "Lots of strange and dangerous people out there." He adjusted his glasses, and added, "And some might have wilderness skills, making them even more difficult to track down."

My detective instincts kicked in as I scanned the article. The details were chilling. "There's an investigative profile of someone who can be very persuasive, able to gain trust easily, a manipulator, using them for his own gain, and to top it off, comfortable in the outdoors."

Sam nodded slowly, his earlier smile disappearing completely, his earlier tone replaced with a tone of caution. "Just be careful, son. The desert can be a tricky place." He paused, then added, thoughtful, "And some folks can be even more dangerous than the landscape itself."

"So, Sam," Alex said, changing the subject and breaking the tension, "how long have you been hanging out here?"

Sam chuckled, his tone instantly shifting back to a friendly campground host. "Oh, I've been here for a good while now, lads. Seven decades and a bit. Seen folks come and go, you know. But this park," he said, his gaze sweeping over the desert, "it's got a hold on me, that's the truth of it."

"Seventy years?" I asked, surprised.

"Ah, that's right, son, and a few more to boot," Sam chuckled, his eyes filled with fond memories. "I've been camping here since the sixties, when it was just a national monument, not this grand park ye see today."

"What brought you here in the first place?"

He leaned back a bit. "First as a wee lad, with me mum and da, then a youth Scout, I was, always drawn to this place, then as a veteran, seeking peace, and now, as a long-term camper, I've come to know every nook and cranny of this place, it's been a part of me life, I suppose."

He glanced at Rusty, who thumped his tail against the ground. "After serving overseas, I just couldn't get enough of being outdoors. It felt like coming home."

"When did you serve?" Alex asked, curious. "My dad served as a pilot in the Vietnam War."

"Korea," he said. "A long time ago. I needed a place to clear my head. My family and I would pack up "Woodie," our old station wagon, bring our dog, and head out here. The peace was just what we needed."

It made sense. He was a man who had seen things, who'd found peace here.

"Sounds wonderful. What was it like back then?"

"It was a different world. Fewer people, more open space. We'd set up camp, cook over an open fire, and watch the stars. The nights were so dark, you could see the Milky Way stretching across the sky."

"How often do you and Rusty camp out here?"

He reached into his pocket and pulled out a worn leather wallet, extracting a card. "I get a great deal with my annual pass," he said, handing it to me. "Active-duty military and their dependents can get a free annual pass to Joshua Tree and lots of other national parks. These days, there are rules, though. For long-term visitors like me, the park has a camping limit each year." He paused, as if considering whether to share more. "Campsites left vacant for twenty-four hours will be treated as abandoned. And they're strict about campfires."

He didn't need to say more. We were all too aware of the delicate balance of this ecosystem, of the responsibility we had to protect it.

Sam looked at us, a serious expression on his face. "It's important to respect these rules. They're here to protect both us and the park."

I nodded. "So, what else can you tell us about Joshua Tree, Sam?"

Sam smiled. "This park, it's more than just rocks and bushes. It's a place of stories, of secrets." He paused, drawing us in. "I've seen a lot in my seventy years here, met all kinds of folks."

"Speaking of folks," I said, "you must have met quite a few interesting people in your time. Any unique encounters you want to share?"

Sam chuckled. "Well, there was this one time, a young ranger, fresh outta training, got himself lost during his first week on the job. Poor fella was wanderin' around near Skull

Rock, scared outta his wits. Rusty and I found him, shivering and mumbling about seeing ghosts."

Alex perked up. "Ghosts? At Skull Rock? Is it really a thing?"

Sam leaned back. "Ah, Skull Rock. Now that's a story. You see, it wasn't always called that. Just another pile of rocks, really. But then folks started noticing how it kinda looked like, well, a skull. Word got around, and the name stuck." He paused. "But the real stories, the spooky ones, those came later. People whispering about strange lights, weird noises, even shadows movin' around at night. Now, I've spent more nights under these stars than I can count, and I ain't never seen nothin' out of the ordinary. But ..." He shrugged. "The desert has a way of playin' tricks on ya. Especially when the moon's full and the coyotes are howlin'." He chuckled again. "So, is there any truth to the rumors? Who knows? But Skull Rock sure does make for a good campground story, doesn't it?"

"Sam," Mitch began, "I brought my portable telescope. I've heard the night sky here is incredible. Any tips or favorite spots?"

"Ah, you're a stargazer too? This place is heaven for gazers because of the minimal light pollution. On a clear night, the Milky Way stretches across the whole sky." He pointed toward the east. "Over there, you'll get a good view of Orion this time of year. I'll be around tonight. Happy to point out a few constellations for ya. Rusty and I, we know 'em all."

Alex was getting restless. "Have you done much exploring in the deeper parts of the park? Those canyons and abandoned mines sound fascinating."

"Used to," he said, patting Rusty's head. "Back when I was a bit younger. Now, I stick mostly to the trails and familiar spots. But I've seen my share, that's for sure."

Mitch leaned forward. "Must've seen some desperate situations too, I imagine. People getting lost, injured ..."

Sam nodded. "The desert can be unforgiving. But it's also a place of resilience, of finding strength you didn't know you had. I've seen folks come out here broken and lost, and somehow, the desert helps them find their way back. It's a humbling experience, this place."

"Thanks for sharing your wisdom and stories," I said, rising to my feet. "We're ready for some adventure now. What do you recommend near Hidden Valley for us to get started?"

"You should check out the Barker Dam Trail and Keys Ranch. Both are great hikes with a lot of history and scenery. A nice warm-up."

"Sounds great!" Mitch said. "Can you tell us more?"

"Sure thing," Sam said, leaning back in his chair. "Barker Dam is an easy one-mile loop. You'll wander through some iconic, massive granite boulders, see plenty of Joshua trees, and pass by the dam itself. It was originally built by cattlemen back in the nineteen hundreds and later raised by a rancher in the forties. It's a great spot for wildlife viewing, especially after a good rain when the reservoir fills up."

"That sounds amazing," I said. "What about Keys Ranch?"

"It's more of a walking tour. Takes you through the old homestead of William Keys—the same fella who worked on the dam. Takes about ninety minutes, I believe. You'll see old buildings and mining equipment and learn a lot about what life was like for early settlers in this area. It's like a window into the past."

"Wow, both sound incredible," I said. "Thanks for the tips, Sam. We're ready for some adventure now."

"Enjoy your day, boys," Sam said. "And remember, the desert is full of surprises. Keep your eyes open, and you might just discover something extraordinary."

* * *

"Barker Dam first, then Keys Ranch," I announced, checking the map. "Sam said they're both nearby."

"Sounds like a plan," Mitch said, looking at the towering rock formations surrounding us. "Those boulders are incredible. It's amazing to think they were formed millions of years ago."

Alex, however, was already bored. "Yeah, yeah, old rocks. Can we get a move on? I'm ready for some action. Maybe we can find a good spot for bouldering after this?"

"Patience, Alex. We've got a whole week for adventure. Let's soak up a little history first," I said.

The Barker Dam Trail was worth it. We wandered through a grove of Joshua trees. The air was still and quiet, broken only by the crunch of our boots on the sandy path.

"Imagine living out here a hundred years ago," I said as we reached the dam. "No electricity, no running water, just the desert."

"Sounds pretty rough," Alex replied, scanning the nearby boulders for climbing potential.

"But also kind of peaceful," Mitch added. "No distractions, just the stars and the silence."

I knew he was picturing himself out here, under the vast night sky, his telescope pointed toward the heavens.

We wandered through William Keys's old homestead, imagining the early settlers hauling water, growing food, and carving out a life here.

"This Keys guy was tough," Alex admitted.

As we walked back toward the campground, our conversation turned to the stories Sam had shared.

"Do you think those ghost stories are true?" I asked.

"Who knows?" Mitch shrugged. "But there's definitely something ... mysterious about this place. I can feel it."

"Boo! It's a ghost!" Alex shouted, jumping out from behind a Joshua tree and giving Mitch a playful shove.

Mitch yelped, then laughed, shoving Alex back. "Very funny, Ace."

* * *

When we returned from our hike, tired but invigorated, we found Sam still holding court at his campsite, a cheerful, yellow umbrella casting a patch of shade over a small gathering. Rusty greeted us with a wag of his tail, his golden fur matching the late-afternoon sun.

Sam was in his element, spinning tails for a captivated audience, two pitchers of lemonade sitting precariously on a small camping table beside him. Sarah and John were perched on folding chairs. Sofia, her ankle now carefully wrapped, was sketching in a notebook in deep concentration. Her parents, Marco and Sofia, looked at us with warm smiles.

"Back so soon?" Sam asked. "I hope the desert treated you well."

I gratefully poured a cup of lemonade from a pitcher, the tart, icy drink a welcome relief after our hike. I quickly spit it out, the drink was more vodka than lemonade!

Sam chuckled, "Two options for ya, one for the kiddies and that's for adults."

"Just surprised me," I responded.

Alex, always ready for action, "I'll drink what he's having," and Sam poured him a cup.

"It was amazing, Sam," I said, settling on a nearby rock. "Barker Dam was fascinating, and Keys Ranch. Wow, talk about a glimpse into the past! You weren't kidding about the history lesson."

"We saw some lizards, a jackrabbit, and even a few quail," Mitch added. "This place is filled with wildlife."

"Yeah, but where are the real adventures?" Alex complained. "All the history stuff is cool and all, but I'm ready for some action! You guys see any good spots for bouldering?"

John, overhearing Alex's complaint, chuckled. "Sarah and I scrambled up some boulders this afternoon. Found a great spot near the Hall of Horrors. Incredible rock formations, challenging climbs. You'd love it."

Alex's eyes lit up. "Bouldering near the Hall of Horrors? Sounds intense! I'm in. You guys up for it tomorrow?"

"We'll see," I said, looking at Mitch. Alex's enthusiasm for adrenaline-pumping activities was always a force to be reckoned with.

"Sofia's ankle is doing much better," Isabella said. "We took it easy today, just a scenic drive around the park. But tomorrow, she's determined to spot a desert tortoise."

"They're pretty elusive," Sam warned, a hint of mystery in his voice. "But keep your eyes peeled, and you might just get lucky."

As the conversation flowed, the sun continued its descent, casting shadows across the campground. The air cooled, and a gentle breeze rustled through the Joshua trees.

* * *

"Who's hungry for some Texas-style barbecue?" Alex announced, his voice booming across the campsite. "I brought all the fixin's in my cooler. Y'all better come hungry!"

"We can use my grill," I said, gesturing toward my camper van. "It's propane, so no worries about the fire restrictions."

Alex took charge of the grill with gusto, expertly flipping burgers and turning sausages. Soon, the delicious aroma of barbecue smoke filled the air, mixing with the earthy aroma of the desert.

As the sky darkened with vibrant colors of orange, pink, and violet, Alex served up his Texas feast. Plates piled high with juicy brisket, smoky pulled pork, and spicy sausage were passed around the circle of eager campers. Sides of creamy coleslaw, tangy baked beans, and crispy potato salad completed the spread.

"Wow, Alex, this is incredible!" Sarah exclaimed, amazed at the sheer abundance of food. "Where did you even fit all this in your cooler?"

"Yeah, man," John added, digging into a heaping plate of brisket, "this is some serious barbecue! You brought half of Texas with you!"

A chorus of applause rippled through the group. Even Sam, who'd seen his fair share of camp meals over the years, looked impressed.

"Son, I haven't feasted this well in years!" he declared, a hearty laugh rumbling in his chest. "You must have a magic cooler."

Alex grinned. "Let's just say, I have my ways. Ordered a delivery to the Airbnb and snuck it all into the van before anyone noticed," Alex smiled. "It ain't your average icebox, that's for sure. That bad boy is practically a portable, climate-controlled food center, perfect for a Texas-sized feast, even in the middle of the desert."

"Sneaky." I chuckled, shaking my head. "It was worth it. This is delicious."

As we ate, savoring the smoky flavors and satisfied sighs and full stomachs stuffed with the delicious dinner, the sun slipped below the horizon, and the first stars began to appear in the darkening sky.

Sam cleared his throat, a shadow of a story on his face. And as he began to speak, the mood shifted, and the carefree atmosphere of the barbecue faded into the growing darkness.

"Let's start with the history of this place," Sam said. "Back in the eighteen hundreds, this area was filled with gold miners. They came here lured by the promise of wealth, but what they found was a harsh, unforgiving land. Disputes over claims were common, and more often than not, they were settled with gunfights. Law and order were concepts yet to reach this part of the world."

We listened in silence, the image of gun-toting miners and lawless chaos painting a stark contrast to the peaceful desert around us.

Sam described the Cholla Cactus Garden, a surreal landscape filled with spiky cholla cacti, where visitors reported strange feelings and eerie encounters. He spoke of the Lost

Horse Mine, where *pickaxe sounds,* and *shadowy ghosts* were said to haunt the area.

Sam's voice dropped to a whisper when he told us about unexplained disappearances within the park. The story of the McStay family, whose bodies were discovered years after they had been buried, sent a chill down our spines. He told us a story about the many UFO sightings.

"Ah, the stories this desert could tell, if only the rocks could talk," Sam continued, a mischievous glint in his eye, as if sharing a forbidden secret. "Over the years, ya see, more than a few poor souls have been found scattered about, buried in these very grounds." He leans in, "I'm tellin' ya, they've dug up bodies here, within these park boundaries, and it's no tale for the faint of heart." He pauses, letting the words settle, swirling the remaining liquid in his mug, as if seeing the images before him.

Sam continued with a low tone, "There was one, just a scatterin' of bones in the rocks, like they'd been tossed about by some angry spirit. Another ... ah, partially buried near the pass, still clutchin' a tarnished locket in its grasp, a lost love or a forgotten secret perhaps." He draws the words out, savouring the drama, his words becoming more pronounced as he gets lost in the tale. "It's enough to make ya wonder about the secrets this old desert keeps, isn't it?"

A chill swept over us as the desert night closed in. The friendly old man with his gentle dog suddenly seemed more dangerous as he disclosed the hidden secrets of the desert.

"Bodies don't bury themselves," Sam said. "Some say desert ghosts wander here ... lost souls, restless spirits ... those who met their end under this unforgiving sky."

He told us about the Lost Ship of the Desert, a Spanish galleon rumored to be buried beneath the sand, its ghostly crew still searching for their lost treasure. A sudden gust of wind rattled the nearby Joshua trees, their branches scraping against each other like skeletal fingers, and Sofia let out a little gasp. Isabella pulled her close, whispering in her ear.

Sam, unfazed, continued. "Then there's the tale of the *Yucca Man*—a creature said to roam the canyons, half-man, half-beast, his mournful cries screaming through the night."

Alex laughed. "Now that's a story I'd like to hear more about!"

Sam told us about unexplained lights in the sky, strange shadows in the rocks, and the chilling discovery of bodies, their secrets buried with them.

But the mood sobered as Sam began his final story. "This desert, as beautiful as it is, holds many secrets. Over the years, there have been disappearances, mysteries, even murders. In the early nineteen hundreds, it was a lawless place where miners killed each other over claims. In the sixties, Charles Manson and his followers left a dark stain on this land. And not much later, Gram Parsons's buddies hauled his body and casket out to Joshua Tree and set it all on fire. Death seems drawn to this desert, and bodies are constantly being dug up here."

Suddenly, a bloodcurdling scream ripped through the stillness of the night. Sofia, her eyes wide with terror, buried her face in her mother's arms. Even Rusty, usually unflappable, let out a low growl, his fur bristling.

"Easy there, folks," Sam said, chuckling, his voice calm. "Just a coyote out for a midnight snack. Nothin' to be afraid of. It's just the desert saying goodnight."

Chapter 7

Alex

Tuesday, December 17—Day three, The Hall of Horrors, Joshua Tree.

"Ready for the Hall of Horrors?" I asked, bouncing on the balls of my feet. I'd already packed up my gear—minimalist style, like Mitch. Unlike Ben, who had enough stuff in his van of his for a month-long expedition.

Mitch looked nervous. "I'm not so sure about all the rock scrambling."

"Don't worry," Ben said, "we'll be careful. Maybe we can split with the others. You can stay on the ground and take some awesome photos."

I grabbed an energy bar from my stash, high performance, of course, and scanned the campground. Sarah and John were already up, their gear neatly packed. Sofia was hobbling around with her parents.

"We're going to take it easy today," Marco said. "Give Sofia another day to rest her ankle."

Just as we were setting off with Sarah and John, a ranger approached us. His face was somber.

"Excuse me, everyone," the ranger said, his tone firm but calm, his face serious. "I need to inform you about a situation that requires your attention while you're in the park. We are currently searching for a person of interest who may be in this area. For your safety, please be aware of your surroundings and take necessary precautions."

"Do you have more details? Ben asked, his investigative instincts kicking in.

The ranger continued, "This person is of medium height, with short, dark hair, and has a tattoo on their arm. He escaped custody during transport, just in town, en route to arraignment. If you see anyone matching this description, or notice any suspicious behavior, please do not approach them. Instead, contact a park ranger or law enforcement immediately."

"Is he dangerous," Mitch asked.

The ranger replied, "Not necessarily. We ask that you be vigilant, and report anything suspicious. Park staff and law enforcement are working to keep the park safe for all visitors. So, stay vigilant, stick together, and enjoy this beautiful park."

* * *

The drive to Hall of Horrors was quick, the desert scenery whizzing past in a blur of Joshua trees and giant rocks. As Ben piloted the van, I thought about the ranger's warning. A person of interest? Hiding out in Joshua Tree? It sounded like something from a movie.

"You guys think we need to worry about that guy?" I asked, skeptical. "I mean, this park is huge. What are the odds we'd run into him? It's like something out of a bad action movie, and we've got front-row seats."

Mitch frowned, adjusting his glasses. "I don't know. The ranger seemed serious. And what about that newspaper article about the missing persons? Maybe that rock climber is using the desert to hide out, too?"

"Chill, Mitch," Alex said, grinning, though his eyes betrayed a flicker of nerves. "We'll be fine. Besides, it'll make a great story later, right?" He then added, "We just have to watch out for bobcats, mountain lions, escaped suspects, and kidnappers."

Ben, his hands steady on the steering wheel, glanced at Mitch, his expression serious. "I think we better take the ranger's warning seriously. It's better to be safe than sorry. We can still have fun, but let's just be extra vigilant, okay?" He paused, then added, "And keep an eye out for anything unusual." He was already assessing the situation, his mind likely working through different scenarios and possible escape routes.

Alex rolled his eyes, but deep down, he knew Ben was right, saying "Fine, *Mr. Responsible*. But if we spot him, I'm calling dibs on taking him down! Think of the bragging rights back home. I can just imagine the headlines: LOCAL HERO TAKES DOWN ESCAPED CRIMINAL IN JOSHUA TREE!"

Mitch shook his head, his anxiety growing with each passing moment, adding, "Or worse, he'll take us down."

* * *

As we pulled into the parking lot, my thoughts shifted from the escapee to the thrill of the Hall of Horrors.

"All right, everyone, let's get moving!" I shouted, jumping out of the van. The towering cliffs were calling my name. "All right, guys, I'm going to do some rock climbing."

Mitch looked at me with concern and disbelief. "Alex, do you even have any training or equipment for this?"

"How hard can it be? I've got plenty of confidence, and it's half the battle, right?"

Ben stepped in. "Alex, rock climbing isn't a game. It's serious business. Did you know rappelling causes the most accidents in the climbing world? It's tricky and dangerous, especially if you don't have the correct setup."

"Come on, how hard can it be? I see people do it all the time."

"And do you even have any gear?" Rock climbing shoes, harnesses, helmets?" Mitch asked.

"Well, no. But I can figure it out."

Ben's expression softened. "Alex, I know you're excited, but this isn't something you can just figure out on the fly. You need proper training and equipment. Why don't we get you signed up for a rappelling course taught by a professional rock-climbing guide? They provide all the necessary gear and teach you everything you need to know."

"But I just want to have some fun."

Ben placed his hand on my shoulder. "I get it. But fun shouldn't come at the expense of safety. Let's stick to the trails for now, and if you're really interested in climbing, we can look into taking a course together."

Mitch nodded. "Yeah. We don't want anything to happen to you. Let's enjoy the hike and maybe tackle climbing another time."

"All right, fine. But I'm holding you to a climbing course, Ben."

Ben smiled. "Deal. Now, let's get back to exploring."

* * *

Ben shared the trip plan with us as the rest of the group had arrived for the hike. "The Hall of Horrors loop trail is less than a mile with virtually no elevation change. It's perfect for a quick adventure."

We started, weaving through the iconic Joshua trees dotting the landscape. The first large rock formation loomed ahead, but Ben pointed out it wasn't where the slots were.

"Around the backside of this rock pile, you'll see a smaller group of boulders," Ben explained. "That's where the entrance to the Hall of Horrors is located."

As we approached the smaller boulders, Ben continued. "The Hall of Horrors is actually two slot canyons, side by side and separated by tall, vertically positioned boulders. The right entrance is the wider of the two, while the left slot is much narrower."

Mitch looked apprehensive. "What about the slot canyons? I've heard they can be pretty tight."

"Yeah, they can be." Ben nodded. "If you have any issues with tight spaces, the slot canyons might not be for you."

"Which one should we start with?" I asked, eager to get going.

"I'd recommend starting with the right slot," Ben said. "It's more open, about four feet in width from wall to wall. If you feel claustrophobic there, the second slot will be a much tighter squeeze."

We reached the entrance to the right slot, and I peered down the long, flat, sandy path. "This looks awesome."

I squeezed against the rock and shouted out as I confidently climbed through. My muscles strained against the weight of my body, my hands gripping the rough, weather-beaten rocks. I moved with the grace of a seasoned athlete, my every motion and muscle prepared after years of physical training.

"Watch and learn, folks!" I called out.

My words were met with laughter and cheers from a group of rock climbers in the distance. Among them were four men and a woman.

"Hey, dude!" one called out. "Be careful, you don't have the proper equipment."

Another person said, "Don't forget to save some energy for the rest of us!"

I laughed. "Don't worry. I'll leave some rocks for you."

As I continued to climb, I found myself in a tight spot between two massive boulders. I tried to squeeze through but got stuck. "Well, this sucks," I muttered to myself, struggling to get free.

The rock-climber group burst into laughter.

"Need a hand, Alex?" Mitch called out.

With Mitch's help and a final tug, I managed to free myself. "All part of the adventure," I said, dusting myself off.

Next, I scrambled up the boulders and made my way into the slot canyon. "Come on, Mitch! It's not so high," I called out as I looked at the towering rock.

Mitch shook his head. "I don't know, Alex. It looks pretty steep."

At this point, John intervened, "It sounds like you might want to avoid the slot canyons," John said to Mitch. "Why don't we take that other route instead?"

"Yeah," Sarah added, "we climbed yesterday and don't have to go into the slot canyons today."

"But the ranger said we should stick together," Ben reminded us.

I sighed. "Fine. Let's split into two groups then. Those who want to climb can come with me. The rest can stay on the ground."

Mitch was relieved. "Sounds like a good plan. I can keep an eye on you guys and take some pictures."

"Hey, over there," I said, pointing to the group of rock climbers scaling the rugged walls. "I'm going to join y'all."

Ben shook his head. "Be careful, Alex. I better join you."

* * *

Ben and I left Mitch and the others behind and made our way to the group of rock climbers. They were a rugged bunch, their weathered faces and calloused hands evidence of years spent conquering these granite giants. A tall guy with a sun-bleached cap and thick beard appeared to be their leader.

"Hey!" I called out. "I bet I can do the climb you're doing. The one with the ropes and stuff."

"You think so?"

"I know so. How about a quick lesson for five hundred bucks?" I pulled out my wallet, already peeling off a few bills.

The climbers exchanged skeptical looks, then laughed.

"Okay, you're on, city boy," the leader said. "You looking to learn some climbing?"

"Absolutely," I replied, puffing out my chest. "What's the best, most badass climb around here?"

He took the bills and introduced himself as Jake. "Well, if you're up for a challenge, we've got some classic routes here at the Hall of Horrors. Ever heard of Exorcist? It's one of the best."

"Sounds perfect." I nodded.

Jake raised an eyebrow, probably questioning my sanity, but didn't argue. "All right, follow me. But remember, this isn't a playground. Respect the rock and know your limits."

As we made our way to the base of the climb, Jake pointed out a few other routes, his voice laced with a hint of pride. "There's Lazy Day, a good warm-up climb. And if you're feeling adventurous, Jane's Addiction is a real test of skill."

We reached the base of Exorcist, and I took a deep breath, the crisp desert air filling my lungs. "Watch and learn, folks," I shouted. "This city slicker's about to show you how it's done."

"Oh, yeah?" someone replied. "We'll see about that."

"You know, back in college, I played football in Texas," I said. "Climbing this rock is nothing compared to facing a blitzing defense."

As I started the climb, I was confident and felt the exhilaration. This was my element, my chance to shine. I moved with the grace and precision of a seasoned climber. I pushed myself harder than necessary, taking risks that made the others uneasy.

Halfway up the rock face, I paused to catch my breath. I looked down at the group below and shouted, "Come on, guys! Keep up! This isn't a walk in the park!"

One of the climbers, a young woman, called back, "Alex, slow down! This isn't a race. We need to be careful."

"Careful is for the weak. If you want to achieve greatness, you have to take risks."

Ben was standing below me next to her. "Alex, listen to her."

I rolled my eyes and continued climbing, my pace more measured.

As we neared the summit, Ben called out from below, "Alex, please be careful. You have nothing to prove."

"Don't worry, I've got this," I replied.

As we reached the summit, I stood triumphantly, looking out over the vast desert landscape. "See? Told you I could do it," I said, a triumphant grin on my face.

"You did great, Alex. But remember, it's not just about reaching the top. It's about making sure everyone gets down safely."

As I started to climb back down, I reached a precarious point on the rocks and noticed a figure out of the corner of my eye—someone was watching me in the distance. I lost focus, just for a moment, the newspaper headline flashing in my mind: ROCK CLIMBER SOUGHT, the ranger's warning about the escaped person of interest.

Was this guy watching us? Or was it just another climber? The desert suddenly felt different, not just a place for a hike, but a place where danger could be lurking behind any rock or Joshua tree. Before I could think, I felt a sudden jolt. My foot slipped and I lost balance. Panic surged through me, but the experienced climbers were quick to act. I felt the sudden, jarring tug of the backup ropes, the taught lines digging into my harness as they caught me mid-fall. The world spun for a moment as I dangled, suspended between the sky and the unforgiving rock face. Slowly, carefully, they began to lower me, the ropes swinging as they eased me back to the ground.

"Whoa, city boy, you okay up there?" one of the climbers yelled..

"As I was lowered, I could hear a mix of heckles and congratulations from the group.

"Nice save!" someone shouted.

"Looks like you almost took a dirt nap there, buddy!" another climber joked.

When my feet finally touched the ground, I stumbled to the side of the rock face, out of view of the other climbers for a minute, catching my breath and trying to regain my composure. My heart was still pounding in my chest, and my legs were shaking from the adrenaline. I could feel the blood rushing in my ears.

I walked back to where Ben was standing. When he saw me, he rushed over, a look of relief on his face. I pulled him into a hug. "Dude," I said, my voice still a bit shaky, "that was awesome!"

"Close call, city boy." Jake clapped me on the back. "Maybe stick to the easier climb next time."

I laughed, brushing the dust. "Nah, where's the fun?"

* * *

Afterward, one of the climbers approached me with a folded map. He handed it to me with a grin and said, "you're going to love this. This is the Chasm of Doom," he said, his voice carrying a hint of danger and adventure. "It's a hidden gem, known only to a few, a place where you first climb up top for incredible views and then descend into a hidden chasm with narrow passages and steep drops. The route is challenging, but if you're up for it, it could be your next great adventure." He paused, studying my reaction. "Not many dare to take it on, but those who do never forget the experience. Just don't get stuck in the Coffin."

My eyes lit up as I unfolded the map, tracing the route with my finger. The Chasm of Doom sounded like the kind of challenge I craved. "Thanks! I'll definitely check it out."

The climbers gathered around, offering tips and sharing their own experiences. "You'll need to be prepared," one of them advised. "Make sure you have the right gear and a reliable partner. It's not a place to go alone."

Another climber added. "The views from the top are breathtaking, but the chambers and passageways inside the chasm is what makes it truly special."

Ben walked to me and looked at the map with a mix of curiosity and concern. "What's that about, Alex?"

I nodded, my mind already made up. "Another interesting adventure. A real test of my skills." The climbers' encouragement and the mystery of the hidden route only fueled my determination.

"All right," Ben said, a smile on his face. "Just promise you'll be careful."

I grinned, feeling a surge of adrenaline. "You got it. This is going to be epic."

* * *

As Ben and I made our way back to the rest of the group, we were greeted with a mix of relief and anger. Mitch was the first to approach, his face flushed with worry and frustration.

"Alex, what were you thinking?" Mitch demanded, his voice trembling. "We saw you fall off the boulder. We couldn't see if you were hurt. Do you have any idea how scared we were?"

I raised my hands in a placating gesture, trying to calm him. "I'm fine. The climbers had everything under control. It must have looked worse from where you were standing."

Laura rushed over, her face worried. "Oh my gosh, Alex," she said. "We thought something terrible had happened."

John added. "That was a close call, Alex." He paused and looked at the group of rock climbers in the distance.

I gave them a reassuring smile. "I'm okay, really. Just a little shaken up. The climbers were prepared and acted quickly."

Ben tried to diffuse the tension. "It was a close call, but Alex handled it well. We didn't realize it looked so bad from your angle."

Mitch's frustration didn't let up. "You need to be more careful, Alex. This isn't just about you. We all care about you, and we don't want anything to happen."

I nodded. "You're right. I'll be more careful."

As we regrouped, Mitch pulled out his camera and showed us some photos he'd taken. "I saw this rock climber guy out there alone. He looked suspicious, and with the person of interest on the loose ..."

I looked closely at the photos. The hiker's face was partially obscured, but there was something unsettling about him.

Ben shifted gears into detective mode, examining the photos. "The person of interest who escaped during transport is medium height, with short, dark hair and ... I cannot see clear enough to see anything else," Ben said.

"Do you think it could be the escapee?" John asked, his voice filled with anxiety.

Mitch nodded, his worry evident. "Yes, it's possible. We need to report this as suspicious activity."

Ben, Mitch, and the others huddled together, scrutinizing the images. The potential for danger had become real.

I found myself drifting from their concerns. The photos of the mysterious climber and the talk of the escaped person of interest seemed distant, almost unreal. My mind was elsewhere, fixated on the map I'd received earlier.

I pulled the map out of my pocket, unfolding it carefully. My friends' voices faded into the background as I studied it. The Chasm of Doom, the name alone sent a thrill through me. I traced the route with my finger, imagining the challenges and the adrenaline rush that awaited. Could I make it alone? The thought was tempting, a chance to prove myself again. I knew I should be paying attention to the potential danger, but the call for adventure was louder.

"Alex, are you listening?" Mitch's voice pulled me back.

I looked up, realizing everyone was staring at me. "Yeah, sorry. Just thinking about our next move."

Mitch's eyes narrowed, but he didn't press further. "Just stay focused, all right? We need to be careful."

"Got it." I nodded, slipping the map into my pocket.

Chapter 8

Ben

Wednesday, December 18—Day four, The Chasm of Doom, Joshua Tree.

Ugh, my back. The usual camping aches and pains. Can't beat the first cup of coffee, though. Especially out here. *Need to get the kettle going.* It was still pitch black, the desert air biting cold against my face as I unzipped the tent. *Man, I miss Jenny and the kids.* But this is good too. Time with the guys, away from it all. Just wish my sleeping pad was a little thicker.

I slipped out of my tent, careful not to wake the others. I fired up the Coleman stove and grabbed the French press and a bag of Noble Coffee's finest dark roast from my camping kit. *Just like home*, I thought with a smile. I carefully measured the coarse grounds, inhaling the rich aroma, almost like being back in Ashland at the cozy coffee shop.

I stretched my neck and shoulders waiting for the water to heat. With the water simmering on the stove, I poured it over the grounds, watching them bloom and release their fragrant oils. After a few minutes, and a slow press of the plunger, my perfect cup of coffee was ready to serve. I filled my mug, the steam warming my hands, and headed out for a hike, enjoying the quiet moments before the others woke up. This was my time, a stolen hour of peace before the day's adventures, just like my early mornings at home before the kids woke up. But here, under the big, blue desert sky, it felt different. I was grateful for this time with my friends, this escape from the everyday, even as a part of me ached for the familiar rhythms of my family back in Oregon.

The desert was beautiful in the early morning light, but I knew it was also dangerous. It'd be easy to get lost out here—or worse. Years of Scouting in the Rockies had taught me to never underestimate the wild. I scanned the landscape, taking in every detail and noting potential hazards. Old habits die hard, even on a casual stroll. The desert demanded respect, and I gave it, even on a simple walk. The cool air filled my lungs. The only sounds were my boots crunching on the ground and a bird calling in the distance. I felt responsible for my friends. I had the training and experience. I couldn't let them down.

As I walked, I thought about Jenny and the kids. Was she already up, getting the kids ready for school? I hoped they weren't too disappointed that I wasn't there to make their lunches. Guilt hit me, but I brushed it away.

I pulled out my phone and saw a new voicemail from Jenny. I must have missed her call last night because of the spotty coverage, but now I had just enough signal to listen. Her voice, tense but loving, filled the quiet desert air. "Hi Ben, we miss you. The house feels empty without you. The kids have been asking about you all day." There was a pause, followed by a soft sigh. "I know this trip is important to you, and I'm glad you're with your friends, but ... please be careful, okay? We need you home safe."

The next voice was my son's, booming with the energy of a seven-year-old. "Dad! Guess what? We learned about Joshua Tree in school today! They said there are all kinds of cool animals. Have you seen any tortoises? Oh, and watch out for tarantulas!" He ended the message with a giggle, his enthusiasm infectious even through the phone.

The last message was from my daughter. Her sweet and curious voice tugged at my heart. "Daddy, are you having fun? Are you camping under the stars? Did you see a roadrunner yet? They're so fast! Wish I could be there with you. I love you, Daddy. Come home soon."

As I listened, I breathed deeply and looked around. The air was crisp and carried the faint scent of sagebrush. The sky was painted with hues of pink and orange as the sun began to rise. The ground beneath my feet was a mix of coarse sand and scattered rocks, crunching softly with each step. In the distance, the massive rock formations of Joshua Tree rose into the sky, a constant reminder of nature's power. A gentle breeze rustled the sparse vegetation, and the occasional call of a distant bird broke the silence.

I thought about my family. I missed them more than words could express. I tried to call my wife back, to hear her voice again, but the call wouldn't go through. I had lost service. A sudden loneliness hit me, but I pushed it aside. I was here now, in this breathtaking desert, and I needed to enjoy the moment. My friends at the campground would be waking up soon, and I needed to get back.

As I made my way back to the campsite, I realized I had wandered further up the trail than I'd thought. Just as I was about to try calling my wife again, I noticed something on the ground I had missed earlier. It was a pair of Ray-Ban designer sunglasses, something Alex would own. I picked them up, thinking Alex must have dropped them on the trail.

* * *

As I neared the campsite, I saw Mitch already up and about, expertly flipping pancakes over the stove. The smell of coffee filled the air. But there was one face missing—Alex's.

"Ben! Where have you been?" Mitch shouted, relief in his voice. "I was starting to get worried." Mitch shook his head. "Well, I hope you're hungry. I have a delicious breakfast waiting for you and Alex."

"Have you seen Alex?" I asked, trying not to sound worried.

"I thought he was with you," Mitch replied, his smile fading.

"No, I haven't seen him since last night. I found this near the trail," I said, holding out the sunglasses. "I think they might be Alex's."

Mitch's eyes widened. "Those are Alex's sunglasses, all right. He never goes anywhere without them."

"Let's check his tent."

I peeked into his tent, a jumble of suitcases, clothes, and gear. My eyes landed on a scrap of paper lying on his pillow. Scribbled in Alex's handwriting were the words Chasm of Doom.

Mitch tried to call Alex, but his cell phone had no signal. He tried texting next, but there was no reply.

A knot in my stomach tightened, but years of Scouting kicked in. I took a deep breath, focusing on the task at hand.

"Yesterday, I overheard one of the rock climbers sharing a map with Alex. I'd forgotten about it until now. I got the feeling the Chasm of Doom isn't a place to be taken lightly," I said.

"What's the Chasm of Doom?" Mitch asked.

"I only overheard bits and pieces, but it sounds like a dangerous place," I replied. "They said not to go there alone."

"Not again," Mitch replied.

"We better go find him," I said. "Pack breakfast to go and grab your pack. We're going to the Chasm of Doom. Stay close and be prepared for anything. This might be a tough one."

* * *

As the gravity of the situation sank, I knew what we had to do. We needed a search party to find Alex. My wilderness first-aid training and years of outdoor experience took over. I took charge organizing the group and distributing supplies. "Mitch, grab the first-aid kit and some extra water. Sarah and John, can you help gather any climbing gear we might need? We have to be prepared for anything."

I took inventory of our supplies, dividing them among us to ensure everyone had a first-aid kit, plenty of water, and some food. I reminded everyone of the basic first-aid procedures we'd learned in Scouts and stressed the importance of sticking together so we don't get separated. Despite the challenges of the situation, I could sense trust in their eyes. I was ready for this leadership role.

We left our campsite, and I saw Sam and Rusty.

"So, you folks headed out, are ye?" Sam asked, gazing at our gear.

"Uh, yeah. Have you seen Alex?" I asked.

Sam leaned forward from his folding chair, showing concern. "Alex, ye say? No, haven't seen him today. Is everything all right, lads?"

"Alex seems to have taken a little detour," Mitch interrupted, his voice strained with concern. "We were just about to go looking for him."

Sam's eyebrows shot up. "A detour, is it now? Well, well. Where'd he wander off to?"

"Actually," I started, debating how much to share, "the Chasm of Doom, I think."

A look of understanding, mixed with a hint of amusement, flickered across Sam's face. "Ah, the Chasm, is it? sure, that's one way to start your morning! Don't you worry your heads, I know the place like the back o' me hand." He turned to his dog. "Rusty, looks like we're going on an adventure, so we do."

I explained the situation, the missing sunglasses, the cryptic note. Sam listened intently, his eyes closed in thought.

"The Chasm isn't a place to be trifled with, especially not alone." He knelt, smoothing the sand with his hand. "Let me show you."

With a few deft strokes, Sam sketched a rough drawing in the sand, his finger tracing the twisting paths and hidden passages of the Chasm. "It's a maze in there. Easy to get turned around, even for experienced hikers. There are tight squeezes, sudden drops, and some say ..." His eyes shined, "some say there are things lurking in the shadows, things that shouldn't be."

A cold sweat broke on my forehead. I had dismissed Sam's tales of the supernatural as harmless campground stories, but now, with Alex missing, they took on a new, unsettling significance.

"So, what exactly did Alex tell you about the Chasm?" Sam asked.

"Nothing. Took off before sunrise," Mitch snapped, shoving his water bottle into his backpack with unnecessary force.

"I overheard a rock climber yesterday telling him about a place that was a secret adventure in the desert," I said, "and he gave him a map."

Sam laughed. "Well, he's not wrong. It's a pretty amazing place, so it is. A bit of a squeeze in parts, mind you. Claustrophobia a no go in there. And mind the shadows, lads, they have a way of playing tricks on ya."

"The rock climber mentioned the route was challenging with narrow passages and steep drops," I said.

"And did he bring water and a flashlight?"

I shook my head. "Knowing Alex, probably not."

Sam rummaged through his gear. "Here," he said, handing me a canteen and headlamp. "Better safe than sorry. And trust me, you don't want to be caught in there without water, not in a place like that." Rusty barked once, as if to agree.

"We need to find him," I said. "We can't just leave him out there."

Sam nodded, his expression determined. "I'll come with you. Rusty and I know these trails better than anyone. We might be able to pick up his scent." Sam disappeared into his tent, emerging moments later with a worn backpack, Rusty's water bowl, and a flashlight. "Can't forget these," he said, securing the pack and filling the bottle from his water supply. He paused, looking at the sky. "The weather's turning. We best move fast." Sam hoisted his worn backpack onto his shoulders. "Let's go," he said, his voice steady despite the worry in his eyes. Rusty, sensing the urgency, trotted ahead, nose to the ground, sniffing at every rock and crevice.

I hesitated, remembering the park rules. "Sam, are dogs allowed on the trails?"

He looked me in the eyes. "Normally, no. But this is an emergency, so it is. There are dangers in this desert, as I've been tellin' ye all along, and sometimes the rules need to bend a bit to keep us safe."

We fell into step behind them, the old man and his dog leading the way, their pace slow but steady. The desert stretched out before us, the sky darkening in the distance.

"Stay close, and watch your step," I instructed, my voice repeating Sam's earlier warning. "This trail can be tricky."

As we followed Rusty and Sam, he gave us a crash course in Chasm of Doom survival. "The key is to stay calm, lads, and follow the path of least resistance, that's what I always say. Don't try to muscle your way through. And if you come to a tight spot, don't be afraid to backtrack and find another way around. There's always another path, if you're willin' to look for it. The entrance is a narrow crevice in the rocks called the Birth Canal," he said with a grin. "Don't worry, it's not as bad as it sounds Just take it slow, and remember to breathe, mind your footing, and listen to the rocks."

"Sounds like fun," I said.

"Oh, yes, it's an adventure, right enough. Just don't get trapped in the Coffin. It's a bit further in, and very tight so you must shimmy as it's very narrow every bit of the way,"

Sam added. Rusty let out a low growl, and Sam patted his head, "Aye, good boy, you know the place well."

I swallowed hard, took a deep breath, and counted to three, focusing on the search plan. Sam's casual approach was unsettling, and my worry for Alex grew stronger.

* * *

"All right, guys," Sam said. "So, the Chasm of Doom isn't exactly marked on the official maps. A local secret, you know? But don't worry, I've been through there enough times to guide you, though not recently. Once we get there, you'll need to scramble up some rocks."

"More rock scrambles?" Mitch asked.

Sam flashed a reassuring grin. "Don't worry, it's a good warm-up. Think of it this way: you're getting your climbing fix before you go underground. 'Cause, trust me, the Chasm itself? More squeezing than scaling. Now, the rock up there is grippy, which is good news. But, even so, always good practice to maintain those three points of contact, you know? Especially you, Ben." Sam clapped a hand on my shoulder. "Gotta protect those knees, right? Once we get there, it's easy to find. The first marker on the map is a picnic table. Then kind of a weird tree. Gnarled trunk, branches all twisted up like a pretzel."

I scanned the area, spotting a particularly contorted tree a short distance away. "Like that? Got it."

"Next, pass under a tree, and keep an eye out for a rock formation that looks like a giant window. You'll want to turn right there and start climbing."

"How steep are we talking, Sam?" Mitch asked.

"Steep enough to make things interesting," Sam replied with a wink. "But the granite's sticky in these parts. You boys got a good grip on those boots?"

"We're good," I confirmed.

"Excellent, excellent. Now, after the window, you'll come across another peculiar tree. This one's a juniper, all twisted up on itself. You'll want to scramble up the base. The view from there is pretty impressive. Once you're up there, you should have a clear view of me down here and a good chunk of the sky above. Look for a lone palm tree. The entrance to the Chasm of Doom is right behind it."

We continued, Sam and Rusty leading the way. But Rusty, that old nose of his had a mind of its own, was more interested in the scents of the desert than the map. He'd veer off the trail, nose twitching, tail wagging, only to be called back by Sam with a patient, "Rusty, search!"

Mitch, his eyes alert, looked at me. "Ben, do you still have Alex's sunglasses?"

I nodded, understanding dawning. "Rusty!" I called, kneeling and holding out the sunglasses. "Find Alex. Good boy! Find him!"

The dog's ears perked up. He sniffed the sunglasses eagerly, then, with a determined bark, bounded ahead, dragging Sam by the leash.

As we ventured deeper into the wilderness, the landscape grew more rugged, the trail winding through narrow canyons and between rocky outcroppings. Rusty, with his keen senses, led us unerringly, his tail wagging with each new scent he picked up.

* * *

After an hour of searching, the sky started changing colors. Dark clouds rolled in, a storm approaching. The urgency of the situation registered immediately, triggering my response instincts.

"Okay, everyone, listen up," I called out, gathering the group. "We're running out of time before the storm hits. I hate to say this, but we need to split into two search parties to be more efficient."

Mitch looked concerned. "Are you sure that's a good idea? What if we get separated and can't find each other?"

I nodded, understanding his concern. "I know it's risky, but we need to cover more ground quickly. Mitch, you go with Sarah and John and head toward the eastern side of the Chasm. I'll continue with Sam and Rusty and head west. We'll meet back at the parking lot in an hour. Make sure everyone has a flashlight."

The sky continued to darken, and the wind picked up, adding to the sense of urgency. I was determined to find our friend and bring him back to safety before the storm hit.

With a final nod, we parted ways. We had to find him. And we had to find him fast.

* * *

We stopped by a large Joshua tree, where I noticed a palm tree not far from where we were. Behind it seemed to be something of interest.

"He's onto something," Sam said, his voice low as Rusty paused, sniffing at the ground. "Stay alert."

With renewed hope, Rusty led us closer, and I realized it was the entrance to a dark cavern. Could this be the Chasm of Doom?

"This is it," Sam confirmed. "But I'm afraid Rusty and I can't go any further. It's too tight in there for us."

The thought of venturing into the dark unknown alone made my heart pound. But I knew I had to do it.

"I'll go in alone," I said, my voice steadier than I felt. "You stay here with Rusty. If I don't come back in fifteen minutes, get help."

I scrambled up the rocks. As I rounded a large boulder, I spotted it: the lone palm tree Sam had described. And there, nestled at its base, a shadowy crevice split the rock face—the entrance. Or, as Sam had so colorfully put it, the Birth Canal.

I stopped and took a deep breath. It was narrower than I'd imagined, barely wide enough for a person to pass through.

"Alex!" I called out, my voice drowned out by the howling wind. "Alex, are you in there?"

Only the drip, drip, drip of water answered, a lonely rhythm in the suffocating darkness.

Taking another deep breath, I squeezed through the opening, the rough rock scraping against my pack. The air inside was cool and damp, heavy with the scent of dust and something faintly metallic made my pulse quicken. I fumbled for my headlamp, the beam cutting through the oppressive darkness, revealing a narrow passage twisted and turned into the heart of the rock.

Oh god, Alex, where are you?

The passage narrowed, forcing me to my knees. I scraped my palms on the rough granite, the sharp edges biting into my skin. The air grew thick and close, making it hard to breathe. Panic, icy and sharp, clawed at the edges of my thoughts.

Calm down, Ben. You can do this. You have to do this.

I pushed on, inch by agonizing inch, my headlamp beam casting a flickering circle of light on the unforgiving rock. Every muscle in my body ached, every instinct screamed at me to turn back. But I couldn't. Not until I found Alex.

Hold on, Alex. I'm coming for you.

I stumbled over a loose rock, my knees slamming into the unforgiving ground. A sharp pain shot through my legs, and I felt the warmth of blood welling up beneath the torn fabric of my jeans. Panic clawed at my throat, the darkness threatening to consume me. I squeezed my eyes shut, fighting for control. *Focus, Ben. Focus.* I took deep, shuddering breaths, the cold, damp air filling my lungs. I couldn't give up. Not now.

I pressed on, deeper into the Chasm, my resolve hardening with each step. *I will find him. I have to.*

The tunnels seemed to stretch on endlessly, the darkness pressing in from all sides. I fought back the creeping uncertainty. *What if I'm too late? What if I can't find him?* The fear of failure repeated in my mind, louder than the drip of water, louder than my own ragged breaths.

Just as I was about to give up, my headlamp flickered and a flash of color caught my eye. A familiar blue sleeve, wedged between two massive boulders.

"Alex!" I cried out, scrambling toward him.

He was lying on his side, his face pale and a trickle of blood matting his hair. His body was contorted, almost folded in half, trapped in the unforgiving grip of the rocks. Relief crashed over me. He did not have a headlamp and likely slipped in the dark, smashing his head against the rock and twisting his ankle. Still, I found him and he was alive.

"Alex, it's Ben. I'm here to help. Can you open your eyes?"

No response. I scanned the area to ensure it was safe before approaching.

I rushed to his side, checking for injuries. He was groggy and disoriented, but thankfully, his injuries seemed minor. He'd taken a nasty fall and hit his head, but there were no signs of any major fractures. His ankle was swollen and bruised, clearly twisted from the fall. I gently shook his shoulder, careful not to move him too much in case of a spinal injury.

A faint groan escaped his lips. "Ben ... it hurts," he whispered, groggy, his eyes trying to open.

"I know, buddy. Hang in there. I'm going to check you for injuries, okay?" I said, trying to keep my voice calm and reassuring. I assessed his airway, breathing, and circulation. His pulse was steady.

"You're doing great, Alex. Just stay with me," I said as I applied pressure to the bleeding wound on his head. "I'm going to get you out of here, but I need to make sure you're stable first."

I carefully examined his body, looking for any other injuries. His leg was twisted and stuck, and I hoped it was sprained and not a fracture. "Okay, Alex, I'm going to release your leg. This might hurt a bit, but it's important."

He winced as I gently adjusted his leg. "You're doing great. Just keep breathing. I'm going to get you out of here."

Chapter 9

Alex

Wednesday, December 18—*The Chasm of Doom, Joshua Tree.*

Darkness pressed in on me from all sides, my throat dry with the gritty taste of dust. I blinked, trying to clear the sand from my eyes but couldn't see inside the cramped space. Every breath scraped against my throat, and a dull ache pulsed behind my eyes. I tried to move, but my legs felt trapped, as if buried under a mountain of giant boulders or inside a coffin. Was I buried alive?

"Alex," a voice called, steady and calm. *Ben.* His voice cut through like a loudspeaker.

I tried to respond, but my throat was parched, my voice a mere whisper snatched away by the desert.

I blinked up at him, vision blurry, the world tilting at an unsettling angle. "Ben? What ...?" My voice came out a raspy croak. "What are you doing here?"

"What does it look like, you idiot?" Ben's words were sharp, but the hand he pressed to my arm was gentle. "I'm getting you out of here. Drink this," Ben said, pressing a canteen to my lips. The water was cool and refreshing, like those sideline breaks during football games, each gulp bringing back memories of bottled water and a rush of clarity and focus before heading back into the game, each sip making me feel more clear-headed.

The water must have done its trick, as fragments of memory started to appear in the darkness. Early morning energy, the smug satisfaction of proving I could handle this adventure solo, the rough paper of the hand-drawn map. Then, the rocks. The press of granite against my chest, my back, the air growing thin. And a rising tide of panic, cold and suffocating, as I realized I was hopelessly, terrifyingly stuck.

A searing pain ripped through my ankle, shooting up my leg like a bolt of lightning. I choked back a groan, my voice reduced to a strangled gasp. "B-Ben ...," I moaned.

I felt him shifting beside me, the scrape of his body against the rock. "Easy, easy," he murmured, his voice closer now, a reassuring presence in the suffocating darkness.

A pressure against my temple, firm but careful. "Just a scratch," Ben lied. I winced as he checked my pulse, his fingers cool against my clammy skin. "Hold still," he muttered, his voice tight.

I tried to shift, to find a less painful position, but every movement sent shards of pain radiating from my ankle, through my head, through my entire body. "Ugh ... help ...," I managed, the word dissolving into a groan. It felt like someone had taken a sledgehammer to my skull, leaving behind a dull, throbbing ache pulsed in time with my heartbeat. Pain slammed into me, my body smashed as if a linebacker had sacked me. I began to struggle, my heart pounding.

"Easy, Alex." Ben's voice was close, calm, cutting through the fog of pain. "You're okay. Just breathe slowly."

I forced myself to take slow, deep breaths, anchoring to the rhythm of Ben's steady voice. I could feel the rocks pressing against me, the unforgiving grip of the aptly named Coffin. But I wasn't alone. Ben was here to help me.

"What hurts?" Ben asked.

"Head ... ankle ... everything." Each word came out as a groan.

"Try to stay still," Ben said. I could feel him shifting beside me, his hand gently probing the side of my skull. "Any numbness or tingling in your arms or legs?"

"N-no ... just pain."

He pressed his fingers against the side of my head, just above my ear. "Tell me if this hurts."

"Ow ... shit," I groaned.

"Good, means you're conscious and responsive. Just try to relax. I'm going to check for any other injuries."

His hands were gentle but firm as he examined my head wound, then moved down to my ankle, his fingers tracing the contours of the bone beneath the swelling.

"Think it's broken?" I asked.

"Too early to tell. We'll deal with it later. We need to get your leg free."

The rock shifted painfully slowly, grinding against my trapped ankle. I clenched my teeth and groaned. It felt like a 300-pound tackle landed on my leg

"Can you move?" Ben asked, his voice closer now.

"Think so." I sucked in a sharp breath. "Just ... give me a minute."

With a combination of rocking, pulling, and the unfortunate sacrifice of my expensive hiking clothes, I felt the rocks relent, inch by agonizing inch. Finally, the pressure eased.

And then, with one final pull, my leg was free.

I rolled away from the rocks, Ben's strong grip a vice around my hand, keeping me steady. I was disoriented, exhausted, and in a world of pain, but at least I was alive.

As I sat there, dragging in deep breaths, shame washed over me. Ben and Mitch ... how could I have been so reckless, so goddamn selfish? It was a pattern as old as our friendship, me charging ahead, them cleaning up the debris of my impulsive choices. And yet, they never hesitated, not once. But guilt was a luxury I couldn't afford, not yet. "We need to get out of here," I rasped, the words scraping against my throat raw and hoarse from dehydration and exhaustion.

Ben nodded, his jaw tight. "Right," he said, the single word clipped and urgent. "Back to the trail."

"Which way?" I said, each breath a shallow victory against the pain biting against my ankle.

"We go back the way Sam described," Ben said, his brow furrowed in concentration. "An up and down passage, hopefully easier, more like a stairway, with more headroom too."

I tried to match Ben's pace, to be more help than dead weight, but my ankle screamed with each step, sending shards of pain up my leg.

"Lean on me," Ben said, his arm wrapped around my waist.

Pride warred with the throbbing in my ankle and the dizziness that threatened to pull me under. "I can ... I can manage."

"Bullshit, you can barely stand," he said, his voice gruff but not unkind. "Just shut up and let me get us out of this death trap."

I clung to him as he half carried and dragged me, his grip surprisingly strong. My head spinning with a cocktail of pain, exhaustion, and a healthy dose of shame. I was the one who was supposed to be strong, the capable one, the quarterback calling the play. Instead, I should be benched. Here I was, a burden, a liability.

Ben was right. The descent, though still painful, was a heck of a lot more than the climb in. The passage widened, giving us a little more room to maneuver, but my ankle throbbed with every step, a constant reminder of my stupidity. Ben's arm around my waist was a steady presence, his grip firm as he helped me navigate the uneven terrain. "Almost there," Ben said, his voice encouraging despite the situation.

"I ... I really screwed up this time, didn't I?" The words tasted like ash in my mouth, thick with shame and regret.

Ben looked at me then—*really* looked at me—and for the first time, I saw a hint of something other than his consistent positivity. Disappointment? Maybe a touch of anger? "Yeah, Alex, you did."

I closed my eyes, a weary sigh escaping my lips. "Thank you, Ben. For coming after me."

He clapped me on the shoulder, the gesture heavy with unspoken things. "We're a team, remember? Always."

* * *

As I wriggled free from the claustrophobic confines of the Chasm, I didn't see the clear blue skies I'd expected. Instead, a bruised, ominous darkness had swallowed the desert. Then a flash! A jagged bolt of lightning tore through the sky, bathing the rock formations in a ghostly light.

"Did you see that?" Ben asked, seconds later, a tense edge to his voice. "That was close."

I did. Then, the close rumble of thunder. The desert was about to unleash its fury.

"Flash flood!" Ben's shout was almost lost to the roar. "We need to move!"

Then the rain hit—fat, heavy drops splattered against my skin like icy needles. As the rain intensified, it became a relentless, driving force soaking everything in seconds. The wind picked up, whipping sand and small pebbles against my exposed skin, each sting a stark reminder of our vulnerability in the face of nature's wrath. The once-dry desert was now a chaotic, muddy field, a raging torrent of murky, brown water. It rushed down the trail, carrying with it a mix of sand, rocks, and vegetation. The water churned violently as it flowed, drowning out all other sounds. The crack and snap of breaking branches and the scrape of rocks being dragged along by the water sounded like the roar of a football stadium. I could barely hear Ben shouting instructions.

My heart pounded as I followed him. We had to survive the muddy, slippery trail. Every step was a struggle, the mud clinging to our boots. But we pushed on, driven by the need to find safety and escape the fury of the flash flood.

The once-familiar trail was gone, swallowed by a churning river. I tasted grit and rain, fear tightening my throat. We scrambled for safe shelter, the deafening roar of the flood closing in, each step a struggle against the current.

As we stumbled through the storm, I thought about how quickly things had changed. I had started the day as a confident, reckless adventurer, leading my friends into danger without a second thought. But now, I was the one being led, the one relying on Ben's calm and steady presence to guide me.

I was no longer the confident adventurer. I was just Alex, a man lost and injured in the desert, hoping for a stroke of luck. All that mattered was survival. And for now, it was not certain.

* * *

The storm raged around us, rain a blinding curtain, wind a howling beast. Ben, ever steady, steered me toward a rocky overhang offering limited shelter. We huddled there, shivering as much from adrenaline as the cold. Safe, for now, but the thought of the others out there ripped at me.

"Mitch...?" I croaked, the words torn from my throat. "The others ... Are they ...?"

Ben's face was grim. "Still out there, Alex. Looking for you."

Guilt hit me harder than the floodwaters. My fault. It's all my fault. "We have to find them."

"No choice," Ben agreed, his voice tight. "Meeting at the parking lot's out. This storm killed the cell signal. We search."

"But Mitch ..." The guilt twisted inside me. "Think he's all right?"

Ben smiled. "If I know Mitch, he's already got a plan. He's always been smart, always thinking ahead. He'll be okay, Alex. We all will."

His words did little to comfort me. We were in the middle of a desert, in a flash flood, with our friend still out there, exposed to the elements. Nothing about this situation was okay. But I had to believe we'd find him, that we'd make it out of this desert alive. Because if we didn't, it would be my fault. The desert wouldn't just be a place of beauty and nature; it would be our grave.

"Alex," Ben's voice cut through the roar of the storm, barely more than a whisper against the wind, "we need to move."

He was right. Staying huddled beneath this rock overhang wouldn't bring Mitch and the others back. Besides, the longer we waited, the colder and stiffer my ankle would get.

I pushed myself to my feet, ignoring the throbbing in my ankle and the dull ache in my head. "Let's go."

The rain was coming down harder now. A relentless torrent blurred the edges of the world. My ankle protested with every step, a sharp, stabbing pain shot up my leg. But I gritted my teeth and kept moving, fueled by a mix of adrenaline and a burning shame.

"Don't push it," Ben said, his hand a steady presence on my arm. "We'll find them."

"I have to try," I muttered, pushing past the limits of what I thought my body could handle. The storm, the pain, the fear—it all faded into the background, replaced by a single, unwavering purpose: find Mitch. Find the others. Don't let anyone else pay the price for my stupidity.

With a shared nod of understanding, Ben and I ventured out from the shelter of the rock-cliff barrier, back into the storm. The rain was relentless. The wind howled, whipping sand and rain into our faces.

We moved as quickly as possible, but our progress was hindered by the slippery trail and the blinding rain. Now and then, a flash of lightning would illuminate the landscape, casting eerie shadows across the desert.

With each passing minute, my worry for Mitch grew. He was the thinker of our group, always the one with a plan. But even the best plans could go awry in the face of nature's fury.

* * *

The storm ended as suddenly as it started. Ben and I struggled ahead in the muddy wasteland. The ground was slick, and the mud clung to our boots with every step. Familiar landmarks were gone, swallowed by the flood. The search was grueling, but the thought of our friends, exposed and vulnerable, kept us going.

Finally, we spotted them huddled under a makeshift shelter. Mitch and the others—wet and cold, but safe.

As we gathered, the relief of finding each other was overshadowed by a mix of anger, fear, and concern. I was tense and stood back, watching as hugs were exchanged, tears were blinked back, and laughter, shaky at first, bubbled up like a spring in the desert. Everyone was soaked, shivering, and a little worse for wear, but we were alive. We were together. And for a moment, that was all that mattered.

The storm's fury broke as quickly as it had begun. One minute we were battling a raging torrent, the next, the sun was a warm caress on our soaked skin. But the warmth did little to thaw the ice, tension had descended over the group.

Sarah and John, usually the picture of laid-back California cool, were practically vibrating with anger.

"Seriously, Alex? This was supposed to be a fun trip, not some kind of survivalist ordeal," Sarah snapped.

John, his usual friendly expression replaced by a thundercloud, nodded curtly. "You pulled a stunt like this yesterday, and again today? It's not just your neck on the line, Alex. We were all out there, risking our necks because of your recklessness."

Sam shook his head. "By the saints, Alex, I've seen more sense from a badger. It's no game, boy! Not even Rusty here was thrilled about our little rescue mission."

"I ... I didn't mean for any of this to happen," I mumbled. The weight of their words, their accusations, crushed me, heavier than any boulder.

Only Mitch, leaning against a boulder, arms crossed, seemed unaffected by the storm of emotions swirling around us. He shrugged, offering, "Could've been worse." But even his usually unflappable demeanor couldn't quite mask the disappointment in his eyes.

"Mitch," I said.

He wouldn't look at me, his eyes fixed in the distance, remembering the storm we had just weathered.

"I'm sorry."

Then, he took a deep breath and nodded, a small smile forming on his lips. "I know, Alex," he said, his voice quiet but firm. "I know."

It wasn't a grand reconciliation, no heartfelt speeches or dramatic gestures. But it was something. At the moment, under the vast desert sky, we understood each other. We were more than just childhood friends, we were survivors, bound by shared experiences and trials.

As I looked around at the circle of faces—faces filled with worry, frustration, and a kind of betrayed affection—the full impact of my actions hit me like a physical blow. I'd been so caught up in my need to prove something, to chase a thrill, I'd put the people I cared about most at risk. And there was no excuse.

"Hey, Alex," Mitch said, opening his backpack. "Let me help you re-wrap that ankle of yours."

Chapter 10

Mitch

Wednesday, December 18—The Chasm of Doom, Joshua Tree.

"Hey, guys," I said, my voice a little shaky. "I'm going to take a short walk along the trail, maybe try to get some cell service and call Aunt May. Let her know we're all okay."

"Okay," Ben replied. "Let me know if you find a signal—I need to check in with Jenny too. And, uh, stick to the main trail, okay? Don't want a repeat of this morning."

"No worries," I assured him, trying to make my voice strong despite the image of Alex wedged in a rock chasm flashing in my imagination. "Hidden Valley Trail—out and back. Twenty minutes, tops."

The desert was quiet, broken only by the crunch of my boots on the sandy trail and the occasional lonely call of a bird I couldn't identify. Inhaling deeply, I tried to draw in the peace that seemed to radiate from the rocks and sand. The desert air, so different from the thin, cool air of the high altitude I was used to, felt strangely calming.

The trail ahead was beautiful, with twisted Joshua trees, towering rock formations, and incredible views. But the raw power of nature was intimidating—a force that had nearly crushed Alex and drowned us just hours earlier. And with every step, the feeling in my stomach worsened, like I was walking straight into a bad sci-fi movie where the nerd gets killed first.

Still, a familiar frustration simmered within me. *Alex*. Why did he always have to push the limits? Why couldn't he be content with a simple hike, a shared experience, like Ben and I? I loved him, I did, but sometimes his recklessness felt like a weight around my neck, pulling me back to childhood fears I thought I'd left behind.

Estes Park. Ten years old. The news of the plane crash. A gaping hole in my life. It never went away. Like a shadow, it followed me on every hike, every trip, every time I looked up, a sky had betrayed me.

Just us guys, the desert, a chance to breathe. Share stories under the stars like we used to. Instead, it was Alex, risking his neck again. The storm. The fear. I just wanted to hear Aunt May's voice, to know somewhere, things were still normal.

* * *

I pulled out my phone, hoping for a miracle. To my surprise, a single bar flickered on the screen. I was excited to call Aunt May, my thumb hovering over the call button for a beat before I pressed it, a nervous habit.

"Hello?" She picked up the second ring.

"Hi, Aunt May, it's me," I said, happy to hear her voice.

"Mitch! Oh, honey, I'm so glad you called. I've been worried sick!" Relief flooded her voice, followed by an undercurrent of anxiety. "Are you all right? I saw those awful storms on the weather channel. They said they were hitting Joshua Tree pretty hard."

"Yeah, we got caught in a bit of a downpour," I said, downplaying it. "But everything's fine. Just wanted to let you know we're all okay."

"A bit of a downpour?" she said, her voice sharp with skepticism. "You know I worry about you boys. Especially you, Mitch, all the way out there …"

Her words, with a familiar protectiveness, comforted me. Aunt May, with her soft heart and an endless supply of cookies, had been my rock after my parents died. I hated worrying her, but I also knew how much she sensed when I wasn't being truthful.

"It was a little more than a downpour," I conceded. "There was some flash flooding. But, honestly, I know what to do in an emergency. Alex went out on his own and got stuck for a bit."

"Stuck?" That got her attention. "What happened?"

"Nothing too serious."

"Really? What else?" she asked.

"It's just … Alex is being Alex, you know? It's like we're kids again, back in the Rockies. He keeps leading us into these crazy situations."

Aunt May was silent for a moment.

"Mitch, you know people don't change overnight. And, remember, you haven't seen each other in years. It takes time to get to know each other again as adults. Try to be patient with Alex."

"But today he pushed it too far, getting hurt and needing a rescue."

Aunt May's voice rose with concern. "Is he all right? Did he break anything?"

"No, no, nothing like that. He'll be okay. Ben was there to help him and patched him up. He's a bit shaken up, but he'll be fine." I hesitated, debating how much to reveal. "He just ... Well, you know Alex. He took a bit of a tumble. Nothing serious."

"Oh, that Alex." Aunt May sighed. "Always the daredevil, isn't he? Just like his dad. Not like yours ..."

Her voice trailed off, and I knew she was thinking about my father. A lump formed in my throat, and I quickly changed the subject.

"So, I met this nice family at the campground—Marco, Isabella, and their daughter, Sofia. And, John and Sarah, both Joshua Tree experts with lots of desert knowledge."

"Oh, lovely! Making new friends ... and speaking of family. How is Ben ... and his family?"

"Yes, he and Jenny are living in Oregon. Two kids now, remember?"

"Of course, of course. Time flies, doesn't it? Must be hard for him, being away from them."

"It is," I said, realizing how Ben hadn't actually talked much about his family. "I know he loves his children and that's why he was so late getting here because he stayed to watch them play in their basketball games, and I know he feels guilty for being away from them."

"He's a good dad," she said. "Like you will be."

"Oh, well, uh, I don't know about that, Aunt May."

Aunt May gently responded, "I am sure you will be great, just a matter of time, be patient."

"It happened fast for Ben and Jenny, alright. Remember how surprised we were when they suddenly got married right after high school?"

"Yes, I remember."

"Jenny got pregnant, and they moved to Oregon to be closer to her parents. It was like he'd just suddenly veered off the path we thought he was on, the one he wanted, the one his father wanted for him. He was supposed to go to the police academy, following in his dad's footsteps, but all that changed."

"Life has a way of its own, Mitch."

"I ... I think he felt like he let his dad down."

Aunt May replied, "That's Ben for you," she says, "Always carrying the weight of the world on his shoulders. Make sure you're there for him, Mitch. He needs someone who understands."

Mitch promised, "I will."

Aunt May's tone shifted to playful. "So, enough about those two. What about you? Met any nice girls out there among the cacti and coyotes?"

I laughed, a little startled by the change of subject. "Well ... there was a woman on the bus with a great smile and rather interesting rainbow shirt ..."

"Oh?" Aunt May was fully in her element now, ready to dissect the potential romantic entanglements of her favorite nephew.

"We had lunch together at the bus stop," I said, unable to keep the smile out of my voice. "We got to talking about astronomy, actually. She's here for a yoga retreat, of all things."

"Yoga and astronomy?" Aunt May chuckled. "That's a combination I haven't heard before. Well, you never know,

Mitch. Sometimes the most unexpected encounters lead to the most ... interesting developments. Remember, be open to possibilities, but don't forget to be careful. The desert, and love, can be full of surprises, some more welcome than others. Mitch, I know you don't want to worry me, but I can tell when you're holding back. Just promise me you'll be extra careful out there. The desert is a beautiful but unforgiving place. People disappear out there, Mitch. Sometimes they're never seen again."

"I will, Aunt May. We're looking out for each other. Besides, Ben's got everything under control. He's like a walking encyclopedia of wilderness survival."

"Good to hear. Ben was always a responsible friend, except that one weekend."

"Well," I replied, remembering his loyalty to Alex and me over the years, "he was a lifesaver today."

"I'm glad you're all safe. Now, tell me more about this beautiful desert you're in. What can you see?"

"It's incredible here, Aunt May," I said, looking at the sunset. "One moment, we were caught in a flash flood, and the next, it's as if the storm never happened. The desert is dry and warm again. The way the light hits the rocks, it's like they're glowing. And the Joshuas ..."

"Tell me about the Joshua trees," she urged, her voice regaining its warmth. "I've always wanted to see them."

"They're kinda strange, with spiky branches reaching to the sky like gnarled fingers," I said, feeling the tension release from my shoulders.

"It sounds magical."

My boot caught on something, a snag in the sand I hadn't seen. Bending down, I brushed away the loose grit to reveal a scrap of fabric, faded denim, stiff and sun-bleached, almost white. It tore easily when I tugged it free, the dry fibers crumbling in my hand. Something about the piece of clothing felt off. As I looked closer, I noticed a strange marking on the ground. My heart started to race. I bent down to take a better look.

"Oh, Mitch, I'm so glad you're all okay," she said. "Please be careful out there. I don't know what I'd do if anything happened to you."

"I will, Aunt May, I promise," I said, distracted. "Hey, listen, I think I need to go. I'll call you later, okay? Love you."

And without waiting for her response, I ended the call.

* * *

My mind, trained to analyze patterns and anomalies, registered the unusual: the fabric's position, the way the edges were frayed as if torn in a struggle. An image of Alex, wedged in the rocky chasm, flashed before my eyes.

I looked at the ground, scanning in a systematic grid like I was searching for a bug in jumbled code. There, just a few feet away, a footprint, faint but distinct in the compacted sand. It wasn't a hiking-boot print; it was smaller, narrower, with a pattern I couldn't quite place.

Then I saw them.

Bones.

At first, it was just a single, white curve protruding from the base of a weathered Joshua tree, almost camouflaged against the pale sand. But as I looked closer, I noticed another small bone, bleached by the sun.

My breath caught in my throat.

I stumbled back. My hand, trembling, I fumbled for my phone. I had to document this, to capture the scene before my mind could distort the reality. *Click. Click.* The shutter sound deafening in the stillness of the desert.

I bolted upright, scrambling back from the bones as if they might reach out and grab me. I braced myself, my heart pounding.

Hidden Valley Trail, I thought, my mind a jumble of fragmented images: bleached bones, a scrap of denim, a footprint in the sand. Stick to the trail. My feet pounded the sand, kicking up a cloud of dust and tasted of fear and something ancient, something primal. With each bend in the path I expected to find ... what? The owner of those bones? The desert stretched around me, silent and vast, a landscape had seen millennia come and go. What was one skeleton, one life, in the grand scheme?

Don't think about it, just run.

* * *

I raced back to the campground, gasping for breath, the sun disappearing as the stars began to light up the dark sky. Ben, Alex, and Sam seemed calmer after the earlier chaos of Alex's rescue and the storm. They were clustered together in a group of camp chairs finishing up the last of the leftovers from the Texas barbecue, and I could smell the strong, spicy scent of the food mixed with the earthy smell of Sam's pipe.

I stumbled to a stop before them, my lungs burning, my mind a jumbled mess of bleached bones and footprints. Then, I noticed the bottles of beer, whiskey bottle in Sam's hand, and, likely the last of the doctored lemonade.

Sam slurred. "Another round, lads?" raising a half-empty cup of amber liquid. "Can't let it go to waste, especially not after the excitement we've had."

Alex, nursing a bruised ego and a bandaged ankle, leaned back in his camp chair, a beer bottle dangling from his hand. "This calls for a toast, to surviving another day in paradise."

"I'll drink to that," Sam replied.

Alex then looked at me from a camp chair. "Man, you look like you've seen a ghost."

"Mitch? What is it?" Ben asked, nursing a chipped mug. "Did you talk to Aunt May?" I need to check in with my family too."

"Yeah, she's ...," I sucked in a breath, trying to slow the frantic pounding of my heart. "She's fine. But I ... I found something."

Ben's expression shifted from curiosity to cautious concern. "What did you find?"

"Bones," I said.

Sam blurted. "Bones, ye say?" blinking his blue eyes trying to focus. "Probably just a washed-up critter. Happens all the time out here."

Alex shifted in his seat. "He's probably right about that, Mitch," his voice surprisingly gentle. "Just a coyote or something. Don't worry about it."

"No," I insisted. "I think they're human."

"Where did you find them?" Ben asked, his detective instincts kicking in.

"I was talking to Aunt May, telling her about the Joshua trees, and then I saw something off the trail."

"What did you see?" Ben asked.

"It was just a scrap of cloth at first," I continued, my voice gaining a bit of steadiness, "faded denim, almost white from the sun. But it was ... out of place. And the edges were frayed, like it had been ripped. I started looking around, and that's when I saw them."

Ben leaned forward. "Did you touch them?"

"No ... yes ..." I said, shaking my head. "Bleached white, scattered around the base of a Joshua tree." I paused, fighting the urge to scrub my hands over my face, to erase the image seared onto my retinas. "I took a couple of photos, here take a look."

"Hmm ... interesting ... maybe we should go back and take another look," Ben said. "Investigate, just to be sure."

Alex, his usual bravado dampened by the throbbing in his ankle, groaned and shifted uncomfortably in his camp chair. "Aw, man, it's getting dark," he complained, "and my ankle's killing me. Can't we just forget about it for tonight?"

Sam, swaying slightly, hiccupped and raised his bottle in a mock toast. "Ah, now, hold yer horses there, lads. We don't want to be messin' with a potential crime scene, do we? Best to let the authorities handle it, so it is."

Ben nodded, pulling out his phone. "Okay I'll try to get a signal and call the ranger, then Jenny."

* * *

As we waited for the ranger to arrive, it was getting darker.

"Mitch, buddy, have a bite, you must be starving," Alex said, handing me a plate with the last of the Texas barbecue. "And here's a peace offering," he added with a grin, offering me a beer. "A cold one to calm the nerves."

I hesitated, "Thanks, Alex," I mumbled, taking the plate and the beer.

Sam sensed the opportunity to share another story. "This land has seen its share of comings and goings," he said. "Folks lured by the promise of gold, of adventure, of a new start. But the desert ..." He paused, a sly grin spreading across his face. "The desert has a way of playing tricks on ya. Makes ya see things that ain't there, hear whispers in the wind."

I felt a chill.

"The desert doesn't give up its secrets easily," Sam continued. "It can swallow a person whole, leaving no trace. Sometimes, the only clues it offers are ... bones."

"But it's not always what it seems." He leaned closer. "Those bones you found, lad ... Well, I wouldn't worry too much about 'em. Probably just a critter, bleached white by the sun."

I nodded slowly, doubt creeping in. Maybe Sam was right. Maybe it was just a false alarm, a trick of the light and my overactive imagination.

"What do you think, Mitch?" Ben asked, breaking the silence. "Do you think they're human?"

I looked at him. "I don't know," I admitted.

* * *

The park ranger arrived as the first stars began to fill the darkening sky. He was tall and lean with a weather-beaten face etched with the lines of a life spent under the desert sun. He moved with the quiet grace of a deer, a turquoise earring under his worn ranger hat.

He approached us, his dark eyes taking me in. "You called about a discovery?" he said, his voice a low rumble, as ancient and weathered as the rocks surrounding us. "Ranger Whitecloud," he added, extending a hand, calloused but firm.

"Mitch," I said, shaking his hand, my palm clammy against his rough grip. "I found them."

He scratched his chin, his gaze steady and assessing. "You found some bones on the trail?"

I hesitated, my earlier certainty wavering under his skeptical gaze. "I ... I think so. There were several of them. And the way they were scattered—"

"Most likely an animal washed up by the storm," Ranger Whitecloud said, his tone matter of fact. "Happens all the time. Anything else?"

"There was a piece of faded denim," I said. "Ripped, like ..." I swallowed, the image flashing before my eyes.

"Like someone might have struggled to get free," Ben finished.

"Anything else?," Ranger Whitecloud repeated.

"But—"

"Wait, Mitch," Ben interrupted, his voice taking on that calm, authoritative tone I'd always admired. "You took some photos."

I blinked, startled. I'd completely forgotten about the photos. "Oh, right," I mumbled, fumbling for my phone. "Here ..."

Ranger Whitecloud took my phone, his eyes focused as he swiped through the images. Then, he looked up, his expression unreadable.

"These bones ... most likely animal remains ... scrap of cloth ... nothing unusual," he said slowly. "The way these bones are positioned ..." He paused, zooming in on one of the photos. "And what about this?"

"It's a footprint," I said, "I found it near the bones."

Ranger Whitecloud nodded, his eyes narrowing. "And who is this?" he asked, pointing to another photo.

It was the picture of the climber that I'd seen earlier, the one who'd been watching us. "A climber," I said. "I saw him on the boulder watching Alex at the Hall of Horrors. He seemed ... weird."

"Weird how?"

I hesitated, trying to find the words. "He was alone ... and he was watching us."

Ranger Whitecloud's expression hardened. "Interesting," he muttered. "It's hard to tell for certain, but his features resemble the escaped person of interest. Hard to tell from this distance."

The escapee? Here? But what was he doing near the bones? And was he the one who'd left that unsettling footprint?

Ranger Whitecloud's expression shifted, concern crossing his weathered features. He nodded slowly. "I'd like to take a look at the site now."

"It's getting dark," Alex said, wincing as he shifted in his seat, his earlier bravado replaced by a grimace of pain as he nursed his beer.

Ben shook his head, his expression firm. "The longer we wait, the more chance the evidence could be disturbed."

Ranger Whitecloud glanced at the night sky. "Yes," he agreed, "but we need to be careful. It's easy to get turned around out here in the dark, even for experienced hikers." He looked at me, then Ben. "Why don't you two come along? Bring your flashlights. The rest of you can stay put."

* * *

The hike back to where I'd found the bones felt different in the dark. The wind, picking up, whispered through the Joshua trees. The familiar landmarks took on an eerie, almost menacing quality.

When we reached the spot that I remembered something was wrong.

Gone.

"They were here," I said. "Just a few hours ago ..."

"Are you sure this is the same location?" Ben asked.

I scanned the area, "I ... I think so. I was right there by that boulder talking with Aunt May when I noticed them."

Ben knelt down, examining the ground, careful not to touch anything. "The sand's been disturbed. Something was dragged through here."

"Or maybe the wind," Ranger Whitecloud said.

"The wind doesn't just pick up a pile of bones and carry them off," Ben replied. "Maybe someone's trying to cover something up."

Ranger Whitecloud surveyed the scene, his experienced eyes missing nothing. "It's possible. But let's not jump to conclusions. Most likely the storm washed them up, and maybe the wind covered them over again. Spread out. Look for anything unusual—footprints, disturbed earth, anything at all, but don't touch anything."

We spread out, scouring the desert for any trace of the missing bones, our flashlights bouncing off the Joshua trees and boulders.

After a while, Ranger Whitecloud called out, "I found something!"

We gathered around him, our hopes rising. Ranger Whitecloud carefully brushed the sand away, revealing a single bone. He held it up, pinched between his thumb and forefinger. It was small, no bigger than the first joint of my thumb, pitted and grooved like a piece of coral.

"It's probably an animal bone," Ranger Whitecloud said, turning it over in his calloused hands. "We get a lot of those out here."

I felt embarrassed. Was this just another reminder of nature's circle of life, where life and death intertwined in an endless cycle?

"There were more here before. Maybe someone took them?"

But Ben wasn't convinced. "Are you sure?" he pressed. "It could be human."

Ranger Whitecloud hesitated, his eyes lingering on the bone. "It's hard to say for certain, but I'll send it back to the lab and have it analyzed."

Chapter 11

Mitch, Ben, Alex

Saturday, August 31st—The fourteen-year-old boys enjoy the end of summer vacation.

The last weekend of summer vacation was like a sparkling firecracker.

It was the perfect summer afternoon. The tree house perched high in the old oak was our hideout. The sun peeked through the leaves, casting a shadow on the place where we played cards, bragged, fibbed, and dreamed up wild adventures. The air was thick with the sweet smell of fresh-cut grass, and the rhythmic buzzing of grasshoppers mingled with the pungent odor of stolen cigarettes.

Ben's dad had helped us build our tree house with hammers and nails, ropes and pulleys, and sweat and tears; a space to hang out, a fort for adventure, and a place where we could be ourselves before high school captured us.

Ben grinned down at us from the tree house entrance. "Climb up, slowpokes."

Alex, a star athlete on the baseball, basketball, and Pop Warner football teams, didn't need any encouragement. Climbing up to the tree house was a challenge, and Alex was always ready for one. He sprinted forward, leaped in the air, and grabbed a branch, the rough bark digging into his palms as he launched himself up. With a swift, fluid motion, he flipped his body and easily landed in the fort. "Piece of cake." He grinned, the thrill of the climb still buzzing in his veins. "Just like a jump up to the rim, slam dunk!"

Mitch was more hesitant, his fear of heights still a struggle.

"Hey, Mitch, come on, don't chicken out!" Alex called down.

Mitch took a deep breath. "I'll be there, just a minute," he replied.

Slowly but surely, Mitch, with his compact backpack strapped on, climbed the rope ladder and stepped into the tree house.

"Welcome to the fort," Ben said, spreading his arms.

The inside of the tree house was our little world. A makeshift bookshelf sat in the corner piled with comics, baseball cards, and detective-mystery novels Ben had borrowed from his dad's bookshelf. A cooler sat in one corner, stocked with our favorite snacks and drinks.

"Dude, what's with the backpack?" Alex asked Mitch, eyeing the bulging pack with a mixture of amusement and suspicion. "You packing for a week in the wilderness or something?"

Mitch shrugged. "You never know when you might need something," he said, unzipping the pack. He pulled out a telescope, compact but powerful looking.

"Whoa, cool! Is that for spying on the neighbor's daughter?" Alex snatched it up, peering through the lens.

"This is a portable refracting telescope. It's for stargazing, dummy," Mitch replied, rolling his eyes. "And birdwatching.

Maybe even spotting crimes, if we're lucky," he added with a smile.

Next came a Swiss Army knife, glinting in the afternoon sun. "This is a multitool knife. It has a blade, a screwdriver, a can opener, and even a pair of tweezers."

"Now this is more like it!" Alex said, flipping open the knife with a flick of the wrist. "Perfect for carving our initials into the treehouse ... or maybe escaping from pirates."

Ben rolled his eyes. "Put it away before you hurt yourself. And, besides, we promised my dad we wouldn't carve up the tree house."

Mitch continued his inventory, displaying a compass, a first-aid kit, an astronomy book, and a fire starter, each item prompting a chorus of questions, jokes, and mock horror from Alex.

"Seriously, dude, are you expecting the Apocalypse?" Alex asked, shaking his head. "What's next, a gas mask? A hazmat suit?"

Mitch, not bothered at all, smiled and patted the neatly packed backpack. "Better to be prepared. You never know when you might need this," he said, patting the first-aid kit. "It has Band-Aids, tweezers, medical tape, and safety pins." Next was a small notebook and a set of pencils. "I like to jot down observations or sketch things I see. It helps me remember details."

A small, knowing smile appeared on Ben's face. "You never know, Alex," he said, his eyes shifting toward the window looking out on the street below, "sometimes even the most ordinary places can hold secrets. And sometimes, those secrets need uncovering."

"Dude," Alex said, shaking his head in mock disbelief, "you're like a walking, talking survival guide! If we ever get stranded on a desert island, I'm sticking with you."

* * *

"Okay, okay, enough with the survival gear," Alex said, tossing Mitch's compass back toward the backpack. "My brain is fried. Let's do something fun!"

"Hey, let's read one of these detective stories," Ben suggested, grabbing a book from the shelf.

"Or," Mitch suggested, "we could finally build a model rocket we talked about. I snagged some tools from the workshop."

Alex groaned. "Ugh, you guys are such nerds. How about a game of poker? Or let's talk about some girls. High school's only a week away," he added, leaning back against the rough wooden wall of the tree house and lighting a cigarette from his shirt pocket. "Besides," he added with a wink, striking a match with a flick, "a little danger never hurt anyone."

Ben, perched on a weathered crate, grabbed a deck of cards fanned out in his hand. "Okay, ante up, boys," he said.

Alex tossed a crumpled bill onto the makeshift table. "Deal me in," he said, his grin wide. "This is gonna be my lucky day."

Mitch, sitting on a wobbly stool, counted his coins. He didn't have much. "How much is the ante?" He loved being in the treehouse. It felt safe, like their own little world.

"You sure you want to play for keeps, Mitch?" Alex teased, nudging him. "Or are you scared of losing your lunch money?"

Mitch's cheeks flushed, but he held his ground. "I'm just being cautious. Besides, I'd rather save my money for something more worthwhile, like college."

Ben chuckled, shuffling the cards. "Man, you're always thinking ahead." He dealt the cards as an old tape recorder played tunes in the background, filling the tree house with the songs of an endless summer.

"Dude, high school is going to be epic!" Alex said, stretching his long legs, sprawled across a pile of cushions, his lanky frame overflowing with energy. He had grown six inches in the previous six months, and his body was still adjusting to the sudden change. "Think of all the chicks! I'm going to ask out Lisa, the cheerleader. She's totally hot."

Ben laughed, shaking his head. "You sure have it all planned out, don't you?"

Alex shrugged, grinning. "Can't hurt to dream, right? Plus, I'm going to try out for the JV football team and maybe even make varsity. And of course, basketball and baseball."

"That sounds great," Ben said. "I'm going to finally get my Eagle Scout badge. Dad says it'll look good on my police-academy application."

Mitch sat cross-legged in the corner, listening. Alex's cigarette smoke curled around him. Mitch clutched his cards close, adjusting his glass, his eyes focused on concentration, realizing he had drawn a full house.

* * *

"Chow time!" Ben announced, tossing a bag of chips at Alex, who snagged it with one hand, never taking his eyes off his cards. "Peanut butter and jelly, the official fuel of champions."

We devoured our sandwiches, washing them down with lukewarm sodas, the tree house filled with sounds of crunching chips, slurping drinks, and good-natured trash talk.

"I just hope we can still hang out like this," Mitch said, "even when we're in high school."

"We will," Ben reassured him. "It'll be just like always. We'll come up here, play cards, talk about girls, maybe even solve a few mysteries."

"Yeah," Mitch said, a moment of doubt in his voice, "but what if things change? What if we don't have time for each other anymore?"

"We'll make time," Ben insisted. "We're not just friends, we're brothers."

Mitch's thoughts drifted to the upcoming changes.

"Hey, Mitch," Ben said. "What are you looking forward to most about high school?"

Mitch hesitated, his fingers tracing the worn edges of his cards. "I don't know ... maybe just learning new things. Exploring new possibilities."

"Come on, man," Alex said, nudging him with his elbow. "You're gonna be the smartest kid in school. You'll ace all the tests, win all the science fairs, and probably invent something that'll change the world."

Mitch blushed, a shy smile spreading across his face. "I don't know," he mumbled, finishing his sandwich and starting to assemble his telescope. The familiar clink of metal and glass, the precise adjustments, was a comforting ritual in the face of the unknown.

"Hey, check out the view," Ben said, pointing toward the two windows. "West for the sunset, east for the city. Almost feels like we can see everything from up here."

But it was the view east that caught Mitch's attention. He adjusted the telescope. What he saw made his heart skip a beat.

"Guys," Mitch said, "you need to see this."

Alex and Ben moved closer, looking into the telescope. Their eyes widened in shock.

Through the lens, the city seemed to draw closer, its streets and buildings coming into sharp focus. And it was there, in a convenience store behind a gas station, where Mitch noticed something strange.

* * *

The crash of breaking glass shattered the sounds of the late-summer afternoon. We froze.

"What was that?" Ben asked, his eyes wide.

Alex grabbed the telescope from Mitch and swung it toward the street below. "Holy crap!" Alex whispered, his eyes glued to the telescope. "Something's going down at the store."

We crowded around, taking turns peering through the lens. Two figures, their faces obscured by shadows, lurked near the back entrance of the convenience store.

"What do you think they're doing?" Alex whispered, his eyes never leaving the store.

"I don't know," Ben replied, lost in thought, "but it doesn't look good."

"It's a robbery," Alex suggested, scanning the area. "Look at the way that guy's acting. He's definitely up to something."

"Or maybe it's a drug deal," Ben added. "I've read about this in my detective books. They often happen in places like this."

"Or maybe they're planning something bigger. Like a heist. Look at that bag. It could be filled with tools or weapons. Think we should tell your dad?" Mitch asked, a nervous tremor in his voice.

"Nah," Alex said, waving his hand. "Let's see what happens first. Maybe we can catch them in the act."

Ben hesitated. "I don't know. What if they're dangerous?"

"Relax, dude," Alex said. "We're safe up here. We're practically invisible."

We continued to watch as one of the men pulled a crowbar from his backpack, the metal glinting ominously in the fading light.

"They're gonna break in!" Mitch whispered.

"Told ya!" Alex said, a thrill of adrenaline coursing through him.

"We need to get the police," Ben said, his voice filled with urgency.

Bang! One of the men smashed the crowbar against the back door.

"Wow! They're doing it!" Alex said, his voice full of excitement and just a hint of nerves.

"Should we tell your dad?" Mitch asked, turning to Ben, whose father was a police detective.

"No," Alex said. "Let's investigate ourselves."

Ben reached for his pocketknife, a gift from his father, a symbol of protection and responsibility. "We need to call the police," Ben said.

But before he could go, Alex grabbed his arm. "Wait," he whispered, his eyes fixed on the scene below. "Let's see what they do."

Another bang rebounded from the street below, making us jump.

"What was that?" Mitch whispered, his eyes wide.

"Sounded like a gunshot," Ben said. He grabbed the telescope from Alex and looked through the lens. "They're coming out! They've got bags of stuff!"

"Wait, look there," Mitch said, his eyes locked on the store's back entrance.

The two men, their faces hidden by ski masks, burst out of the store, their arms filled with what looked like stolen goods.

"Let's go!" Alex shouted. "We gotta follow them!"

"Alex, no!" Mitch yelled, grabbing his arm. "It's too dangerous!"

"But this is our chance!" Alex protested. "We gotta get down there before the cops show up and ruin everything!"

"My dad's a cop, remember?" Ben said. "We don't want to ruin anything, we want to solve it. But we need to be smart about this."

"We can be careful," Alex argued, his eyes blazing with determination. "We'll stay hidden, be like ninjas!"

"Look," Mitch said, pointing to a spot near the alleyway. "There's a ski cap. One of them must have dropped it."

"Good eye, Mitch. And there … see there? Looks like a knife. We should tell my dad," Ben replied.

"But they're getting away!" Alex yelled, his voice full of frustration. "Look, they're driving a GTO!" Alex bounced with excitement. "A dark-green GTO, just like the one in that movie!"

Ben jotted down the description in his notebook. "Okay, good. We've got something. Now, let's call my dad."

But Alex was already halfway down the rope ladder. "Are you guys coming or what? Those dudes are gonna be long gone!"

Ben hesitated, torn between his sense of responsibility and the urge to follow his friend. He looked at Mitch, who shrugged.

"Fine." Ben sighed, already knowing he was going to regret this. "But we stick together. No heroics, got it?"

Ben and Mitch scrambled down the rope ladder and raced toward the store. When they arrived, the GTO was gone, only shattered glass in the store window.

Alex kicked at a stray piece of glass. "We missed them," he groaned.

"We did the right thing, Alex," Ben said. "It was too dangerous."

Mitch scanned the area. Near the door, he noticed a dark stain on the sidewalk. "Hey, look," he said, pointing. "Is that blood?"

"Looks like it." Ben knelt down and carefully retrieved the cap and the knife, wrapping them in his handkerchief. He also carefully marked the bloodstain spot with a rock. "We should take this to my dad."

Alex, still buzzing with frustrated energy, started poking around near the dumpster. "Check it out," he said, holding up a crumpled backpack with a worn hoodie stuffed inside. "Looks like our robbers were trying to be incognito."

We spent the next few minutes gathering any potential clues they could find: a discarded cigarette butt, a muddy footprint near the alleyway, and a crumpled receipt.

"My dad's gonna be impressed. We're like real detectives!"

* * *

The boys raced back to the tree house, excited to have the evidence.

Ben's father was waiting for them by the tree house's rope ladder. He was a tall man with a stern face, his police radio crackling with static. "Where have you been?" he asked with concern. "Are you okay? I heard what sounded like a gunshot, or did you boys shoot off a firecracker?"

"We're okay, Dad," Ben said, his heart still pounding from the night's events. "We ... We have evidence of a crime." Ben hesitated, then pulled out the handkerchief containing the cap and knife. "There was a robbery at the convenience store," Ben said, his voice gaining confidence. "We saw the whole thing from the tree house." He pointed to the blood-stained rock. "There was blood on the sidewalk too. And Alex saw the getaway car—a dark-green GTO."

Ben's father looked at the bloodstains, his fingers careful not to disturb the evidence, his eyes lingering on the blade. He then turned to the boys, his stern look returning. "And what were you doing at the scene?"

"We ... we were just there," Alex replied, trying to sound confident.

Mitch nodded, his eyes filled with fear. "We just saw what happened and thought we should do something."

Ben's father paced, his face a thundercloud of disapproval. "What were you boys thinking, charging into the crime scene? Interfering with evidence-collection protocols? Do you have any idea how dangerous it was?"

They boys stood before him, heads bowed, shame burning in their chests. Even Alex, usually so quick with a comeback, was silent.

"You're not cops, Ben," his father said, his voice softening slightly. "It's not your job to apprehend criminals. You could have gotten yourselves hurt—or worse. Do you understand how much damage you have done to the investigation?"

They mumbled apologies, their words lost in the weight of his disappointment.

He sighed, running a hand through his salt-and-pepper hair. "Look, I know you were trying to help. And I'm ... relieved you're all safe." He paused, his eyes meeting Ben's. "But this kind of recklessness has consequences, Ben. You're grounded for a week. No hanging out with your friends, no tree house, no investigations. You're going to spend that time reflecting on your actions and learning about the importance of following the law."

Ben nodded, his face pale. A week of grounding felt like an eternity, but he knew he deserved it.

Chapter 12

Mitch

Wednesday, December 18—Hidden Valley Campground, Joshua Tree.

I was back in the recurring nightmare that had haunted me since my parents' tragic plane crash. I was ten years old seated in the plane, the turbulence shaking me as I reached for my parents. But then there was a flash, and the scene shifted. I was fourteen again with Ben and Alex, their laughter filling the tree house. Suddenly, a scream pierced my dream like a dagger in the dark.

I woke up with a start, my heart pounding. I sat up in my sleeping bag. The scream felt so raw, so real. The dream—the plane, the turbulence, the screams—clung to me. It was always the same. A moment of helpless terror, the feeling one time, there would be no waking up.

I slipped out of my tent and stumbled around the campsite, the desert sand cold against my feet. I laced up my boots, trying to shake off the lingering reminders of the nightmare, but the scream stuck in my mind. The desert was quiet, except the hoot of a distant owl and the rustle of a critter in the underbrush. I glanced at the other tents. Ben and Alex were still asleep, their steady breathing a comforting rhythm in the quiet night.

The sky was filled with stars, guiding me as I walked away from our campsite. I tried to understand the dream. It had been so vivid and real, and that scream sounded so familiar. A clue something was wrong? But what?

I scanned the campground, searching for any sign of disturbance. The other tents were silent, their occupants lost in slumber. And then I saw them—prints in the sand, circling the campsite.

They were fresh, the edges sharp and clear, as if someone or something had just been there. My heart hammered as I looked at them, my mind racing. *Was the scream real? Was something there ...?*

The footprints led me deep into the desert darkness. With no moonlight, the stars were my only guide, illuminating the path ahead and revealing a trail of disturbed sand. It was as if someone, or something, had passed through the area in a hurry, leaving a trail of chaos in their wake.

Something is out there. I better get back to my tent.

* * *

Crawling back into the tent, I zipped myself into a cocoon of nylon and down. Sleep wouldn't come easily. The scream, the footprints, the unsettling feeling of being watched—it all swirled in my mind like the desert dust, refusing to settle. I tossed and turned, thinking about the bones, the ranger, and Sam's stories—it all felt like a bad dream I couldn't wake up from. The dream had shaken me, and I couldn't get the sound of the scream out of my head, but the memories were real.

My mind drifted back to my parents' plane crash, the moment shattered my life. I saw their faces, their smiles frozen in time, hearing their voices in my memory. *Why? Why did they have to die?*

The memories played on like a projector, a relentless slideshow of happier times. The smell of my mom's home cooking, the sound of my dad's laughter, the warmth of their hugs—all stolen away. Anger flared, hot and bitter, not at them but at the unfairness of it all. I clenched my fists, the thin fabric of the sleeping bag offering little comfort.

Finally, just as the first rays of dawn were beginning to light up the sky, I fell into a fitful sleep.

* * *

"Mitch? You, okay?" Ben's voice, soft and concerned, broke through the fog of my sleep.

I groaned, my voice rough from the dryness of the desert air. "Yeah," I mumbled, "just a bad dream." I blinked, searching for Ben's face.

Ben peaked into my tent and leaned toward me. "I heard you scream last night. Wanna talk about it?"

I shook my head. The last thing I wanted was to burden Ben with the weight of my grief, to ruin our camping trip. "I'm fine," I insisted, forcing a weak smile. "Just need some coffee."

A moment later, Alex's long arm appeared, stretching into my tent with a steaming mug. "Here ya go, buddy," he said, his usual boisterousness tempered by genuine concern. "A little caffeine boost is all you need."

I took the mug, the warmth a welcome contrast to the chill I'd felt during the night. The first sip of the bitter brew jolted me awake, and I managed a grateful, "thanks." I climbed out of the tent and sat in the camp chair next to my friends in silence as we drank our coffee.

"Hey, Mitch," Ben finally said, his voice gentle. "We're here for you. You know that, right? Whatever's going on, we're in this together."

Alex nodded. "Yeah, man. You can tell us anything."

"I know. It's just ... it's hard sometimes. The memories, the what ifs. They never go away."

Ben reached in and squeezed my shoulder. "I know, buddy," he said. "But you don't have to carry it all alone."

I nodded, a tear tracing a path down my cheek. I knew my friends were right. I wasn't alone. I had Ben and Alex, my brothers in all but blood.

But a lingering feeling remained, a sense something wasn't right. As we ate breakfast and planned our day, I scanned the campground, searching for anything out of the ordinary. The other campers seemed oblivious, their laughter and chatter a stark contrast to the turmoil within me. The bones, the scream, the footprints, it all added up to something.

"Maybe it's the escaped person," I blurted.

Alex clapped me on the shoulder. "Come on, Mitch, you're letting your nightmares get the best of you. We're here to have fun, remember?"

I looked at him, my mind still on the scream and the prints. "I know. But I can't shake this feeling something's off."

Alex rolled his eyes. "You're always overthinking things. It's probably just some desert critter, like the ranger said."

"But what if it's not?" I pressed. "What if someone's in trouble?"

Alex sighed, running a hand through his hair. "Look, I get it. Your parents' death was tragic, and I know you have these fears and nightmares. But we can't let them ruin our trip."

"This has nothing to do with my parents, Alex."

"Doesn't it? You've been on edge since we got here. You're letting your fears control you."

Before I could respond, Ben intervened. "All right, guys, we're *family*, remember? Let's not fight."

Alex and I exchanged a look, then nodded. "You're right," I said, taking a deep breath. "Let's focus on enjoying Joshua Tree."

* * *

"Hey guys," Ben said, leaning back against a weathered rock, "we need to review our trip plan, remember? We talked about a day of rest. How about it?"

"A rest day?" Alex replied. "That's not exactly my style, Ben. What brought this on?"

"Well ...," Ben said with a thoughtful look, "after yesterday's ... adventures, I think we could all use a little downtime. Recharge the batteries, you know?"

Alex was sprawled on a picnic bench, nursing his ankle with an ice pack. "Okay, okay," he said. "A rest day it is. What do you have in mind?"

"How about a good old-fashioned poker game?" Ben suggested.

"Sounds good to me," I said.

"Well then ... winner takes all," Alex added. "And don't worry, Mitch, I can loan you some funds if you need it."

"It's settled," Ben said. I'll grab grub, drinks, cards, and poker chips from my van. We can chill out, play some cards, and relax."

* * *

Ben, Alex, and I were gathered around the picnic table, a deck of cards between us.

"So, gentlemen," Ben said, picking up and shuffling the cards. "What'll it be? Texas Hold'em? Five-card draw? Seven-card stud? Or maybe we should invent our own game—Desert Poker?"

"Seven-card stud," Alex replied. "Y'all know who the stud is and the winner gets bragging rights for the rest of the trip."

"In your dreams, Alex," Ben replied.

"Let's keep it simple, five-card draw," I suggested.

Alex grinned. "You're going down, Mitch. I've been practicing my poker face."

Ben laughed, shaking his head. "Don't get cocky, Alex. Remember what happened last time in the tree house?"

We all laughed, the memory of our disastrous poker game in the treehouse fresh in our minds. It had been years since we'd last played together, years since we'd just been Ben, Alex, and Mitch, three friends with nothing but time and adventure on our minds.

"You know," Ben said, dealing the cards, "it's good to be back together like this. Just us guys ..."

Alex nodded. "Yeah, it is. It's like we're kids again, back in the treehouse, dreaming up wild adventures."

"Speaking of wild adventures," I said, "what exactly were you thinking, Alex, venturing off into that chasm alone?"

"I know, I know. It was stupid. But I just wanted to prove something, to myself I guess." Alex paused, then added, "I'm not that reckless kid anymore, Mitch. I've grown up."

"Have you?" I countered. "Or are you just better at hiding it?"

"Maybe a little of both," Alex said. "But seriously, guys, I'm glad we're here together. I've missed this."

Ben nodded. "Me too, Alex. Me too."

With the stakes set, we dove into the game. The cards flew, the chips clinked, and the trash talk flowed. We were like kids again, lost in the thrill of the game, the years melting away with each hand.

* * *

"Okay, gentlemen," Alex drawled, leaning forward. "How about we make this more interesting? Let's raise the stakes. Winner gets to pose a challenge."

"A dare?" Ben asked.

"Exactly," Alex said. "That's what makes it fun. Winner gets to come up with a dare for one of the losers. And the loser has to do it. No backing out."

I hesitated, glancing at Ben. "Common Alex," let's just play cards.

"Come on, man up, Mitch!" Alex replied.

"Truth or dare?" Ben asked. "That takes me back to our middle school days."

I sighed, knowing I was outnumbered. "Fine," I conceded, "but let's keep it PG-13, okay? No dangerous stunts or public humiliation."

"Deal," Alex said, leaning forward.

Ben shuffled the deck. "Alright, gentlemen, five-card draw, winner picks the truth or dare."

"Five-card draw, huh?" I said, placing my chips on the table. "This might be more my speed. I can actually calculate some probabilities." I'd always preferred the logic of it, unlike the chaotic nature of the other games.

Alex smiled confidently. "Probabilities, schmobabilities, *Professor*. This game's all about guts and a little bit of luck."

Ben dealt five cards face down to each of us. I picked up my cards and looked at them. Ugh. Not good. I shook my head and pushed three cards toward the center of the table. Ben asked for two new cards, and Alex, only asked for one card.

"I'm out. I fold," I said quickly, not wanting to waste any more time on this hand. I knew when to cut my losses and move on. I had a feeling that this game would not end well for me.

Ben glanced at his cards. "Okay, I'll open with a small bet," he said, putting more chips into the pot.

Alex looked at his hand and laughed. "I'll see that bet and raise you, *Scoutmaster*." He tossed more chips onto the table.

I watched them both and waited.

The two friends revealed their hands. Ben had a pair of aces, and I thought he had it for sure, but then Alex slammed his cards on the table with a triumphant grin. "Boom! Three kings! Looks like I win this round," Alex declared.

"Well played, Alex," Ben said, his voice good-natured. "Looks like the cards were in your favor. So, who gets the truth or dare this time?"

"Alright, Mitchell Donovan," Alex asked. "Truth or dare? Still a virgin?"

I hesitated. "Dare."

"Okay, here's your dare: drop and give me twenty pushups."

"That's it? I thought you were going to make me do something embarrassing or dangerous."

I dropped to the ground, positioning myself for the pushups. I focused on my form, pushing through the first few reps without much difficulty, but by the tenth pushup, my arms were starting to feel the strain. I could feel my face getting red, but I pushed through, finishing the last few pushups with a grunt.

"Eighteen ... nineteen ... twenty!" I said, getting up off the ground.

Alex shuffled the deck, a look of surprise on his face, impressed. "Wow! You're stronger than you look! Alright, gentlemen, let's see if *QB One* can win two hands in a row."

Ben laughed. "Don't underestimate me, Alex. You might be surprised."

I looked at my cards, they were better than the last hand, but not great. I thought about the odds of pulling a straight after drawing one card. I decided to try it. Ben and Alex both decided to draw two cards each, their faces unreadable. Ben opened the next round of betting, and Alex called.

"Two pairs, aces and deuces," Ben announced. He'd won the hand.

"Well done, *Scoutmaster*!" Alex said, throwing his cards down with a dramatic gesture. "Looks like you had a lucky hand. Who is your victim?"

"Alright, Alex, it's your turn," Ben said. "Alex, run a lap around the campground or tell us what happened that summer after high school."

"Seriously?" Alex glanced down at his ankle, wincing slightly, which was still a bit sore.

Alex hesitated. He looked away from Ben and then back. "Man, that summer was tough, okay?" He looked down and sighed before continuing. "After my decision to play football in Texas over the Air Force ... and the accident ... that was a rough summer." He paused. "You know, that night ... I was sure he'd kill me. My dad—strict Air Force guy, you know? Failure wasn't an option. And for a while, I thought that was it. Like, I'd ruined everything between us. But it didn't. That's when things got better."

"What changed?" Ben asked.

"Honestly? Time. He was furious, yeah, but he eventually came around. I think he realized I was just a kid trying to live up to impossible expectations. And I realized I needed to stop trying to impress him and just ... be me. That's when things got better."

"Sounds like he really loved you, even if he didn't always show it," I said.

"Yeah, he does," Alex paused. "It was tough for a while, but ... we worked it out, eventually. I wouldn't be here today without him ... even though he was strict and had all those plans for my life. He's always been there for me, even when I didn't deserve it." Alex smiled. "You know ... I was so proud when he came out to Texas for my football games. So ... you happy now, *Scoutmaster*? Did I pass the truth test?"

"I wish I could say the same about my dad," Ben said.

"What do you mean? Your dad was, like, the coolest guy ever. A detective, always solving crimes and telling those crazy stories. He even helped us build the tree house!"

"Yeah, he was. But I don't think he ever got over the fact that I didn't follow in his footsteps. He had my whole life mapped out—the police academy, detective work. Then Jenny got pregnant, and all of that went out the window."

"You think he's disappointed in you?" I asked.

Ben nodded. "I do. He had all these dreams for me, and I took a completely different path. I let my dad down in so many ways. I had to get a job, any job, to support my family.

I looked at him, surprised. Ben had always been the responsible one, the one who seemed to have his life figured out. "What do you mean?"

"I always thought I'd be a cop, like him," Ben continued, sadness in his voice. "But then Jenny got pregnant, and we moved to Oregon, and I just ... I guess I lost my way."

Alex reached out and touched Ben on the shoulder. "You didn't lose your way, man. You found a different path."

"You're a great dad, Ben. And a damn good friend," I said.

Ben smiled, a grateful look in his eyes. "Maybe you're right."

"Ben, listen. I know we're not the best at talking about this kind of stuff, but ... maybe that wall is in your head. You're assuming he's disappointed, but have you ever actually asked him?" Alex asked.

"No. I wouldn't even know where to start," Ben replied. "We barely talk anymore. I even forgot his birthday this year. It's the same day as Alex's, for God's sake."

"Wait, you forgot my birthday too? That's not like you, man," Alex joked.

"Maybe start with his birthday. Call him, apologize, and tell him you miss him."

"Mitch is right. Your dad might surprise you." Alex said.

"Maybe. I'll think about it," Ben replied.

"Good," changing the subject Alex said. "You're the dealer, Mitch."

I took the deck, trying to appear casual as I shuffled. I dealt the cards one by one, glancing at my own hand. I instantly knew I had a winner—a full house. This was it. I carefully arranged my cards, feeling the slight tremor in my fingers and adjusted my glasses.

I watched Alex and Ben pick three new cards, their expressions impossible to read. I reminded myself to keep my breathing steady, to not fidget, to not let my eyes dart to my own cards.

"Winner, winner chicken dinner," I announced victorious at last.

* * *

"What do we do next?" Alex asked, his energy restored after resting for hours playing poker and eating the last of the leftovers from the cooler. Alex stretched out his long legs, his ankle seemingly forgotten now his stomach was full. "Remember the rock formation we saw on the map? Skull Rock? Let's check it out. It's supposed to be epic for photos."

Ben held up a hand. "How about this, we do a shorter hike, something not too strenuous for Alex's ankle.

We set off again, this time following a well-marked trail wound through a grove of Joshuas. My senses felt heightened, every shadow seemed to hold a potential threat, and every rustle in the bushes sent a jolt of adrenaline through me. I lagged behind Ben and Alex, constantly scanning the landscape.

"Hey, Mitch, you coming?" Ben called back to me.

"Yeah," I said, quickening my pace.

We continued for another twenty minutes, the trail becoming steeper and more uneven as we approached the site of the boulders. Here, the terrain felt otherworldly—like a natural labyrinth of stone. The largest boulders rose several stories high, their surfaces etched with streaks of mineral deposits. Beneath them, the shadows deepened into narrow crevices and hidden alcoves.

Suddenly, another scream pierced the air. This time, it was real.

"Someone, help!" a woman cried.

"What the ...?" Alex started, but before he could finish, Ben was already sprinting toward the sound, his face grim, his detective instincts replaced by the urgency of a first responder.

We scrambled after him, our hearts pounding. As we rounded a cluster of boulders, the source of the commotion came into view. A group of hikers huddled around a figure sprawled on the ground, their faces a mixture of shock and horror.

"Call 9-1-1" someone yelled.

"Give her some air!" another shouted.

Ben pushed through the crowd, his voice cutting through the chaos. "Back away, give her some room to breathe."

Chapter 13

Ben

Wednesday, December 18—Hidden Valley Campground, Joshua Tree.

I saw the woman sprawled on the trail ahead, her body twisted at an unnatural angle. My heart thundered as I scrambled over the rocks, adrenaline surging through me. Towering cliffs framed the scene, their sharp edges silhouetted against the sky. A dark streak on the rock face above caught my eye—had she fallen from up there?

My mind zipped through the wilderness first-aid training, now second nature. *Scene size up*, I reminded myself. Is it safe? Rocky, exposed. Limited resources, no cell service. The desert was indifferent, offering no immediate threats.

"Scene safe," I muttered, my eyes darting around. I dropped to my knees beside the woman, my training kicking in. Her face, pale against the red dust, her lips swollen.

"Everyone, stay back!" I yelled. "Give her space!" The small group of hikers scattered. "Ma'am, can you hear me?" I asked, gently touching her shoulder. No response. Her eyes were closed, her breathing shallow. Blood trickled from a gash on her forehead.

"Okay, let's see what I'm dealing with," I told myself. *Airway, breathing, circulation,* training repeated in my head. I tilted her head back, listening for any sign of breath.

ABCDE ... just like the training.

Airway. I gently tilted her chin up, checking for any obstructions. "Clear."

Breathing. Shallow and rapid, but present. Good sign.

"Ok, she's breathing," I said.

I heard a gasp, not from her, but from someone nearby.

Circulation. I pressed into the cold skin of her wrist, searching for a pulse. The seconds sped by, like a clock ticking fast and loud in my head, a relentless reminder of the stakes. Pulse weak and thready. Need to control that bleeding. *No time to waste.*

Disability. Unconscious, possibly a head injury. Need to keep her spine stabilized.

Evacuation decision. "She's alive," I announced to the anxious faces surrounding me, "but we need to keep her stable until we can get her out of here."

"I think she fell. Hit her head pretty hard," a woman's voice came from behind me.

"Mitch, get your kit! And help me stabilize her neck and spine." I barked orders. Every second counted.

Mitch scrambled to my side, his backpack hitting the ground with a thud. "Got it," Mitch fumbled with the zipper, his fingers shaking. "Here's the first-aid kit!"

"Good man" I said, grabbing the gauze pads and pressure bandage. "Now, listen carefully. I need you to hold her neck steady. Don't let it move an inch. Got it?"

Mitch nodded, his touch surprisingly firm. "Don't worry, Ben. I won't let go."

Gauze pads, pressure bandages ... I carefully cleaned the wound on her forehead, the blood clotting quickly. Then, I gently positioned her, keeping her head and neck aligned, into the recovery position.

"We need to keep her warm," I said, looking around for anything that could serve as a blanket. A woman quickly offered her jacket. I draped it over the injured hiker, tucking it around her body.

"Can someone call for help?" I asked.

"No cell service out here," Alex said. "We're on our own for now."

I continued to monitor her vital signs. We were miles from any help. *She's stable, but barely,* I thought, my fingers tracing the faint pulse in her wrist. *We need to get her to a hospital, and quickly.* Despite all my training, I was worried. Her life was in my hands, and I was miles from any real medical help, deep in the heart of Joshua Tree. *But I can't give up,* I told myself, focusing on the task at hand.

"What happened?" someone asked. "Is she going to be okay?"

What happened? My mind raced through the possibilities. Despite all my training, I felt helpless. Her life was in my hands—a woman unconscious and badly injured under mysterious circumstances.

"Come on," I urged. "Don't give up on me. Do not die today."

* * *

A figure emerged from behind a boulder. It was a man, compact yet rugged, with a calmness that seemed out of place in the chaos. He knelt beside me, his deep brown eyes meeting mine, filled with a weariness that spoke of hard days and sleepless nights. A thick stubble covered his cheeks. He looked like he belonged here, a creature of the wilderness, his presence as natural as the rocks and sand surrounding us.

"Let me see," he said, his voice calm but firm, cutting through the panic. His eyes swept over her, taking in her shallow breaths and swollen face, and the head wound. "I'm a paramedic," he added, his hands already reaching for her wrist to check her pulse.

I hesitated. A paramedic? Out here, in the middle of nowhere? *He's good*, I thought, watching as he expertly assessed her airway and breathing.

"Her pulse is weak," he said, his voice low and urgent.

"We need to get help. *Stat!*" He took charge, barking orders. "Switch positions," he instructed me to take over for Mitch bracing her neck. "Go get help. Call for emergency responders," he said pointing at Alex and Mitch.

Alex and Ben, their initial shock giving way to action, scrambled to follow his commands. I watched as his hands, calloused but gentle, moved with trained precision as he examined her.

Suddenly, Mitch stopped, turned, and shouted, "Hey, catch!" and tossed his backpack toward the paramedic. It landed in the dirt. "This might help!"

"Let's see what we've got in here," he said, unzipping the pockets. A familiar assortment of gadgets and gear spilled onto the sand—Mitch's incredible *just-in-case* kit.

The paramedic blew a low whistle. "Not bad, kid. Not bad at all." He held up the water filter, a look of approval in his eyes. "This could be a lifesaver. And this survival blanket ..." He unfolded the lightweight fabric, his eyes sweeping over the surrounding landscape. He paused, lingering on the first-aid kit. "No IV supplies, but we can at least monitor and care for her until help arrives."

I was grateful for Mitch's meticulous preparation. His backpack, usually the source of good-natured teasing, offered much needed hope.

"I'm Ben," I told the paramedic, breaking the silence.

He nodded with a smile. "I know," he replied, his voice soft. "I heard your friends call you earlier."

I raised an eyebrow, curious about this stranger who had appeared out of nowhere to help save a life.

He seemed to understand my unspoken question. "I was climbing not too far away when I heard the commotion. I came to see if I could help. I didn't expect to find her here like this."

We looked at each other, a silent understanding.

"We need to figure out what happened to her and get her to the hospital," I said. "We owe her that much."

He nodded. "Agreed. But we're limited here. No medical devices, no way to transport her quickly. First, we need to stabilize her and assess the extent of her injuries."

He worked quickly, checking for any hidden injuries. Gently, searching for fractures or dislocations. and carefully examined her scalp for more signs of head trauma.

"Good work stopping the bleeding" he said. "But we need to keep her warm and hydrated."

Her leg was at an odd angle. "I think her ankle might be injured."

The paramedic nodded. "If only we had a splint kit. For now, let's try to immobilize it as best we can."

As we worked together, the paramedic's calm, authoritative presence guided me through each step, turning a chaotic situation into a coordinated rescue effort.

"She's stabilizing," the paramedic said, a note of relief in his voice. "Now we need to keep her comfortable until help arrives."

He paused, looking over the surrounding landscape. "I hope those men will be able to get help. Cell service is spotty out here, but they might get lucky. We need to get her professional medical attention immediately."

I placed a reassuring hand on his shoulder. "Don't worry, they'll do everything they can. Mitch is incredibly resourceful, and if anyone can find a signal, he can. And Alex? He can run like the wind. They'll get help."

I saw confidence in his eyes. "Good. In the meantime, we need to keep an eye on her. Any changes in consciousness, breathing, or pulse, let me know immediately."

We continued working together in a silent practice of emergency-rescue procedures and switched positions as I monitored her airway, ensuring it remained clear. He checked her pupils, noting their sluggish response to light. We searched for any signs of external injuries, snake bites, scrapes, fractures.

"We need to get her out of the direct sun and wrap her to keep her body warm," he said with a sense of urgency.

He pulled the foil emergency blanket from Mitch's backpack. Carefully, he unfolded it and wrapped it around her, tucking it snugly to trap her body heat. Then, I noticed the glare of the bright sun was still beating down on her face. I grabbed a jacket that someone offered, and gently draped it over her head, making sure it didn't block her airway.

I looked over at the paramedic, thinking of us two strangers, thrown together by the dangers in the desert but united in our purpose.

Suddenly, her eyelids fluttered open, revealing dazed, unfocused eyes.

"Can you tell me your name?" the paramedic asked, leaning close to her ear.

"Ev ... Evie," she whispered, her voice barely audible.

He nodded. "Any pain? Dizziness? Nausea?"

She shook her head weakly. "Th ... thirsty."

The paramedic sighed. "We need to get fluids into her, but without an IV kit, we're limited." He looked around, his eyes on Mitch's backpack. "We'll have to rely on oral rehydration for now."

I rummaged through Mitch's pack, finding a few electrolyte tablets and a half-full water bottle. "Here, this is all I have," I said, offering them to him.

He nodded. "Good. Let's get these dissolved and see if we can get her to sip some. We also need to elevate her legs, help prevent shock."

I gathered some rocks and propped her legs up.

"Okay, Evie," he said. "We're going to get you some help. Just hang in there."

"Evie, can you tell me what happened?"

She winced, a flicker of pain crossing her face. "I ... I don't remember. I ... we...were. ... hiking ... then everything went black."

"Ben, look at her face, it's swelling too."

* * *

Just as a sense of cautious optimism began to settle, the situation took a turn for the worse. One of the bystanders, who had been watching our frantic efforts with wide, anxious eyes, suddenly swayed on her feet. Her face became pale, and she crumpled to the ground with a gasp, hitting the dirt with a thud.

Before I could react, the paramedic was on his feet, moving with the speed and precision of an experienced professional. He knelt beside the fallen camper, his hands already assessing her condition.

"Ben," he barked, his voice sharp and commanding, "stay with Evie. Monitor her closely."

I nodded, my heart pounding. The situation was spinning out of control.

The paramedic turned to the other onlookers, his voice booming through the desert air. "Someone assist me here! The rest of you, head back to camp. Get to a phone and call 9-1-1. Tell them we need a rescue chopper. We have two people down."

The remaining hikers sprang into action, some rushing to the paramedic's side, others scrambling back toward the campground. I was left alone with Evie, her shallow breaths the only sound in the vast expanse of the desert. Fear surged in me. Could we keep them both alive until help arrived?

"What happened to her?" I asked, glancing over my shoulder as he worked on the second woman.

"Looks like she fainted," he replied without missing a beat, his hands steady as he tilted her head back. "Probably a panic response to everything going on. Fear can do that—triggers a fight-or-flight reaction."

I nodded, my eyes never leaving Evie. "She's stable for now, but we need to keep her hydrated."

"Agreed," the paramedic said, his eyes shifting between the two patients. "We'll need to improvise. Any more water?"

I shook my head. "That was the last of it."

"Ma'am, are you all right?" His voice was gentle. "Can you tell me your name?"

"Rose," the older woman replied, her voice weak. "Oh my, what happened? I'm so embarrassed."

I leaned closer to Evie, my voice a soothing murmur. "Evie, can you hear me? It's Ben. Try to focus on my voice."

Her eyelids fluttered, her eyes unfocused.

"You collapsed, Rose," the paramedic explained. "But you're safe now. We're here to help you."

"Evie," I repeated, my tone patient. "Can you open your eyes for me? Do you remember what you were doing before you collapsed?"

"Hiking ... climbing ..."

"Were you alone, Evie?" I asked.

"No ... with ... a friend," Evie mumbled, her eyes drifting closed.

"Do you remember their name?" I asked.

"Umm ...," she replied, her voice growing weaker.

"Evie," I said urgently, "can you hear me? Stay with me, Evie. Can you tell me your friend's name?"

A flicker of recognition crossed Evie's face. "A ... man ...," she whispered, her voice barely audible. "I need my ... meds ..."

"Meds?" I pressed, my heart pounding. "What kind of meds, Evie?"

"All ... allergies."

"Possible anaphylactic shock," the paramedic said, more to himself than me. "We need to act quickly. If only we had an epinephrine auto injector, just in case she had an allergic reaction."

I checked her pulse ... weak. Her skin was clammy, and her lips and cheeks were swelling like a balloon. There was a rash on her face. *Shock,* I realized. *And possible head injury.* Her eyes closed, her breathing shallow and labored. Something was terribly wrong, and time was running out. Her breathing grew shallow, her pulse fluttering beneath my fingertips. A wave of panic washed over me. "She's fading," I said.

The paramedic looked at her, his expression determined. "We need to keep her talking, Ben. Keep her engaged."

His use of my name, the directness of his attention, and something in the way he spoke sparked a glimmer of recognition. He wasn't just a skilled paramedic; he was like me, I could tell. A man helping someone in danger. I wondered if he was also a dad.

"Thank you ...," I said, extending a hand one more time, a silent offering of trust, a fragile bridge.

He hesitated, his eyes searching mine, then grasped my hand, his grip firm. "Kai," he replied, his voice a low murmur.

And in a brief exchange, a bond formed, a silent understanding between two men, perhaps two fathers fighting against the odds, united by a desperate hope, a shared prayer for a miracle in the unforgiving heart of the desert.

"Evie," stay with me.

* * *

Evie's pulse faltered. Her breathing was weak. Evie was slipping away from us.

"We need to start compressions," Kai commanded.

Thirty chest compressions. "One, two, three, four ..." I counted to maintain the rhythm. A bead of sweat trickled down my face, mixing with the dust. Each compression was a desperate plea, a race against the clock. But she was unresponsive. Was it too late?

We worked together, our actions synchronized as if we'd done this a thousand times before. Back and forth we went, our efforts a desperate dance against time. Sweat trickled down my forehead, stinging my eyes. My arms ached from the exertion, but I pushed through the pain. The man was a rock, his resolve unwavering. He didn't falter, didn't hesitate. His confidence was infectious, and I drew strength from it. We were a team, united by a common goal: to save a life.

"She's young and strong," he said. "Keep fighting!"

And then, just when I thought we might lose her, he let out a triumphant cry. "She has a pulse! It's faint, but it's there."

Hope surged through me, but I knew our work was far from over.

Chapter 14

Alex

Wednesday, December 18—Hidden Valley Campground, Joshua Tree.

My heart thundered as Mitch, and I raced away from the scene. The stranger's words repeated in my mind, *Go get help!* His command was as harsh and unforgiving as the desert itself.

The man wasn't a hulking figure, like the left tackle back in Texas when I played college ball. But his presence was intimidating, his command absolute. I was worried about the woman we'd stumbled upon. But there was no time for fear. We had a mission. I thought back to my football days: the adrenaline rush, the focus. This was no different.

My athletic build, toned from years of playing football, propelled me forward. My breath came in ragged gasps, each breath tasting of the trail's grit and the fiery kick of hot sauce and fear. I glanced over my shoulder, shouting at Mitch to keep up. But Mitch wasn't built for such physical exertion. He lagged, his face a mask of determination and exhaustion. I remembered our childhood races, how we used to compete for everything. But this was no game, this was real.

I pushed forward, my muscles straining with each stride. Pain shot through my ankle, a sharp reminder of my tumble earlier. I gritted my teeth, pushing through it. This wasn't some college game, this was real life, and there was no chance for a time-out. The campground, a touchdown waiting to happen in the distance, was my end zone. This time, the cheers of the crowd would be the silent prayers of my friends. The desert was a harsh and unforgiving place, but I was no stranger to challenges. I had outrun linebackers twice my size on the football field, and I would tackle this challenge too. The end zone wasn't a painted white line on a green field this time but the campground, our base, our hope. I remembered the cheers of the crowd, the thrill of the game. But this was no game, this was survival.

I could feel the sun on my back, the dry air sucking the moisture from my lips. But I kept running. I had to. There was too much at stake. I wasn't just running for myself but for Mitch, for Ben, for the woman whose life hung in the balance. I thought about our past adventures, the close calls, the laughs. This was different, this was serious.

The desert sand crunched beneath my boots, each stride a desperate push against the unforgiving trail. The sun shined overhead, a relentless adversary in this race against time. Mitch was falling behind.

I skidded to a stop, dust swirling around my ankles. "Mitch, keep up!" I shouted, glancing over my shoulder. His face was pale with exertion. "What are you doing?" I barked, frustration edging into my voice.

He stumbled to a stop, doubling over, gasping for air. "Faster ... to throw ... the ball," he wheezed, pointing at his phone.

It took me a second, then it clicked. Mitch, the brains of our outfit, had a plan.

"But how will you get reception?"

He pointed to a cluster of towering rock formations in the distance. "I need to ... climb ... to the top," Mitch said.

Of course, I thought, proud. Mitch, our friend who'd always been terrified of heights, was gonna climb a mountain to save a life.

Fear flickered in his eyes, but it was quickly overshadowed by resolve. He was going to do it, no matter the cost. A lump formed in my throat. This was more than just a rescue mission, it was a demonstration of our friendship and trust in each other.

"You got this, Mitch," I said, my voice filled with newfound respect. "I'll get back to the campground. You make the call."

I turned and ran, the desert blurring around me. The familiar rhythm of my strides, the burn in my lungs, it all felt different now. I wasn't the quarterback anymore, calling the shots, expecting everyone to follow my lead. I was the receiver, running a route Mitch had drawn up, trusting him to deliver the perfect pass. The campground was the end zone, and I was determined to catch a touchdown.

* * *

As I ran, I thought about how this trip had taken a chilling turn. What was supposed to be a reunion had turned into a high-stakes game of survival. But I couldn't afford to dwell on it now. Now I had to run.

The desert stretched before me, vast and unyielding. But I was undeterred. I was a man on a mission. And I wouldn't stop until I got help.

I rounded a large boulder, the campground coming into view. I was close. I could see the familiar tents dotting the landscape, searching for the old man and his dog, the park ranger, someone to help. But as I neared the campground, my relief turned to dread. The reality of the situation hit me hard. The campground was a whirlwind of activity—families packing up their gear, kids chasing each other, blissfully unaware of the life-or-death situation unfolding just a few miles away.

"Help!" I shouted, my voice raw, my throat burning. "Someone's hurt! We need help!"

A few heads turned, but most people just stared at me, then went back to their leisurely activities. Frustration gnawed at me as my heart pounded. Each beat a reminder of our race against time.

I sprinted from tent to tent, my desperation rising.

A few heads turned, curiosity flickering in their eyes, then just as quickly turning away, dismissing me as some kind of overreacting drama queen. Frustration surged through me, hot and bitter.

"Please," I begged, grabbing a woman's arm as she packed up her camping chairs.

She pulled away, annoyance replacing the fleeting concern in her eyes. "Look, I saw what happened earlier. You guys need to be more careful. Just go find a ranger."

"Yeah, call the ranger," a man muttered from inside his tent, his voice muffled. "It's what they pay them for."

The words stung, a reminder of my own recklessness, the burden I'd placed on Ben and Mitch.

The ranger! I frantically scanned the campground, my eyes landing on a man in a ranger's uniform, talking urgently into a radio. I stumbled toward him, hope reigniting.

As I got closer, I caught snippets of his conversation. "A ... a hiker ... unconscious ... needs immediate assistance ..."

Mitch had done it! He'd gotten through. Relief washed over me, mingling with the sweat stinging my eyes.

"Ranger!" I gasped, collapsing in front of him. "Thank God! We need your help!"

He looked at me, surprise quickly replaced by recognition. "You're with the group who called in?"

I nodded, words tumbling out in a rush. "My friends, Mitch, Ben ... a woman ... collapsed. We need to get back there!"

The ranger's face hardened. He barked into his radio, issuing orders with a calm authority that reminded me of Coach during a crucial game. The ranger instructed me to follow him. I jumped aboard his off-road buggy, equipped with emergency supplies, and held on with all my strength. I was no longer alone. We had a plan, a leader. And I was ready to follow, to do whatever it took to get back to them.

* * *

The jeep bounced and swerved, the ranger's strong hands gripping the steering wheel while navigating the treacherous path. Suddenly, a flash of color caught my eye.

"Mitch," I shouted, pointing toward the distant figure perched atop a massive rock formation. "You did it!"

Mitch waved, a triumphant grin on his face. The ranger slowed the jeep, maneuvering closer to the base of the rocks.

"Mitch, climb down! We'll pick you up ahead!" I yelled, my voice barely audible over the roar of the engine and the wind whipping past us.

Mitch gave a thumbs-up and began his descent, his movements surprisingly agile for someone who'd just conquered his fear of heights. The ranger and I exchanged a look of relief. One hurdle cleared, but the biggest challenge still lay ahead.

The ranger pushed the buggy to its limits, the engine roaring as we tore through the desert. The wind whipped past us, carrying the scent of sagebrush and dust. I gripped the roll bar, my knuckles white, my eyes fixed on the horizon.

"So," the ranger's voice cut through the noise, "what exactly happened out there?"

I swallowed, trying to gather my thoughts. "We were hiking and found a woman collapsed on the trail. Bens with her and the other stranger now, trying to keep her stable."

"And the other guy?" the ranger asked.

Mitch and I exchanged a nervous glance.

"We don't know who he is. He just showed up, said he was a paramedic, and started helping Ben. The ranger nodded, his jaw set. "A paramedic? Interesting, did he have a tattoo on his forearm?

"I couldn't see closely," Mitch replied.

"No worries. We'll get to the bottom of this."

As we rounded a bend, the scene came into view. The huddled figures, the tension in the air, but our path was blocked by a large boulder. *Please let her be okay.*

The jeep skidded to a halt, sending a cloud of dust billowing into the air. I jumped and my boots hit the ground. The scene before me was a tangle of emotions. Ben kneeling beside the unconscious woman, the blanket flapping in the wind, and the mysterious man—the paramedic—frozen for a moment before taking one look at us and racing away, disappearing around the rocks.

"That's him." The ranger's voice was tight, his eyes on the man. "The escaped suspect, the person of interest."

The words hung in the air, heavy and ominous. *Escaped suspect?*

We ran toward the woman on the ground wrapped in an emergency blanket, her face the only thing visible. Her face was obscured by the coat covering her head, but something about her stirred a distant memory.

Mitch's voice cut through the tension. "I know her! She was at the restaurant on the Palm Springs tram!"

The ranger joined Ben on the ground by her side, his skilled hands checking for a pulse, his radio crackling with urgent instructions. Ben, looking exhausted but relieved, stepped back, his eyes meeting mine.

"She's alive," Ben said, his voice hoarse. "But struggling ... the paramedic ... Kai ... suggested anaphylactic shock from an allergic reaction."

The ranger's voice was sharp. "Any known allergies?"

"Her lips and face are swollen, and she mentioned medicine before she lost consciousness."

The ranger's expression shifted, his jaw tightening as his eyes locked onto us with intense focus. "Could be an allergic reaction in addition to the fall. We need to act fast." He reached for his medical kit, his movements swift and efficient. "This should help open her airways and stabilize her blood pressure." He administered an EpiPen.

Minutes ticked by, each one agonizingly slow.

Then, finally, a flicker of life in the woman's eyes.

"She's stabilizing," the ranger announced with relief. "But we need to get her to a hospital."

As the woman stirred, I stepped closer, my mind reeling. The escaped criminal, the woman from the restaurant, what was the connection?

The ranger turned to us, his expression grave. "The man who helped you, he's dangerous," he warned.

"That can't be possible," Ben looked shocked. "But he helped us. Why did he run?"

"He's an escaped person of interest," the ranger repeated, his voice firm. "We need to find him. And we need to figure out what happened here."

I turned to Mitch. "Wait a minute." A jolt of recognition shot through me. "The couple at the tram restaurant! The ones I paid for dinner?" The memory of that night, the extravagant gesture, the subtle tension between the couple, it all came rushing back.

"Yeah, that's her, I'm pretty sure," Mitch confirmed.

"I didn't get a good look at her then," I admitted, my mind racing. "But ..." The image of her elegant attire, the way she'd barely touched her food, the man's cold, calculating eyes, it all started to come into focus.

"Can you tell me anything else about the woman?" the ranger asked Mitch. "Did she mention where she was staying or who she was with?"

Mitch shook his head. "No, we just had a brief conversation at the restaurant. But she did seem a bit ... on edge. Quiet. She was with a man, and their interaction felt off."

The ranger nodded, scribbling notes in his worn notebook. His attention then shifted to me. "Alex, do you remember anything about her?"

"I mostly remember the man. At first, he had a certain... presence that impressed me. But over time, I didn't like him much."

The ranger's expression hardened. "Any details you can remember might help."

I hesitated, the image of the man's cold, calculating eyes flashing before me. "He was tall and well-dressed, sporting an expensive watch. His name was Randy ... Randall. But it seemed like he cared more about his real estate ventures than his date."

"Randall Thorne," Mitch added.

The ranger nodded again. "We'll do our best to identify her and notify her family." His voice was heavy with the weight of responsibility.

Meanwhile, Ben had been monitoring the woman while listening. He turned to the ranger. "Can you tell us more about the man who helped me, Kai? Who is he?

The ranger looked at Ben. "His name is Kai Nguyen. He was being held at a nearby county jail and escaped during a transfer to the courthouse for arraignment, along with another suspect."

"That cannot be possible," Ben replied.

The ranger sighed. "I wish it weren't."

"We need to figure this out," I said.

Mitch nodded, his face pale. "We will."

The sound of helicopter blades cut through the silence, a rhythmic thumping bounced off the rocky landscape. I watched it land in a nearby clearing. The dust kicked up by the rotor wash stung my eyes.

Two responders jumped out of the helicopter, their movements swift and sure. They raced toward us, medical bags in hand. They knelt beside the woman, checking her vitals and assessing her injuries.

The ranger was by their side in an instant, relaying information, guiding them. He had taken charge of the situation from the moment we'd found the woman, his calm and steady presence like a rock-solid captain on the field.

We watched as they carefully immobilized her neck and back, then moved her onto a carrying platform, securing her with straps. Every movement was precise, every action calculated. They were professionals, and they were here to save a life.

They loaded her into the helicopter, the ranger giving them a final nod. Then, with a roar of the engine, the helicopter lifted off, disappearing into the sky. We watched until it was nothing more than a speck in the distance, its rhythmic thumping fading.

The dust settled, the echo of the helicopter fading into the vast desert. It wasn't just the adrenaline of the climb, or the rush from the rescue. Something had shifted. The desert, my playground of epic adventures, had shown its true nature. I knew then, we weren't just three guys on a camping trip. We were a team, a force, a unit.

Chapter 15

Ben

Thursday, December 19—Day five, Cholla Cactus Garden and stargazing, Joshua Tree.

The past few days were a blur of danger and near tragedy, ending with the frantic helicopter rescue. As the sun rose, the usual campground sounds—conversations, chirping birds—seemed louder, sharper. It was like the desert was holding its breath, waiting for the next crisis.

"Good morning, Ben, how about a cup of joe?" Alex asked, handing me a warm mug.

"Just what I needed," I replied, inhaling the aroma, gulping the delicious coffee, and warming my hands. I sat in the camp chair next to Alex while Mitch flipped pancakes.

"Yep, here's a pancake, looks just like you." Mitch grinned, passing me a plate with a pancake shaped like Superman with a cape.

I looked at the dirt with mixed emotions. "I'm not so sure."

"Morning, hero!" I looked up to see Sarah, her usual sunny smile a bit shaky. John stood behind her, nodding. "We heard what happened yesterday. You guys were amazing. You saved the woman's life."

Warmth crept up my neck, but it wasn't the sun. "It was a team effort," I said, taking a bite of the delicious pancake.

"Yeah, *Team Awesome!*" Alex boasted, already on his second pancake. "Mitch, you were a rock star, scaling the cliff to get a signal. Ben, you were practically a surgeon with your first-aid expertise."

"And you," Mitch added, handing Alex another pancake. "You sprinted like your college days to find the ranger."

"Not bad for a twisted ankle, huh?"

Sofia tugged at my sleeve. "Did you see the helicopter?"

"Yep, I did." I smiled.

Her parents, Marco and Isabella, were quick to thank us too, their relief clear. The campground felt like one giant emotional hug. For a moment, I let myself be swept up in it. We were heroes. It felt ... strange.

I spotted Sam approaching, Rusty trotting beside him, his nose locked on the sweet smell of maple syrup rising from my pancake. Sam stopped before us, his usual easygoing smile replaced by a frown.

"Morning, folks. Before you head out, I thought you should know. Got an update from the ranger about the woman you found." He paused. "She's still in the hospital. Alive ..."

"I hope she recovers," I said.

Sam nodded. "Seems she doesn't remember much."

Alive. Thank God, I thought. But Evie was lost in the fog of forgotten memories.

"The desert keeps its secrets," Sam said. "Sometimes, those secrets come at a cost." He paused, his eyes glancing between us. "They're searching for the man who helped you, Ben. He's now a person of interest—maybe even a suspect.

There's a chance he's the one who hurt her in the first place. A good deed, sure, but they're still investigating."

Sam's news hit me hard—relief, grateful the woman was alive, and a feeling of cognitive dissonance.

"Kai helped save her," I said, my mind replaying how he had taken charge, his hands sure and steady during the rescue. A part of me wanted to dive into this whole thing and investigate, just like my dad would have.

Mitch frowned. "He's an escaped suspect in a crime, Ben. Helping her doesn't erase it."

Alex shrugged. "Let the cops sort it out. We've got a desert to explore. Come on, guys, those stars aren't going to gaze at themselves."

Sam studied my conflicted expression. He placed a weathered hand on my shoulder, his touch surprisingly firm. "You boys did your part. Sometimes, the best thing you can do is step back and let the authorities handle things. Don't let this ruin your trip. The desert's still full of beauty. The sky will be spectacular tonight. You've earned a little peace."

Mitch nodded. "He's right. These stargazing conditions are perfect tonight after the storms."

I looked up at the sky. My dad's voice sounded in my memory. *Everyone has a story. Even the bad guys.* Was Kai's story one of desperation, of a good man forced into impossible choices? Or was he simply a wolf in sheep's clothing, using his skills to manipulate and deceive?

"Go on, son," Sam said. "These moments with your friends, under these stars ... they're precious. Don't let them slip away."

He was right. We had been through enough. And those stars ...

"Ben?" Alex was watching me. "What's our plan, *Scoutmaster*?"

"Okay, give me a minute," I forced a smile. "I need to get something from my van first."

* * *

That's weird, I thought, I was sure I locked the camper van door last night. Typical Alex, snacking in the middle of the night. As I opened the van door, I saw Kai hiding in the back. We stared at each other for a long moment, not speaking.

"You need to turn yourself in," I finally urged.

"I can't, it's too late," Kai replied, his voice rough with despair.

"No, it's never too late," I insisted, stepping closer. "Look, I trust you. Let's walk and talk for a minute."

Kai hesitated, then nodded. We walked into the maze of boulders, away from the campground, the silence broken only by the crunch of our boots on the sand. We found a large boulder and sat, the desert stretching out around us, vast and indifferent.

"Come on, what's your story?" I asked gently, trying to build a connection.

Kai began to share his story. "It started when I was desperate. My son was diagnosed with cancer, and the medical bills were piling up. I didn't know where to turn. I took a job—a risky job—transporting some ... sensitive materials. I thought it was the answer to my prayers. A way to pay for the surgery, to save my son's life." His voice cracked, the weight of his past heavy on his shoulders. "But it all went wrong. The cops showed up. There was a shootout. I didn't hurt anyone, didn't even have a gun. It was the other guy. But I panicked. I ran." He looked at me, his eyes filled with regret.

"I understand," I said, my voice soft. "The things we do for family ..." I thought of Jenny, the kids, the sacrifices we'd made over the years. "It's not always easy. My wife just started working again, we finally have health insurance. But for a while there, it was just me, contract work, spotty health coverage. It can be scary."

Kai nodded, a flash of trust in his eyes. "It is. You feel so ... responsible. Like you have to protect them, no matter what."

I nodded in agreement. "You do. It's what dads do."

Then, Kai revealed something that made my blood run cold. He had seen a man arguing with the woman up on the boulders while he was climbing. "I think he did something to hurt her," Kai said.

"A man and a woman?" I asked.

"He was tall, rough-looking, the way he held her, it wasn't right. He was ... he was practically dragging her along the trail." Kai's voice shook slightly. "They were arguing, and he seemed like he was threatening her, like he might push her."

"Threatening her?"

Kai nodded. "I didn't know what to do. I was...well, I was trying to stay hidden."

"Wait ... the woman on the trail...the one we found, the one you helped. Was it Evie?"

Kai nodded slowly. "I think so...I think it was."

The newspaper story about the missing women, the rock climber, flashed through my mind. It all started to make sense.

"You need to turn yourself in," I said, my voice firm but compassionate. "Report what you saw. I'll vouch for you in court if necessary."

Kai looked at me, a flicker of hope in his eyes. "You'd do that for me?"

I nodded. "We all deserve a second chance."

* * *

We stood there for a moment, the significance of Kai's decision hanging in the air. Then, with a nod, Kai turned and headed towards the ranger station, his shoulders squared with a newfound determination. I watched him go, a mix of admiration and relief spinning within me. As I turned back towards the campground, I saw Alex and Mitch waiting for me.

"*Superman*," Alex exclaimed, "Dude, what took you so long? I was about to lead a search party for you!"

Mitch added. "Yeah, Alex was ready to grab his search binoculars. Figured you were off solving the mystery of the century or something."

"Not quite, but close. I ran into Kai—our paramedic on the run."

"You *what*?" Alex asked.

"He decided to turn himself in," I explained. "We talked for a while, and he shared his story with me—what he witnessed. A man arguing with the woman, practically dragging her along the trail. He said the man looked rough, like he might hurt her, and Kai's been hiding ever since, scared to come forward. But after our talk, he realized he needs to tell the authorities everything he knows about what went down."

Mitch let out a low whistle. "Man, that's wild."

"He wants to set the record straight," I said. "Honestly, after talking to him, I think he's doing the right thing. Feels like a weight's been lifted."

"Good for you, Ben. Another mystery solved, huh?" Alex paused. "Well, are we just going to stand around and talk all day, or what? I'm ready for some actual fun!"

"Alright, team," I said. "How about we get back on track to our original plan?"

Alex laughed. "You mean the plan we ditched when all hell broke loose?"

"Exactly," I said. "Let's take the van over to the Cholla Cactus Garden, check it out for a bit, and then hike up to stargaze. It's time we make the most of this trip."

"Sounds good to me," Mitch said. "But if we run into any more mysteries, I'm officially retiring from amateur investigations."

I swung open the door of my van. The familiar scent of sun-warmed upholstery and camping gear welcomed me. We were going to trust Kai, Sam, the authorities, and each other. For now, it was time to get back to our trip.

"Load up the van and pile in, guys," I called, tossing our gear and packs into the back.

Alex smiled, slinging his fancy camera bag over his shoulder. "You mean you won't let me get behind the wheel of your baby?"

"Not a chance, hotshot," I replied, grinning as I slid into the driver's seat. The engine roared to life, and I shifted into gear, the familiar feel of the stick in my hand grounding me. "Let's explore!" I pulled out my well-worn park map as we rumbled out of the campground in the van. "Next stop, a cactus garden.

* * *

The Cholla Cactus Garden lived up to its name—a spiky, sprawling forest of teddy-bear cholla. As we stepped onto the trail, the crunch of gravel under our boots felt oddly satisfying. I scanned the landscape, noting trail markers and potential hazards. Old Scout habits die hard.

"See these cacti here?" I pointed to the teddy-bear cholla that dominated the landscape. "They look soft and fluffy, but they're covered with hundreds of thorns. They're called teddy-bear cholla."

"Those cacti are pretty amazing," Mitch said, snapping photos with his phone camera.

"Amazingly prickly," I added. "One wrong step, and you're a human pincushion. They're called teddy bears because they look soft and cuddly, but those spines, man, those will get you."

Alex squinted at the cacti. "They do look like teddy bears. But I wouldn't want to cuddle with one."

Mitch chuckled. "Definitely not. They're also known as *jumping cholla* because the segments can break off and attach to people and animals."

As we continued our hike, I pointed out other plant species. "There's a hedgehog cactus over there, and if you look closely, you can see the desert lavender. The garden attracts a variety of wildlife, even in winter," I said, pointing to a small wren perched on a branch, its sharp eyes scanning the ground for insects. "These birds are year-round residents, perfectly adapted to the harsh desert climate."

We explored the trails, each at our own pace. Alex, as usual, was a blur of energy, his camera clicking nonstop, capturing the strange beauty of the twisted cacti. Mitch was not just looking at the desert blooms, but also scanning the sky and muttering about the unique atmospheric conditions that make winter stargazing in Joshua Tree so exceptional. Me? I was feeling better. More relaxed than I'd felt all week. Saving a life, helping a dad, and being with my best friends in the desert was calming and reassuring.

My thoughts drifted back to Kai, his face filled with desperation as he spoke about his son. It could have been me, I realized. Any one of us, driven to desperate measures by the fear of losing a child. *Speaking of dads ...* I glanced at Alex, a sudden memory jolting me. "Hey, it's almost your birthday, isn't it?"

Alex looked up, surprised. "Yep, Saturday, you remembered."

"December 21st, right?" I asked. "Same as my dad's." I finally remembered what I had forgotten.

"That's right."

Almost forgotten ... Dad's birthday. "I forgot my dad's birthday."

"Alex nodded, "I get it," he said. "Family stuff can be complicated."

"Yeah," I said, staring at the desert. "It can be."

"No, it *is* complicated," Mitch interjected, his voice unusually forceful. "But that doesn't mean you give up. Ben, you need to call your dad."

I looked at Mitch, stunned by his sudden outburst. He was usually so quiet, so reserved. But there was a fire in his eyes now, passion.

"It's his birthday on Saturday, right?" Mitch continued. "Call him. Make a plan to meet up. Life's too short."

His words hit home. He was right. Life *was* too short. I'd learned that lesson the hard way, seeing that woman lying lifeless on the trail.

"I would give anything for one more day with my parents," Mitch said. "One more conversation, one more hug ... Don't waste the time you have, Ben."

Mitch, who had lost so much, was teaching me the value of what I still had. "You're right, Mitch," I said. I'll call him." I knew one thing for sure: my dad would have been proud of me. He would have been proud of the man I'd become, the life I'd built, the friends I'd kept. And he would have been damn proud of the life I'd saved.

A smile brightened Mitch's face. "Good," he said. "Now, let's go enjoy this beautiful day."

* * *

We found a nice spot to set up for lunch. Alex pulled sandwiches and refreshments from his expensive backpack.

"This is kinda nice," I said.

"No helicopters, bones, or collapsing hikers," Alex joked.

Mitch looked at Alex, surprised. "When did you make these?"

"I made them earlier while you two were packing up. Thought we'd need a good meal for today."

I laughed, shaking my head. "You're full of surprises, Alex. I'm starving," I said, gratefully accepting a sandwich. "This ... right here ... is something we should do every year. For moments like these."

"To moments like these," Alex said, raising his can of iced tea. "And to more adventures together."

We clinked our cans, the sound acting strangely in the vastness of the desert. For a moment, we just sat there, the silence comfortable, the food settling in our bellies, the sun shining on our faces. It was good, this feeling of just being.

"Remember when I nearly fell off those rocks? I thought I was a goner," Alex said. But those rock climbers ... they were amazing. Saved me in the nick of time."

I laughed, the memory of Alex's near miss still fresh. "You sure know how to keep things exciting," I said, shaking my head.

Mitch added, "And, let's not forget about my backpack. Everything we needed, when we needed it. It's all about being prepared."

I agreed. "That backpack of yours is something else. You've been a lifesaver more than once with your *just-in-case* items."

"You know, this reminds me of when we were kids," Mitch said, a nostalgic smile on his face. "Camping in the tree house, solving mysteries ... We've come a long way since then, haven't we?"

Alex nodded. "I missed this ... just being out here with friends. Despite all the setbacks, I'm having a blast."

"You know," I started, looking at them, "after all these years apart, I'm grateful to be here with you guys. Even if I miss Jenny and the kids too. I wish you could meet them."

Alex nodded, his usual swagger fading. "Yeah, I'd love to. Family ... It's a whole different game. After my divorce ..." He shook his head. "Let's just say, I realized what I'd been taking for granted."

Mitch was absentmindedly adjusting his glasses, his fingers fidgeting with the frame. "I met someone on the bus ride here," he mumbled, his cheeks flushing. "We talked about the stars ... about this trip."

Alex and I exchanged a look, a mix of surprise and hope. "Great, Mitch," I said, giving him a nudge. "You gonna tell us her name?"

Mitch's cheeks flushed, and he mumbled something.

"What was that?" Alex leaned forward, a look in his eyes. "Come on, buddy, spill the beans."

Mitch took a deep breath, his eyes fixed on a distant rock formation. "Her name's Jamie."

"Jamie ...," I repeated, trying to picture her. "What's she like?"

He shrugged. "We just talked ... about astronomy, the desert ..."

"Astronomy, huh?" Alex chuckled. "Sounds like your kind of girl."

"She's here for a yoga retreat," Mitch added.

"Yoga and astronomy?" I smiled. "That's an interesting combination. You get her number?"

Mitch shook his head, looking at the ground. "No."

"Dude." Alex groaned. "Classic Mitch move. Always overthinking. Maybe you'll run into her again. Yoga retreats are pretty popular here. You could always, you know, just happen to be hiking in the same area."

Mitch blushed even deeper, shaking his head. "Nah, statistically it's not likely."

I gave Mitch a reassuring pat on the shoulder. "Hey, you never know. Small world, this desert."

Mitch nodded. "Yeah, maybe."

I smiled, thinking about my Jenny, her warm laughter, and our chaotic mornings back home, juggling breakfast, backpacks, and permission slips. *Yes, I miss you.*

I pulled out my phone, hoping to catch a signal. No such luck. But I managed to send Jenny a quick text: *All good here. Miss you guys.* I attached a selfie of Alex, Mitch, and me, grinning in front of a Joshua tree.

A few seconds later, my phone buzzed with a reply: a single red-heart emoji.

* * *

"All right, gang," I announced as we pulled away from the Cholla Garden, as the prickly landscape disappeared in the rearview mirror. "Next up: phase two of our *Desert Adventure,* off the grid on the east side of the park." I clapped my hands together. "We've got a plan, and it's gonna take all of us working together like the good ol' Scouts we are. Tonight's stargazing extravaganza awaits, but we're going off the grid. Buckle up."

"Mitch, fill Alex in on what we're in for."

Mitch, who'd been humming to himself, gazing at the clouds as if they held constellations, perked up. "Off the grid in the eastern section? Excellent choice, Ben." He looked at Alex, excited. "This time of year, the skies out there are at their absolute darkest, especially with the new moon. It's prime stargazing season. Joshua Tree is an International Dark Sky Park, you know, which means minimal light pollution."

"So, what does all that mean in English?" Alex asked, tapping his fingers impatiently on the dashboard.

"It means we're going to see more stars than you can imagine. Millions upon millions. We might even catch a glimpse of

Andromeda, a whole other galaxy spiraling millions of light-years away."

"Andromeda?" I said, trying to picture it. "A whole other galaxy, huh? Sounds like something out of *Star Wars*."

"It's better," Mitch said, his voice filled with passion. "It's real. We might even be lucky enough to see the Zodiacal Light after dusk, a faint glow caused by sunlight reflecting off dust particles in space. It's pretty rare." Mitch pulled a small notebook from his backpack. "You know, guys, the late fall and early winter are some of the best times for stargazing in Joshua Tree National Park."

I looked at him, intrigued. "Really? Why?"

Mitch smiled. "Well, during this time, the skies are at their absolute darkest, especially on or around the new moon. This allows for the greatest number of stars to be visible. Plus, the night sky changes throughout the year. So, what we see looking east in the late fall or early winter will be different from what we see in summer."

"Okay, okay," Alex said, his tone shifting from skepticism to genuine interest. "This is starting to sound pretty cool. But how do we make sure we get the best view?"

"Well," Mitch said, adjusting his glasses and ticking off points on his fingers. "First, we need to climb up high so dress warmly. Layers are your best friend. Second, keep those flashlights pointed down at the trail—don't want to ruin our night vision. And lastly," he paused for dramatic effect, "get ready to be amazed, relax and enjoy the show. It's going to be spectacular with my telescope."

"All this talk of the sky and stars is making me thirsty," Alex said. "I hope we have enough supplies to last us through this epic adventure."

"Relax, I've got us covered," I said, patting the dashboard. "This old girl is stocked for a week in the wilderness. Besides, after the barbecue feast you whipped up, I trust your packing skills."

"We should scout a good spot near Cottonwood Spring Oasis," Mitch said. "There's a loop trail nearby with great views, and it should be far enough from the campground to avoid any light pollution."

The van hummed, the miles melting away. I kept my eyes on the road, but my mind drifted to those starry nights back home in Oregon, watching the constellations with Jenny and the kids. It felt like a lifetime ago, those days of peaceful routine.

* * *

As we reached the trailhead, the air was already cooling. I parked the van, and we gathered our gear.

"All right, team," I announced, hefting my pack onto my shoulders. "One last push. Think of it as a Stairmaster to the stars."

Alex groaned. "Do I have to? My quads are already screaming from the Cholla Garden hike. And I swear, if I see one more cactus ..."

Mitch laughed, giving Alex a friendly nudge. "Quit whining. You're the all-star here. I bet you could carry two packs and still beat us to the top. You'll thank me later. The view is going to be mind-blowing."

As we began our hike, the weight of our gear seemed to double with each step. The path was steep, the terrain rugged.

"Watch your step, guys," I warned, navigating a particularly rocky patch. "We don't want any more twisted ankles."

Alex grunted in agreement, his focus on the path ahead. "And keep an eye out for wildlife, in case we encounter a bobcat or coyote."

Mitch nodded, adjusting his gear. "Noted. And if we're lucky, we might spot some desert bighorn sheep high up on the rocks."

Reaching the summit, we were met by a blast of wind, cold and exhilarating.

"Worth it, right?" I said, my breath fogging in the air as I dropped my pack.

"I'm speechless," Alex said, for once, not complaining. He seemed awed by the panoramic view.

We set up camp. I pulled out some blankets, pillows, and set up a kettle for a thermos of hot cocoa from my backpack, creating a cozy outdoor living room. "I thought we could use a bit of comfort."

Mitch was already setting up his telescope. "Conditions are perfect," his eyes glued to the sky, where the first stars were beginning to appear, tiny pinpricks of light against the fading blue.

I watched him and remembered a younger Mitch, wide-eyed and full of wonder, always eager to search for the stars. Some things never change.

The air grew colder as darkness deepened, those pinpricks multiplying into a dazzling canopy of stars. Alex, after a few initial grumbles about the lack of central heating, was silent, his eyes fixed on the sky. He watched the stars with the same intensity he once had when searching for receivers deep in the end zone during his college football days.

And then, the Milky Way, a river of silver fire, blazed across the expanse above. It was a sight that stole our breaths, made us feel small and insignificant, yet somehow connected to something infinitely vast.

"There," Mitch whispered, his voice filled with awe, pointing toward a cluster of stars. "Orion. See his belt? Those three stars in a line? And just below, a faint smudge. There's the Orion Nebula. A stellar nursery, where stars are being born."

"Stars being born," Alex repeated, his voice soft, reverent. "Crazy."

Mitch, like a conductor leading an orchestra, guided us through the constellations, sharing stories and scientific facts. We saw Gemini, with its twin stars, Castor and Pollux, Taurus with its fiery eye, Aldebaran, and Sirius, the Dog Star, blazing like a diamond in the heart of Canis Major.

Alex joked. "Sounds like we're in an MIT lecture, not a national park."

Mitch grinned. "Well, you're stuck with *Professor* Mitch tonight." He then pointed toward another constellation.

The hours slipped by, marked by shooting stars, the distant hoot of an owl, and the hum of our voices. We talked, laughed, and told stories of good times together, the weight of the past few days finally lifting.

We all sat back and stared at the stars as Mitch finished his impromptu lecture, inspired by the beauty and complexity of the night sky. Despite Alex's jokes, we were all grateful for Mitch's knowledge, which added another layer of wonder to our stargazing experience.

"You know," I said, leaning back against a rock, a mug of hot cocoa warming my hands, "this is what it's all about. This view ... you guys."

"Remember that night as Scouts in the Rockies?" Mitch asked, breaking the silence. "We thought we could see forever."

We were together again, safe here, at least for tonight.

Chapter 16

Alex

Friday, December 20—Day six, Ryan Mountain, Joshua Tree.
"Ugh, my foot!" I yelped, jolting awake as something—or someone—collided with my big toe.

"Rise and shine, Sleeping Beauty." Ben's cheerful voice invaded my sleep. "Or should I say, Sleeping Beast?"

I groaned, rolling over and burying my face in the pillow. Every muscle in my body ached, a flurry of protest from nights sleeping on the hard ground. Man, I missed my king-size bed back in Dallas, those Egyptian cotton sheets, the perfect temperature control.

"Breakfast is ready, but only if you get up right now!" Mitch said.

"If you two don't quit your yapping, I swear, I'm gonna—"

"You're gonna what?" Mitch's voice, already annoyingly chipper, came from outside the tent. "Turn into a grumpy grizzly bear and devour us whole? Get up, Alex. We've got a schedule to keep."

I lifted my head, shivering as a blast of icy wind hit my face. "A schedule? Dude, it's Friday. We're on vacation."

Ben, already zipping up his backpack with annoyingly efficient Scout-leader precision, shook his head. "No dice, Alex.

Ryan Mountain, remember? And if we want a prime spot at the campground, we gotta get moving."

"More driving? My delicate rear end is begging for a break."

"Patience, young man." Mitch said, pointing to a place on the map.

I groaned. "Why can't we just find a pull-off with a view, pop a cold one, and watch the stars from the comfort of the van?"

Mitch added. "Because, this campground is first come, first served. No reservations. Plus, it's right at the trailhead. Ben's got a killer hike planned."

My luck. Mitch and Ben were planning this with the the meticulousness of an Eagle Scout and the precision of a rocket scientist. *Killer views. Right. Ben's grand finale.* As much as I loved the idea of those wide-open desert skies, the thought of another strenuous climb made my ankle throb.

"Here." Mitch appeared beside me with a steaming mug. "Fuel for the adventure."

Real, brewed coffee, not the instant crap we'd choked down at Scouts camp.

I took the mug, the warmth seeping into my hands, the rich aroma filling my senses. And as I took the first sip, the world didn't seem quite so bleak. Maybe this mountain climb wouldn't be so bad after all.

"All right, all right," I said, forcing myself to sit up. "Let's do this."

* * *

"Next stop, Ryan Mountain!" Ben announced, turning to me with a grin from the driver's seat. "Ready for some serious elevation gain?"

"A mountain?" I snorted. "Hiking up a mountain sounds more like a punishment to my ankle."

Ben focused back on the road, the van humming along the desert highway. I was perfectly content to stay right where we were—sprawled out under last night's star-dusted sky, those incredible constellations still locked in my memory. But Ben, our fearless leader and trip organizer, had a schedule to keep.

I fiddled with my camera, happy that I'd captured some amazing shots of the Milky Way last night, but my legs were already protesting the thought of another hike.

"It's a classic, Alex," Mitch added from the back seat, his nose already buried in his hiking guide. "Short but challenging. About three miles round trip with a good bit of elevation gain. The views from the top are supposed to be spectacular with three-hundred-sixty-degree views of the entire park. You can see everything from the top—the San Jacinto Mountains, the Salton Sea, even the Coachella Valley on a clear day."

I sighed. "Okay, okay. You've twisted my arm. But if I end up needing another helicopter rescue, I'm sending you both the bill."

Ben chuckled. "Deal. Just try to keep up, old man."

Despite my grumbling, I was excited. Those panoramic views did sound epic. And maybe, just maybe, I'd actually manage to stay on the trail.

* * *

As Ben maneuvered the camper van along the winding route, I was lost in thought. The hum of the engine, the scent of desert filtering through the open windows, the easy banter between Ben and Mitch, it all created a comforting backdrop.

We'd spent the last few days navigating danger, facing down storms, and staring death in the face. And through it all, Ben and Mitch had been there—steady, reliable, always having my back. Even when I'd been a reckless idiot, charging headfirst into trouble.

The incident from high school, a memory I'd tried to bury for years, kept resurfacing. I'd been a star athlete back then, my future bright with the promise of a football scholarship. But one stupid mistake nearly cost me everything.

Ben, always the responsible one, had stepped in and protected my future, even though it meant risking his own. It was a debt I'd carried with me ever since.

Ben slowed the van, pulling in to park. I needed to say something.

"Hold on a sec, guys," I said, my voice catching in my throat. "Before we head up the mountain, there's something I need to say."

Ben turned off the engine. Mitch watched me from the back seat.

I took a deep breath. "I ... I owe you both a lot. Especially you, Ben. Back in high school, you saved my ass, and I ... I never really thanked you. You saved my chance at a scholarship, at a future. I wouldn't be where I am today without you." I paused, feeling a lump in my throat. "And Mitch," I continued, turning to him. "You've always been there, the voice of reason, the steady hand. I appreciate you, man. Both of you."

Ben just smiled his easygoing smile that always made me feel like I was back in the tree house, safe and carefree. "It's what friends do."

Mitch nodded. "Right back at you, Alex."

Feeling a weight lift from my shoulders, I went on. "I also want to apologize for being such a jerk on this trip," I said, meeting their eyes. "I've been pushing it, taking stupid risks, not listening ... I promise, from now on, I'll be more careful."

They nodded.

"And, to show my appreciation, I'm inviting you both to Texas, VIP treatment, the whole nine yards. We'll catch a Cowboys game, tour The Star in Frisco, and feast like kings at Hard Eight BBQ. My treat, of course. What do you say?"

"Dude, you're on!" Mitch said, his eyes wide with excitement. "Just as long as I don't have to fly. Trains, automobiles, maybe a horse ... anything but a plane."

Ben chuckled, shaking his head. "Oh, it's about time you finally invited us to see why you rave about Texas so much. Let's see if it lives up to the hype."

* * *

"All right, guys," Ben said, clapping his hands after securing the last available campsite. "Ryan Mountain awaits. Just a heads-up, this trail's a bit of a leg-burner. Starts with stone stairs, and it's pretty much a constant climb all the way to the top."

I groaned, my ankle already sending up warning signals.

Mitch patted me on the back. "Think of it as a cardio workout with a view. And just imagine those photos you'll get from the summit!"

"Yeah, all right," I said, adjusting my camera bag. "But if I collapse halfway up, you two are carrying me the rest of the way."

"Dude, slow down," I gasped during the hike. "Man, you weren't kidding about the constant climb." Even my athlete-trained lungs were working overtime.

Ben chuckled, stopping to wait for me. "Sorry, Alex. Old habits die hard. Scout's pace and all." He gestured toward the view unfolding behind us. "But check it out. Worth the burn, right?"

"Keep your eyes peeled for bighorn sheep," Mitch said as he caught up to us. "This is their territory."

Sheep? I was more concerned with not twisting my ankle again. But even I had to admit, this was something else.

As we climbed, the landscape started to change. Desert bushes gave way to towering rock formations. The trail was relatively easy to follow, leading us up stone stairs that wound their way up the mountain. The views were already breathtaking, the vast expanse of the park stretching out below.

We reached a bend in the trail, the wind picking up, whipping around us. I pulled my jacket tighter, feeling the chill cut right through me.

And then it started snowing.

At first, it was just a few flakes, swirling in the air. But then, the wind picked up, those flakes turning into a flurry, a white curtain obscured the view.

The stone stairs were now covered in snow, sparkling in the occasional sunlight managed to peek through the heavy clouds. It was like looking at a black-and-white photograph, the snow highlighting the contours of the landscape.

"Guys ...," Ben's voice, usually so steady, had a slight edge to it now. "This doesn't look good. Maybe we should turn back."

I squinted toward the summit, so close, yet suddenly so far. "Come on, Ben. We're almost there. We can't turn back now. Right, Mitch?"

Mitch was already pulling a pair of non-slip gripper spikes from his seemingly bottomless backpack. "I think we can make it," he said, his voice calm and reassuring. "But we need to be careful."

He handed us each a pair, showing us how to strap them onto our boots. "These will give us better traction on the snow. Just take it slow, watch your step."

As we continued our climb, the snow fell harder, transforming the desert landscape into a surreal winter wonderland. The trail was slippery, the air biting, but it didn't faze me. Nothing beats conquering the wild with my childhood friends by my side.

We saw other hikers turning back, their faces frozen and worried. But we pressed on, fueled by an unspoken pact—we were in this together, come hell or high water, or in this case, a freak snowstorm in the desert.

The uphill section, which would have been difficult in the summer, was quite nice in the winter. The snow provided a cooling effect, and the white landscape, despite the cold, had its own rugged beauty and almost distracted me from the burning in my legs.

And then, finally, through the swirling snow, we saw it—the summit. A jumble of frosted rocks, a weathered signpost leaning against the wind, and a view stopped me in my tracks.

"Unbelievable," Ben whispered.

Mitch just stood there, his breath misting in the air.

I fumbled for my camera, its weight suddenly heavy against my chest. I'd been so caught up in the moment, in the sheer physicality of the climb, I'd almost forgotten. I raised the lens, framing the shot, but even my high-end equipment couldn't quite capture the magic of it all.

* * *

We lingered on the summit for as long as we dared, the cold seeping through our layers. But the view, man, it was hypnotic. As the light started to fade, the adrenaline rush wore off, and my ankle throbbed like crazy. The cold was really setting in, and wouldn't you know it, *Mr. Invincible* here started to actually feel a twinge of worry. *Imagine that.*

"All right, guys," Ben said, "time to head down. This storm doesn't look like it's letting up anytime soon."

The descent was a different beast. The snow was coming down harder, the wind whipping it into our faces, obscuring the trail. Every step felt treacherous, the rocks hidden beneath the snow.

"Watch your step, Alex," Ben warned, his voice barely audible above the wind's howl. "Those stairs can be tricky, even without the snow."

I nodded, my heart pounding. "Think we're still on the right track?"

Ben squinted at the swirling snow, his face plastered white. "Should be ... but I can't see the trail anymore."

We pressed on, the snow deepening, the light fading. The temperature had plummeted, that desert chill amplified by the wind, seeping through our layers like icy fingers.

"I don't like this, Ben," I said, my teeth starting to chatter. "We're lost, aren't we?"

He didn't answer, but the grim set of his jaw was answer enough. We were lost. On a mountain. In a blizzard. And the sun was setting fast.

"We need to find shelter," Mitch said, his voice steady despite the situation. I could see the worry in his eyes but also determination. He was right—we couldn't afford to spend the night in the open.

"Any ideas?" I asked. My ankle was screaming, my fingers were numb inside my gloves.

Ben, his jaw clenched, shook his head. "Just keep moving."

We pushed on, each step a gamble. The snow drifted in places and hid the uneven terrain. I slipped, cursing as pain shot up my leg.

"Easy, Alex," Ben said, catching me by my arm.

Another hour crawled by, marked by the relentless wind, the sting of snow against our faces, and the growing fear. The last sliver of sunlight disappeared, leaving us in a world of gray and white.

Just when I thought my legs would give out, Mitch yelled, "Over there! Look!"

He was pointing toward a rocky outcropping, barely visible in the gathering darkness. As we stumbled closer, I saw it—a gaping hole in the side of the mountain, besides the cliffs.

"An old mine," Ben said. "Might be our only chance."

We scrambled toward it, a desperate dash for survival. The entrance was narrow, choked with snow and debris, but beyond it, the mine shaft opened into a tunnel, then a room, a cavern of darkness, a promise of shelter from the storm.

I squeezed through, relief flooding me as the wind's howl faded to a muffled roar.

Inside, the air was cold and damp, heavy with the scent of earth and something metallic, something ancient. But it was still. Safe. For now.

"Thank God," I gasped, leaning against the rough rock wall, my chest heaving.

We huddled together. It wasn't much, but it was shelter. It was survival from the dangers in the desert.

* * *

As we huddled in the abandoned mine, the reality of our situation began to sink in. It was dark and freezing outside. I could feel the cold seeping into my bones, despite the layers of clothing.

"Okay, guys," Ben said, "let's not panic. We just need to assess the situation and come up with a plan. Remember the rule of threes? It's a good starting point."

I groaned, leaning back against the rough rock wall. "Rules, Ben? Now? Can't we just huddle and pray for a miracle?"

Mitch was already rummaging through his backpack. "Three minutes without air? We're good, there's plenty of ventilation," he said, his voice muffled by the pack. "Three hours without shelter? Check. Three days without water? We have our water bottles, and we can melt snow if we need to." He paused, pulling out a folded silver square. "And for warmth ..." He unfolded the square, and it magically transformed into a large thermal blanket.

"Whoa, Mitch," I said, my jaw chattering. "What is that thing? Some kind of high-tech space blanket?"

"It's a thermal reflective blanket. It traps your body heat and reflects it back to you. Learned about it at MIT. Figured it might come in handy."

He opened the blanket, and we wrapped it around our bodies, the warmth radiating through us like a welcome embrace. It was like we were all tucked into one of those massive Texas burritos, wrapped up tight and held together, keeping us warm and safe from the cold, each of us an essential part of that binding. I had to admit, the guy was a walking survival kit.

"And for sustenance," I said, pulling out the remaining energy bars from my pack, "we've got leftovers. Not exactly a first-class dinner, but hey, at least it's a meal for three stranded adventurers."

"Looks like we're not the only ones who've sought refuge here," Ben said, pointing to a pile of ashes and a few discarded cans. "Someone else was here recently."

"Hopefully they made it out okay," Mitch said, his voice low.

We ate in silence, the only sounds were the crunch of bread and the howling wind. Despite the cold, the darkness, the uncertainty, we were together, had resources, and a plan, thanks to Ben's Scout wisdom and Mitch's tech-savvy preparedness.

The storm raged on, but inside the abandoned mine, we felt a familiar bond. It was just like those nights in the tree house years ago—huddled together, telling stories, and daring each other to face the darkness. We were kids again, only now the stakes were higher and the shadows a little more real.

As I drifted off to sleep, the warmth of Mitch's blanket enveloping me, the taste of energy bars lingering on my tongue, a single thought sounded in my mind: *We'll make it through this. We always do.*

Chapter 17

Mitch

Saturday, December 21—Day seven, abandoned mine, Joshua Tree.

The bus swerved, horns blared, and a woman screamed. Then, the world dissolved into a blizzard of chaos. The familiar terror of the plane crash, the weightlessness, the sickening crunch of metal ...

I woke with a gasp, the dream clinging to me, its weight as suffocating as being buried under an avalanche. Each breath felt like a struggle to dig myself out from the icy depths of my subconscious. I wasn't on the bus, I wasn't falling from the sky. But the feeling of being trapped, the weight pressing on me, was the same.

Then I realized what was holding me—the thermal blanket I had wrapped around us. It wasn't just draped over us anymore; it was bound tight, constricting, a cocoon of warmth turned into a prison. And then I felt the ropes. Thick, sturdy ropes, like the kind climbers use, wrapped around the three of us, holding us as securely as a rock climber's harness. Someone must have tied us up when we were asleep, and the darkness had allowed him to move without us waking up exhausted from the snowstorm.

Panic clawed at my throat. I strained against the ropes, but they held firm, cutting deeper with every movement. My legs, bound together, were useless. It was like being in a deep chasm, the darkness closing in, the air growing thin.

"Ben? Alex?" My voice came out a hoarse whisper, the fear of a metallic tang in my mouth.

"Here, Mitch." Ben's voice, closer than I expected, strained with effort. "We're ... we're tied up."

"No shit, Sherlock," Alex muttered, his usual bravado subdued, replaced by a raw fear mirrored my own. His voice was muffled, coming from somewhere beneath the blanket. I couldn't see him, but I knew he was there, as trapped and helpless as I was. "Not what I had in mind for my birthday."

Then, I saw him. A tall, rugged man with a face weathered by the desert and eyes as cold as the weather outside. He towered over us, his body tense and coiled like a predator ready to strike. His grip on a large knife was firm, the edge looking wickedly sharp. Every movement he made radiated danger.

My mind, usually my most reliable tool, was spinning, a jumble of fragmented thoughts and flashing images. *Who is this man? What does he want? Why are we tied up?* I forced myself to breathe, slow and deep. *Airway, breathing, circulation.* But what good were those protocols now? We weren't injured—not physically, at least. We were captives.

I scanned the man's face, searching for a clue, a flicker of recognition. Nothing concrete. And yet, something about him, the way he moved, stirred a distant memory. It was like a puzzle piece that almost fit—something familiar, but just out of reach in my memory bank.

While Ben kept talking, my eyes darted around the mine, taking in every detail. The rough walls, the low, timbered ceiling, the piles of rubble and rusted mining equipment—a scene from one of those old Westerns. But the harsh cold of winter made it feel more like a survival film. But there was nothing glamorous about this situation. This wasn't a movie. This was our lives.

Think, Mitch, think.

Ben, steady and calm, cut through the panic. He talked to the man, trying to reason with him, buying time to assess the situation.

Three minutes without air ... three hours without shelter ... three days without water ... The rule of threes, Ben's mantra, a guideline hammered into us since our Scouting days. It was intended to help us prioritize and stay calm in a crisis. But what about three days tied up in an abandoned mine at the mercy of a knife-wielding stranger? There was no rule.

Escape routes? I scanned the mine shaft, searching for a way out, a hidden passage, anything. The entrance, a narrow gap in the rock face, was our only way in or out. And the man was standing right in front of it, his silhouette a dark, menacing shape.

Weapons? I shifted to get a better view of the mine's interior. A rusty pickaxe leaned against the wall, but it was out of reach. A pile of loose rocks, a few old, wooden crates... Nothing could help us against a man with a knife.

Think, Mitch, think. There had to be a way out of this.

Ben's detective instincts were kicking in as he traced his fingers along the rough fibers of the rope bound his wrists.

"This is climber's rope," he said, his voice carefully neutral, testing the waters. "You're a climber?"

The man chuckled, a low rumble ricocheted off the mine walls. "Good eye," he said. "Used to be a guide, back in the day. Taught city folks like you how to climb, how to survive." He crouched, his silhouette a menacing shadow in the lantern light. "And let's just say I've learned a few other tricks over the years." He gave the rope another tug, making sure it bit deep. "These knots won't come loose. I didn't hide out here with my escape plan to let some hikers ruin my plan."

"Who are you?" Ben's voice trembled, but there was a steely edge, a familiar determination I'd always admired.

The man laughed. "You don't need to know my name. What you need to know is you're in my way."

"We ... we didn't mean to be in your way," Ben said. "We got caught in the snowstorm and needed shelter. We'll be gone as soon as the weather clears. We're sorry for the intrusion."

The man's eyes narrowed, suspicion flickering in their depths. "You expect me to believe you? You're hiding something."

There was something about the man, his voice, his stance, a nagging familiarity I couldn't quite place.

"We're not hiding anything," I said.

"Look," Ben said, his voice taking on a calm, reassuring tone he used with his kids, "we're not a threat to you. We just want to get out of this storm. If you let us, we can even help you. We have supplies, food, and water in my van. We could drive you somewhere if you need a ride."

"Help me? You? Do you think I need help from a bunch of punks? You're the ones who need help. Stuck out here, freezing your asses off."

He took a step closer. But Ben didn't flinch.

"We're more resourceful than you think," Ben insisted. "We could be useful to you. Just tell us what you need."

The man hesitated, his eyes darting between Ben and me, a muscle twitching in his jaw. He was a study in contradictions—hulking but graceful, his eyes both weary and sharp, his voice a mix of gruffness and a strange, almost unsettling confidence. It was like he was two different people—a hardened, paranoid survivalist and someone else, someone calculating, almost predatory. It was the second look that made my pulse beat like a drum and my senses go on high alert.

"Could we at least have some water? We're dehydrated."

The man's expression softened a fraction. He reached into his backpack and tossed a canteen toward us. It landed with a thud on the dusty ground, just out of reach.

"Alex," I whispered, my voice barely audible. "Can you ... reach?"

Alex shifted beside me, the blanket rustling as he tried to inch closer to the canteen. It was no use. We were bound too tightly.

Then, I felt it—a gentle pressure against my side, the warmth of Alex's breath against my ear. "I know him," Alex whispered. "I think ... I think I know who he is."

Before I could ask him what he meant, the man's head snapped up, his eyes narrowing. He let out a harsh, barking laugh that echoed through the mine. The laughter morphed into a hacking cough, his large frame shaking, his eyes blazing with a manic energy. Then, his fist shot up, a blur of motion stopped just inches from my face. A thick gold watch, heavy and expensive, glinted in the dim light, looking ridiculously out of place against his rough, dirt-stained clothes.

"You know me?" He spat the words out, his eyes searching for Alex, who was now perfectly still. "Funny. Because I don't know you. And trust me, you don't want me to."

* * *

It hit me like a jolt of electricity. I recognized the watch. I did know him. Not just from the restaurant but the tram. *The Palm Springs Aerial Tram*. He was the guy with the expensive watch, the one who'd been flirting with those women while his date sat there, practically invisible.

But he looked different now. Haggard, his face shadowed with stubble, and the manic glint in his eye replacing the cool, calculated demeanor I'd observed at the restaurant. He had shaved off his mustache, and instead of the fancy suit, he now wore weathered hiking clothes. And where was the woman? The one he'd been with? The one we'd found on the trail … the one Ben had helped … Evie … Evelyn.

And perhaps we'll run into each other again in this vast desert playground, he'd said. And then, that line, delivered with a wink, seemed more like a threat.

The memory of the night at the tram restaurant, the man's words, his tone, it all came flooding back.

He'd called himself Randy then, all charm and swagger, flashing an expensive watch and a predatory smile. His words, at the time, had just seemed like harmless bravado, the kind of thing a guy would say to impress a couple of out-of-towners. But now … now they felt different. Ominous. Prophetic.

He'd been with the woman that night, and now she was in the hospital. He was the one who'd left her there. But why? And what was he planning to do with us? We were in grave danger, I knew it. But a different kind of certainty joined the fear—the unshakeable knowledge we were in this together. We were a team. We'd faced challenges before and had clawed our way out of impossible situations. We'd do it again. We had to.

My mind, a tangled mess of adrenaline and fear, raced, trying to grasp his motive. Revenge? Greed? Desperation? But figuring out why wasn't enough. We needed a plan. A way out.

I glanced at Ben, his face pale but determined, his voice a steady stream of calming words as he tried to reason with the man. Then, I imagined Alex, hidden under the blanket, his jaw clenched, eyes blazing with defiance. And in the moment, I felt a surge of strength—not my own but ours. Ben's quick thinking, Alex's fearlessness, my ability to analyze, to find the weak point, the bug in the code. We had everything we needed. We just had to use it.

Ben was still trying to reason with the man. "Look, we're not going to tell anyone about this. Just let us go, and we'll forget this ever happened."

"You think I'm stupid?" the man sneered, pacing like a caged animal. "You think I'm just going to let you walk out of here?"

My heart hammered against my ribs, a trapped bird desperate for escape. I had to do something.

Then an idea sparked, like a shining star piercing through the suffocating darkness. It was a long shot, but it was all we had.

"Psst, Alex," I whispered. "Remember the knot-tying trick we learned as kids? At Ben's birthday party? The magician, the one with the loose loop?"

Alex nodded in understanding.

The trick was simple but required teamwork. Together we needed to push and pull with our legs. If I could just get the right angle, I could create enough slack to slip free.

"I think I can get my hands free," I whispered, my mind picturing the knot, the way the magician's fingers had danced, creating an illusion of impossible escape. "Maybe I can loosen the ropes enough to reach the canteen."

Ben, sensing our hushed exchange, glanced at me. I gave him a quick nod, a silent message to distract the man. He understood.

"So, what's your plan?" Ben asked the man, his voice carefully casual, buying us precious seconds. "What are you going to do with us?"

The man grinned, a cruel, predatory expression. "Let's just say, you won't be needing those hiking boots anymore."

"Come on, man, we're just some hikers. We're not a threat."

While Ben kept talking, I subtly shifted my weight, testing the limits of the ropes. Alex, mimicking my movements, began working on his bonds. We were a team, always had been, even without speaking a word.

Almost there, I thought, my fingers inching closer to the canteen.

Inch by agonizing inch, I worked the knot, my fingers numb, my heart pounding. Alex had loosened the rope around his legs just enough to create a bit of slack. The thermal blanket, our cozy refuge just hours ago, was now a suffocating weight.

Ben kept the man engaged. "You know," he said, his voice taking on a storyteller tone he used to captivate his kids, "this place is historic. Old mines, ghost towns, lost treasures ... Did you ever hear any of those stories growing up?"

The man, his attention momentarily diverted, grunted. "Stories are for fools! Only thing that matters in this desert is survival."

But Ben pressed on. "My grandfather used to tell me about a lost gold mine, hidden somewhere in the desert ..."

I tuned him out, focusing on the task at hand. The canteen was just inches away now. My hand, finally free, brushed against its smooth surface.

"Got it," I whispered, sliding the canteen closer to Alex.

With agonizing slowness, I inched my hand toward my backpack, my fingers fumbling for the familiar shape of my phone. I was unlikely to get a signal down here, but it was worth a shot.

Ben, meanwhile, was in full storyteller mode. "There was this one legend about a miner who stumbled upon a vein of pure gold—"

"Quiet!" the man snapped, his patience wearing thin.

Ben shouted, "What? Did you hear something?" He pointed toward the back of the mine, his eyes wide with a feigned alarm.

The man turned to look. It was our chance.

In a flash, I slipped free of the ropes. "Alex, now!"

Alex, springing to his feet with the agility of a quarterback evading a blitz, raised his arm and threw the heavy canteen at the man. It connected with a sickening thud, the icy water exploding against the back of his head.

The man staggered, a startled grunt escaping his lips. I scrambled out from under the blanket, my phone clutched in my hand, and darted toward a narrow crevice in the mine, hoping for a signal.

Ben, still tangled in the ropes, struggled to get free. "Alex! Mitch ..."

The man, shaking his head, dazed but recovering quickly, turned back toward us. And then, recognition dawned. "It's you!" he roared, his eyes fixed on Alex. "The tram! The restaurant! You meddling, little prick!"

He lunged at Alex, tackling him with the force of a raging bull. They rolled in the dirt, a tangle of limbs, the knife visible in the dim light.

* * *

I scrambled backward, adrenaline surging. The rough rock scraped against my skin, and the mine shaft narrowed, pressing in on me like a tomb, but I didn't care. I *had* to get out of there and find help.

"Come back here," the man snarled, but I was already squeezing through the narrow passage, my heart thumping. "You can't hide!"

I burst out of the mine entrance, gasping for air. The cold desert wind hit me like a slap, but the snow had stopped, thank God. For a moment, I just stood there, my lungs burning, my legs trembling, the vast expanse of the desert sky around me.

Then, from deep within the mine, I heard Alex yell, a sharp, strangled cry cut short. A sickening thud followed, then silence.

I hesitated, torn. The urge to go back to help was overwhelming. But another, more primal instinct took over—survive.

Get help, Mitch. You're the only one who can.

I fumbled for my phone, my fingers numb with cold and fear. No signal. Damn it! I had to get higher.

I looked up. Towering rock formations loomed, their jagged edges menacing. My stomach lurched. *Heights.* My old nemesis. Panic clawed at me—doubts, images of falling, shattering bones.

But I couldn't let fear paralyze me. Not now. Not when my friends' lives were at stake.

I scrambled up a nearby boulder, my hands and feet gripping the rough granite. The world tilted beneath me, the ground seeming to sway. I squeezed my eyes shut for a moment, willing the dizziness to pass.

Just keep climbing, Mitch. One foothold at a time.

And somehow, I did. I climbed, driven by a primal need to survive, to save my friends. Each step was a victory over fear. And as I finally reached the summit, my phone searching for a signal, I knew the real battle, the fight for my friends' lives, had just begun.

At the top of the boulder, the wind whipped at my face, stinging my eyes. I held my phone high in the air, praying for a signal. And then, a miracle, a tiny bar flickered on the screen.

"9-1-1, what's your emergency?"

The words tumbled out in a rush—the mine, the man, the woman, the fear. "He's going to kill them! Please, you have to hurry!"

"We're sending help, sir. Just stay on the line and tell me your exact location."

As I relayed the details, relief washed over me. Help was coming, but it wouldn't be fast enough. I had to get back to Ben and Alex, to make sure they were okay.

I scrambled down the boulder, my fear replaced by a surge of adrenaline-fueled determination. I raced back toward the mine entrance, a voice urging me to stay safe.

But as I plunged back into the darkness, the mine seemed strangely quiet. The sounds of struggle had ceased. I stumbled forward.

Ben was gone. Alex was on the ground, not moving, the blanket tangled around him. And the man ... he was gone too.

"Ben? Alex?" I said.

No response.

And then, as I knelt beside Alex, the world tilted, a wave of darkness crashing over me, the only sensation a sudden smash against the back of my head.

Chapter 18

Mitch, Ben, Alex

Saturday, June 30—Eighteen-year-old high school graduates celebrate in the Rockies.

Alex sat behind the wheel of the classic '67 Mustang, gunning the rebuilt 289 engine. The Stang was a beast of chrome and muscle, the metallic-green paint reflecting the dim overhead light in his dad's garage.

A faded poster of "Dandy Don" Meredith, a Texas football legend, watched over the garage. Scratches on the concrete floor marked the countless times the engine had been hoisted, disassembled, meticulously cleaned, and inspected, while empty oil cans remained scattered. Rock music from the seventies, Boston, Led Zeppelin, and The Eagles, crackled from an old transistor radio. The garage carried the scent of oil, gasoline, and WD-40; stories of long nights, scraped knuckles, and the shared triumph of bringing this classic back to life.

Alex's dad, a retired air force pilot with a voice that could rival a jet engine, barked instructions; *clean the carburetor, time the distributor, rebuild the engine.*

Ben and Mitch became honorary members of the *Mustang Crew*. We worked tirelessly for days and weeks stretched into months to restore the pony car. The engine rebuild was a monumental task that tested patience, skills, and friendship and brought the 289 V8 back to life. The excitement peaked on painting day with the sharp scent of paint filling the garage.

Alex eased the Mustang out of the garage, the morning sun glinting off metallic-green paint job. His dad called it "British racing green"—a color fit for a champion. And this car truly was a champion. The rumble of the rebuilt engine vibrated a victory song after all those long summer days and late nights spent in this garage, elbows deep in grease and dreams.

But the Mustang was more than just a car to us. It was a labor of love, countless hours of tinkering and fine-tuning. It was also a battleground. With his booming laugh, calloused hands, and an endless supply of pilot stories, Alex's dad had a vision for Alex—the Air Force Academy, a football scholarship, and a career soaring through the skies. But Alex's dreams were grounded in a college-football escape plan in Texas. Everything was bigger and better in Texas, especially football, from Friday night under the lights, college football on Saturday, and the Cowboys on Sunday.

The Mustang was more than a car to the boys. It was an escape plan for our last summer vacation in the Rockies. The beautiful, powerful machine was also a symbol of rebellion against a future Alex's dad wanted. And yet, his dad was there, every step of the way, teaching, guiding, and helping. It was a twisted kind of love, a contradiction we couldn't quite understand.

* * *

Alex floored the accelerator as the Mustang raced onto the mountain road, the gears shifting smoothly, feeling every curve and bump in the road, the power of the rebuilt motor purring. This was freedom. This was an adventure.

Alex whooped, his sunglasses perched on his nose. Beside him, Ben laughed in the shotgun seat, leaning out the open window, his hair blowing in the wind. In the back seat, Mitch gripped the door handle, his knuckles white.

Alex's left hand turned the steering wheel, his right gripping the stick shift, one foot on the accelerator and the other managing the brake and clutch. Downshifting into turns, the engine roared as the RPMs climbed, taking the curve a little too fast, the tires squealing in protest. The experience surged adrenaline, like scoring a touchdown.

A sign warned of a hairpin turn ahead. Alex smiled. This was it, the ultimate test, man and machine against the mountain. He eased off the gas and gripped the wheel tighter, feeling the g-forces pressing us into our seats as the Mustang hugged the curve. The engine growled, the tires held, and the car surged forward, a wild horse unleashed.

"Mitch, you okay back there?" Alex asked, pressing the accelerator as the road straightened out.

"Yeah, just ... wow!" Mitch replied. "You know how to handle this beast."

To the right, Ben was leaning back in the shotgun seat. "Man, this is awesome! I'll miss this car when you head off to Texas."

"Don't worry, you'll get to drive it when I visit," Alex promised.

"Hard to believe we've finished high school," Ben said, shaking his head.

"Yeah, but this week is gonna rock in the Rockies!" Alex replied.

"End of an era, though," Ben said, his eyes drifting toward the rear-view mirror. "The *Mustang Crew* era."

Mitch, who'd been lost in his book, looked up. "It's not the end," he said. "Just ... a new beginning."

As the Mustang crested the summit, the world seemed to open up. The road dropped into a valley, the landscape sprawling out in a breathtaking view of towering peaks and lush forests.

The opening guitar riff of "More Than a Feeling" roared from the speakers. Alex turned up the volume. "Perfect song for a road trip, don't you think?"

"Definitely," Ben replied. "Especially considering where you're headed, Mitch."

Mitch rolled his eyes. "Yeah, yeah. I'm going to Boston, I get it."

As the song faded, Alex looked in the rearview. "Mitch, you're about to start one hell of an adventure. MIT, Boston ... it's gonna be a whole new world—maybe a little intense—but dude, you've got this. You're the smartest guy I know, and you'll crush it. But remember, college isn't just about hitting the books. It's about meeting new people and trying new things. So, step out of your comfort zone, and enjoy the ride. And no matter how far you go, we've got your back."

"Thanks, Alex," Mitch replied. "I know it will be a big change, but I'm ready. And don't worry, I'll try to remember to have some fun too, not just bury myself in books and code."

The Mustang cruised into a valley, the road straightening, the air thickening with the scent of pine and damp earth.

Sunlight reflected off rushing streams, the water surging by melting snow high above. In the distance, the surface of a lake reflecting the blue sky appeared nestled among the trees. Everything seemed to come alive with sound—the chirping of birds, the rustling of leaves, the distant bleating of sheep.

"So, Texas in the fall, huh?" Mitch said. "Must be pretty stoked about the scholarship."

Alex grinned. "Yeah, man. Texas forever, baby! It's gonna be epic."

"Just don't forget about us little guys when you're a big football star," Ben added.

"Never, man. You guys are my team, always."

"What about you, Ben?" Mitch asked. "Police academy, right?"

Ben nodded. "Yep. Following in Dad's footsteps."

"Awesome," Alex said. "You'll be a great cop, I know it."

* * *

We pulled into the campground, and the Mustang rolled to a stop, kicking up a cloud of dust. The sun was high in the sky, warming the mountain air, but a cool breeze whispered through the pines, a reminder this wasn't Texas. It was the perfect spot to lose yourself in nature, forget about the pressures of everyday life, and just be..

"All right, boys," Alex said, shutting off the engine. "Welcome to paradise. Let's set up camp and hit the lake Ben told us about."

A group of girls walked from a nearby campsite. They were tanned, toned, and cute. One of them, a tall, athletic brunette with big brown eyes caught Alex's attention.

"Hey there," Alex said, leaning against the Mustang. "Name's Alex. What brings you lovely ladies to this neck of the woods?"

"I'm Jessica," the brunette replied. "These are my friends Lisa and Kim. Got here this morning. It's amazing, isn't it?"

Lisa added. "We're escaping Denver for a few days. Needed a dose of fresh air and mountain magic."

"You came to the right place," Ben said. "Best hiking trails in the Rockies."

"Hiking, huh?" Kim jumped in. "We're planning on hitting the trails right now. You guys are welcome to join us."

"Thanks for the offer," Mitch said, glancing at her friends, "but we need to get our camp set up. Maybe later?"

"Sure, we'll be around all week," Jessica said.

* * *

We unloaded their gear and pitched their tents. It was a routine we knew well, setting up the poles, stakes, and tangled nylon, having done it many times together on camping trips.

"Not bad, guys," Alex said, surveying the campsite. The tents were up, gear stowed, everything in its place. "But I gotta say, I'm a little bummed we missed out on the hike with Jessica and her crew." He playfully shoved Mitch. "You and your shy-guy routine, man. You could've at least tried to charm the redhead."

Mitch looked at his worn hiking boots, his ears burning red.

Ben put a hand on Mitch's shoulder. "Hey, don't worry, Alex. There's an awesome lake, not too far but hidden in the woods. Pure, crystal-clear water, perfect for a swim."

"Let's go!" Alex yelled.

The trail, though, was a challenge with switchbacks winding through the forest and stunning views. By the time we reached the lake, we were hot and sweaty.

The lake was nestled in a valley, surrounded by towering pines reaching for the sky. Their dark-green needles contrasted with the brilliant blue of the water, a scene straight out of a postcard. A small waterfall tumbled over a rocky outcrop on the far side.

"Race you to the water!" Alex shouted, already stripping off his shirt, his lean, muscular frame filled out after years of football.

"Cannonball!" Ben yelled, launching himself off a nearby rock, a massive splash erupting as he disappeared beneath the surface.

Mitch waded in, his skinny legs pale against the dark water.

"Come on, Mitch!" Alex shouted, already splashing toward him. "The water's fine!"

Mitch screamed as Alex dunked him.

The next hour was a full-on water war—splashes, dunks, and underwater wrestling.

Later, we collapsed on the shore, exhausted and exhilarated, the sun warming us.

"This ... this is the life," Ben said.

"Yeah," Mitch agreed. "It's hard to believe it's almost over."

"Over?" Alex scoffed. "This is just the beginning, man. We're the Mustang Crew, remember? We're unstoppable."

* * *

That night, after a dinner of charred hot dogs, s'mores, and campfire stories, we lay on the ground, looking up at stars in the Milky Way.

"Remember," Alex asked, "where we'd spent hours plotting adventures, solving imaginary mysteries, and hiding from adults? Or when we snuck into the drive-in, hiding in the back of Ben's dad's old pickup?"

"Yep," Mitch added. "Hours spent in Alex's garage, rebuilding the Mustang, piece by piece."

"Right!" Ben added. "You can repay us when you go pro!"

"Glory days," Alex said.

"It's going to be weird, not seeing each other," Mitch said.

"Yeah," Ben agreed. "But we'll always have these trips, right?"

"You know, guys," Mitch said, "high school ... it changed us, didn't it?"

"What do you mean?" Alex asked.

Ben shrugged, his eyes focused on the trail ahead. "I mean, we've all changed, haven't we? We've grown apart in some ways. I mean, Alex, you were always with your sports buddies and cheerleaders. And Mitch, you were always buried in your books and gadgets. And me ... well, I guess I was just trying to follow in my dad's footsteps."

"You're right," Mitch said. "We have changed. But it doesn't mean we've grown apart. We're still friends, aren't we?"

Alex nodded. "Yeah. And we always will be. No matter where life takes us."

We made a pact that night under a billion stars. We swore to stay connected. Texas, Boston, Denver—it didn't matter. We were the *Mustang Crew,* and the bond, forged in those late nights in Alex's garage, went way deeper than geography. We would find a way, every year, no matter what, to get together. For adventures, for poker nights. For life.

* * *

Waking up the next morning, the sun was already warming up the campground. Our muscles ached, but it was a good feeling, the kind you earn after a day of hanging out with your best friends.

After a quick breakfast of granola bars and fruit, we were ready for another day on the trails. As we were packing our gear, the three girls from the other campsite, with Jessica in the lead, walked over.

"Morning," Alex said. "Wanna go swimming? We found a killer spot yesterday."

"Actually," Jessica said, "we're checking out a waterfall. You guys up for it?"

"Sure, let's go!" Alex replied.

Ben and Mitch exchanged a look and nodded.

We spent the next few hours hiking through the forest. The waterfall was even more impressive than Jessica had described, a roaring torrent of white water cascading down moss-covered rocks. A perfect location for Alex to show off, splashing and swimming in the pool below the falls.

Later that evening, we continued to enjoy the night with a campfire dinner. Kim had brought her guitar and led the group in campfire songs with Alex and Jessica sitting together under the full moon.

Over the next few days, a pattern emerged. Alex, Ben, and Mitch would have breakfast together, but then, as soon as Jessica and her friends appeared, Alex would shift gears and hang out with the girls, drawn to their energy, their laughter, and their smiles. Alex loved the attention and looked forward to Texas, a world of football games, parties, and endless possibilities.

One afternoon, after a particularly grueling climb, we were all sprawled out on a rocky ledge, catching their breath and gazing out at the panoramic view. The girls were laughing, comparing photos on their phones. Ben and Mitch sat a little apart, talking quietly.

"It's just like high school all over again, isn't it?" Mitch said, watching Alex toss a football with the girls.

"Yeah. He's found his crowd."

* * *

It was the last night of the camping trip. Alex, Ben, and Mitch hiked together after another outing with the girls.

"Hey, Jessica told me there's a college party going on over on the other side of the lake," Alex said. "What do you say, guys?"

Ben hesitated. "I don't know. It's getting late, and the road's dangerous in the dark."

"Don't be such a buzzkill," Alex said. "Live a little! What about you, Mitch? You in?"

"It's our last night together," Mitch replied.

"Look, we talked about this," Alex urged. "Mitch, you promised to take some chances in college. This is your chance. Ben, come on, you're my wingman."

"Sure," Ben replied. "I got your back."

"Okay ...," Mitch said.

Alex eased the Mustang onto the lakeside road, the engine a low rumble, purring in the darkness. The headlights cut through the darkness, illuminating the winding path ahead. He downshifted smoothly, the gears meshing with a satisfying click, the tires gripping the pavement as he took the curves. The windows were down, letting in the cool night air. Moonlight reflected off the lake, and a driving beat of music pulsed along. The drive to the party was smooth. Alex was the designated driver, Ben rode shotgun, and Mitch sat in the back.

Alex glanced at Ben, then Mitch in the rearview mirror. "College life, here we come. Get ready to party like rockstars, boys."

Before we knew it, we were there. The Mustang screeched to a halt in the gravel driveway, its headlights momentarily blinding a group of college kids standing around a keg. The party was in full swing with a kid shooting bottle rockets over the lake, loud music thundering inside the house, and a booming bass shook the ground.

"Told you it'd be worth it," Alex shouted, grabbing the keys. He was already out of the car, his eyes scanning the crowd. He spotted Jessica, laughing near the pool, and walked towards her, his swagger back in full force.

"Dude, wait for your wingman," Ben muttered.

The place was a mansion, a sprawling log cabin with windows overlooking the lake, and a swimming pool with a big guy diving off the diving board and splashing everyone on purpose.

Inside, it was pure chaos. People were dancing under the strobing lights, music blasted from massive speakers, a wall of sound made conversation impossible. It felt hot and sticky with sweat, spilled beer, and something sweet and smoky coming from the barbecue just outside the kitchen on the deck.

Ben and Mitch roamed the rooms, dodging elbows and half-empty cups. It was a whole new world, a glimpse into the college life Alex craved.

"Where'd Alex disappear to?" Ben shouted.

Mitch scanned the room, observing and analyzing the situation, but Alex was nowhere to be found.

* * *

Ben and Mitch finally found Alex in a corner, a beer in one hand, his arm around Jessica's shoulder. Empty cans littered the floor around them.

"Alex, maybe you should slow down," Mitch said. "You've had a lot to drink ... you're our designated driver."

"Relax. It's just a few beers."

"Dude, you're putting away those beers like it's water," Ben said. "Don't you think you've had enough?"

Alex laughed. "Ben. It's a party! We're celebrating!"

"Celebrating what?" Ben asked. "You ditched your wingman and ditched us all week for a bunch of girls you just met."

"Come on, don't be like that," Alex said, his words slurring slightly. "You guys are my best friends. We'll always be tight. But this ...," he gestured toward Jessica, "this is different."

"Different?" Ben said. "Yeah, it's called being a jerk."

"Dude, chill," Alex said, his voice rising. "I'm just having some fun. Besides, it's our last night. We gotta make it count."

"Maybe we should head back to the campsite," Mitch suggested. "It's getting late."

Ben reached for the car keys, which Alex had tossed carelessly onto a nearby table, but Alex was faster. He snatched them up, a flash of anger in his eyes.

"I'm driving," Alex said, his voice slurred but insistent. "You guys can walk if you're so worried about it."

Alex stumbled toward the door, pushing past a group of laughing girls.

"Alex, wait!" Ben called out, but Alex was already gone, the screen door slamming shut behind him.

Ben and Mitch ran after Alex. He was already behind the wheel of the Mustang, the engine roaring to life.

"Get in!" he yelled. "We're going for a ride!"

The tires screamed in protest as Alex wrestled the Mustang around the curves, the headlights scattering light across the trees. The speedometer climbed, the numbers blurring, a reckless combination of speed and chaos.

The drive back was a nightmare.

Ben gripped the dashboard, his knuckles white. "Alex, slow down!"

And then it happened. The Mustang hit a patch of wet pavement, tires losing grip. Alex fought to regain control, but it was too late. The car skidded off the road, crashing into a tree with a sickening crunch of metal and the abrupt, terrifying silence.

* * *

"Alex! Mitch!" Ben yelled, scrambling out of the passenger's seat, helping Mitch and Alex escape the vehicle, the smell of gasoline filling the air. "Are you okay?"

Alex fumbled with the seat belt. "Yeah, I think so."

The Mustang's front end was crumpled against a massive pine tree, its headlights shining into the darkness.

Alex, slumped to the ground, head in his hands, let out a groan of despair. "I'm so screwed," he said, his eyes filled with tears. "My Stang ... it's smashed. Dad ... he's going to kill me."

Another car, its headlights cutting through the darkness, pulled up. A middle-aged couple got out and approached.

"Are you boys all right?" the woman asked. "We saw the accident and called 9-1-1. The police are on their way."

Alex didn't look up.

Ben, his jaw clenched, eyes flickering between Alex and the crumpled wreckage of the Mustang, made a decision. He took a deep breath, picked up the keys on the ground beside Alex, and walked toward the approaching police car, its flashing lights painting the trees in a strobing dance of red and blue.

"Ben, what are you doing?" Mitch whispered. "What about the police academy?"

"I have to, Mitch," Ben said. "I can't let him throw his life away."

Chapter 19

Alex

Saturday, December 21—Abandoned mine, Joshua Tree.
The memories of that summer night in the Colorado Rockies weighed down on me, heavier than any barbell I'd ever lifted. Ben, taking the fall for me, those cops interrogating him ... the image played on a loop in my mind, a constant reminder of my cowardice. The sound of tires, the sickening crunch of metal, the Mustang smashed against the tree. And then silence, broken only by the sound of my sobbing. I'd frozen, paralyzed by fear, while Ben had stepped up, taken the blame, and shielded me from the consequences of my stupidity.

My head throbbed, each pulse a hammer blow against my skull. More pain came after I tried to lift my arm. Was I asleep—no, somewhere deeper and darker than sleep—and when I floated back to the surface, I was rocked by waves of dizziness. I was lying on my back, not in a bed, on the ground, but on something hard. And cold. My head felt like it was being crushed against a hard surface. Where was Ben? A wave of nausea rolled over me, the taste of blood and dust thick on my tongue.

I was back in the goddamn mine, the darkness pressing in like a suffocating blanket. Mitch was beside me, but Ben ... *God, I hope he's okay.*

Our captor was still here somewhere. We were his hostages, pawns in a game we didn't understand. The dim light filtering through the mine entrance cast shadows on the walls. I stared at those shadows, trying to make sense of the past few hours, trying to reconcile the image of a polished, sophisticated guy from the restaurant—Randy, he'd called himself—with the wild-eyed, unpredictable man who now held us captive. It was like looking at two different people, two sides of the same coin, both equally unsettling.

Randy Thorne.

How the hell could that guy be this guy? One minute we're sharing a bottle of wine at the restaurant in Palm Springs, boasting about his latest real estate deal. Now I'm tied up in some abandoned mine.

This wasn't chess, a game where Mitch excelled, or one of Ben's Scouting badges. It wasn't a football game either where I could call a play and stand safely behind my offensive line on my way to victory or a woman I could charm, or a business deal I could negotiate with a cocky grin. This was different. This was a game of survival where the stakes were higher than any I'd ever faced. And for the first time in a long time, I felt a surge of something other than fear—a sense of responsibility and a fierce protectiveness for my friends. The old Alex, the one who always took the easy way out, the one who let others clean up his messes, was fading. A new Alex was emerging, ready to face his demons and fight for what mattered.

Most importantly, we needed to do this together. With Ben's leadership, Mitch's brains, and my courage. This time, I wouldn't let them down.

* * *

Dry, crusted blood filled my nostrils, a sharp coppery scent mingling with the musty odor of damp earth and old iron permeated the mine. I tasted it too, a bitterness on my tongue. My head throbbed, a dull ache pulsing behind my eyes, a souvenir from my failed attempt to play hero.

I was back on the ground, my wrists and ankles bound tight with damn climbing rope, the cold seeping through my clothes, my body shivering. Mitch was beside me, his face pale, his glasses crooked. We were huddled in the dark, our bodies pressed against the cold rock wall.

The lantern was gone. I vaguely remembered grabbing it and swinging it at the face of our captor in my failed escape. I realized Ben was gone too.

"Mitch?" My voice came out a whisper. "You okay, man?"

He groaned, shifting, the ropes creaking. "Yeah, except for my throbbing head, the cold, and the fact we're still tied up in an abandoned mine with a homicidal maniac." His voice was weak, but there was an edge, a spark of something gave me hope.

"What happened?" I asked. "I got out ... You came back. Why?"

"I got out. Called 911. They're sending help. A helicopter ... but ... they need our exact location."

A surge of hope, then a crash of despair. "But we're stuck down here. How are we going to—"

"We'll figure it out," Mitch said, his voice stronger. "We always do."

He was right. We always did. At least, Ben and Mitch did. I was usually the one screwing things up, then they had to clean it all up.

"Mitch," I said, my voice thick with shame, "I'm so sorry. For all of it. The Chasm ... all the stupid things."

Mitch didn't move, but I could hear him breathing.

"Remember that night in the Rockies?" I rasped, the words scratching my throat like sandpaper.

Mitch's shoulders tensed. "How could I forget?" he whispered, his voice hoarse with terror and the lingering effects of dehydration.

"I never took responsibility or even thanked you for not saying anything to the cops. For protecting me."

Mitch shook his head. "We were kids. We made mistakes."

"Yeah, but you and Ben, you always had my back. Even when I didn't deserve it. You know what? You're the real hero."

Mitch shook his head. "No, not me. I wasn't there for my parents, for you and Ben when you needed me."

I shook my head. "No, Mitch. You were always the smart one, the one with the plan. Remember back in high school when we got caught sneaking out? You were the one who figured out how to get us back in without getting caught."

Mitch chuckled, a hint of his old self returning. "Yeah, and you were the one who almost got us killed climbing the fence."

"Hey, I made it over, didn't I?" I grinned. "Besides, you were always the one with the backpack full of gadgets, prepared for anything."

He rubbed his shoulder against mine. The feeling of closeness was more than any words could say. "It's okay, Alex. We're past it. But right now, we need to focus on getting out of here alive. Speaking of which, I learned something important in my MIT physics about friction and energy. I think I know how we get out of these ropes."

"Wait, hold on," I interrupted, a grin spreading across my face. "Before we get into the intricacies of MIT-level physics, there's something we need to address." I leaned closer, lowering my voice conspiratorially. "It's my birthday, old friend, even if we are currently tied up in an abandoned mine."

Mitch groaned, then smiled. "Fine, fine. Happy birthday, you old jerk. Now, about those ropes ..."

"Ok, that's better," I leaned back closer, shoulder to shoulder, eager to hear his plan.

"It's all about generating heat. By rubbing the ropes against the rough rock, we create friction, which converts kinetic energy into thermal energy. Heat weakens the fibers of the rope, helping us to get free."

I stared at him in awe. "Damn, Mitch. You're a genius."

"Just putting my education to good use."

The sound of heavy footsteps jolted me. I can't let him know I'm scared; he'll use that to his advantage. I know I act tough, but I'm freaked out too.

"He's coming back," I whispered. "We gotta do something now."

"Just keep working on the rope. I've got a plan."

We pressed our bound wrists against the rough rock face, the rope biting into our skin. It was slow, agonizing work, but with each back-and-forth motion, a tiny bit of heat built, a faint glimmer of hope.

The footsteps grew louder and closer. Then, the man's silhouette appeared at the entrance, his massive frame blocking out what little light remained. Beside him, Ben stumbled, his face contorted with pain, his arm hanging at his side.

"What the ...?" the man snarled. His eyes, wild and bloodshot, darted between Mitch and me. "You think you can escape? You think you're smarter than me?"

He shoved Ben to the ground, the impact causing a painful groan.

"Need to spread out, separate you little bastards." His hands worked quickly as he bound Ben's wrists and ankles with more of that damn climbing rope. He positioned Ben a few feet from us. "Easier to keep an eye on you now."

The lantern light flickered. For a moment, the man just stood there, chest heaving, his eyes darting between us like a snake sizing up its prey. Then, as he held the lantern closer, his eyes locked onto mine.

I tried to buy us some time. "So ... Randall Thorne, is it?"

"So, you do remember me," Randy said. "Good. Let's see how much you remember about the night at the restaurant. Let's see how much you remember Evelyn. And you," he turned to Mitch, his sneer widening, "the quiet one, the *Professor*. Always watching, always judging. Well, you've seen too much now. You've all seen too much."

"Let Ben go," Mitch begged. "He needs medical attention. His arm might be broken."

Randy just laughed. "You're in no position to make demands, kid. You're all pawns in my game now. And this game is just getting started."

He took a step closer, the knife glinting in his hand, the threat hanging in the air like a thundercloud.

"Right now, we need to stop thinking about the past and find a way to preserve our future," Mitch said.

Randy raised the knife. "You leave me no choice," he growled. "You've seen too much. You know what I'm capable of."

Mitch swallowed hard. "We won't tell anyone. We'll just ... disappear. No one will ever know you were here."

Randy laughed. "You think I'm stupid? You're city boys. You'd run straight to the park rangers or the cops, blabber about everything you saw."

"It doesn't matter what we saw," Ben said, his voice surprisingly strong despite the pain in his wrist. "Whatever you're running from, whatever you've done, it has nothing to do with us."

"Right," Mitch added. "We're just passing through. This is your territory. We respect it. We can help you."

For a moment, the tension in the air seemed to dissipate. The man lowered the knife, his eyes darting between us with a flicker of uncertainty.

"You don't understand," he muttered, his voice rough, almost pleading. "You don't know what I've been through. What I've had to do."

"We don't need to understand," Mitch said, his voice soft, almost hypnotic. "We just want to get out of here and back to our lives."

A long silence stretched between us. I held my breath, praying Mitch and Ben's words had gotten through, perhaps they'd planted a seed of doubt in his mind.

Then, as if a dam had burst within him, he threw back his head and roared, "It's too late! You know what I did! You know I killed her!"

"Who?" Ben asked.

"The woman from Palm Springs," Randy snarled, his eyes focused on me. "The one with the fancy clothes and the platinum credit card. You remember her, don't you, Alex?"

"So, it was you," Ben said, his voice low and steady, cutting through Randy's manic energy. He'd been so quiet, his presence almost forgotten in the darkness, but now his words had a sharp, incisive edge, like a detective closing in on his prey. "You drugged her and pushed her off the cliff. But why?"

Randy's eyes widened, his fury rising. "No!" he yelled in anger.

"You are the kidnapper from the papers," Ben accused.

"She was ...," he stammered, his voice losing its luster, the carefully constructed facade of control crumbling. "She was going to expose me. Ruin everything. I had to! I had no choice."

"No choice?" Ben replied. "There's always a choice, Randy. You chose to hurt her. You chose to take what wasn't yours. You chose to run."

"I killed her," Randy repeated, his voice a broken whisper. "I had to run ... escape ... hide. But the confession, instead of bringing him release, seemed to weigh him down, the shadows around his eyes deepening.

Mitch jumped in. "It doesn't matter now. What matters is what you choose to do next. Let us go, Randy. We can help you. We can get you a lawyer, a new identity—"

"It's too late," Randy muttered, his eyes dropping to the floor, the manic energy draining away, leaving behind a hollow shell of a man. "They're already looking for me. The police, they know. They'll never believe my story."

"She's alive," I said, surprising myself. My head was pounding, but a strange clarity was starting to emerge from the fog of fear. "Ben saved her."

"What?" the man's head snapped up, his eyes widening.

"It's true," Ben confirmed. "She's alive. She's in the hospital. And she'll be able to tell them what really happened."

"No! It's not possible." His anger returned. Randy stepped toward Ben, threatening him with the knife. "Still, there is no evidence. It's her word or mine."

Suddenly Mitch remembered the photos that Alex took at the restaurant. "We have evidence of your relationship ... on Alex's camera from the restaurant."

His face turned dark red with fury and anger. "Let me have it!" he yelled and moved towards Alex.

* * *

I knew this was my chance for redemption. I was ready to be the man, the friend, and the hero in my own story. "Mitch, we're going to escape, rescue Ben, and end this nightmare, once and for all."

Mitch looked at me with surprise and readiness.

"Okay, we need to squeeze together, then create leverage on this rope," I said. "We can do this!"

The man's face contorted with rage, his eyes burning with a fiery intensity, his grip tightening on the sharp knife in his hand.

"Now!" I shouted, twisting my arms and pushing Mitch with all my might. "Hey, asshole, pick on someone your own size!" I yelled.

Panic flared in my chest, a cold sweat erupting on my skin. Randy's eyes burned with a terrifying intensity, the blade glinting as he advanced toward us.

But just as I braced myself for the inevitable, a low rumble resonated deep within the earth. The ground shuddered and a tremor escalated into a violent shaking. The mine groaned in protest with dust and debris raining down from the ceiling like a vengeful storm. Cracks spiderwebbed across the rock walls, and a deafening roar filled the air, drowning out Randy's enraged shouts.

Earthquake. It was a gift from the unforgiving desert, a chance to break free.

And in a moment of chaos, as the ground buckled and swayed beneath our feet, I felt a strange sense of ... rightness. As if the desert, this ancient, unforgiving land, was revealing its true nature, its power to both conceal and expose, to protect and punish.

"It's an earthquake!" Mitch shouted, his voice drowned out by the deafening roar of the shifting earth.

The ropes binding our wrists had loosened in the tremor.

"Mitch!" I shouted. "The ropes! The jagged edge of that rock—use the friction, the energy from the shaking!"

Mitch nodded, his face a mask of grim determination.

"Ben, we're coming!" I yelled. "We're getting you out of here!"

The ground bucked again, sending us sprawling. But we were no longer helpless victims. We were fighters, fueled by desperation and the primal urge to survive.

Seizing the moment, we launched into action. Mitch, with newfound agility, moved toward the sharp edge of a protruding rock, the rope biting into his skin as he sawed against it with frantic movements.

Ben, despite his injuries, braced himself against the wall, ready to join the fight and help us escape.

With a final, desperate yank, Mitch broke free.

The sound of Randy's shouts boomed through the mine. He was charging right at us.

"Thirty-Two Dive!" I barked, my football instincts taking over. "Mitch, go low! I'll hit him high!"

With a synchronized burst of energy, we executed the play. Mitch dove low, his shoulder slamming into the captor's knees. I followed with my shoulder, a battering ram aimed at the man's chest. The impact sent Randy reeling backward and to the ground.

I grabbed Mitch's arm, and we bolted from the mine. We followed the twisting tunnel, the cold air biting at our exposed skin.

"Let's go!" I yelled, pushing Mitch toward a narrow passage. We scrambled through the darkness. The man's enraged shouts echoed behind us, urging us to run faster and push harder.

I looked back, and a movement caught my eye.

"He's coming!" I shouted, pushing Mitch as we raced for cover, finding a hiding spot behind a cluster of boulders.

Randy came out of the mine holding Ben in a violent grip. "I'll kill him too. Give me your camera."

Without thinking, I stood tall away from the rock and shouted, "Let him go!"

Then I turned to face Randy, bracing myself for the onslaught. He lunged at me, his knife aimed at my chest. I dodged, my years on the field honing my reflexes, and grabbed his wrist, twisting it with all my might. The knife clattered to the ground, and a feral snarl erupted from his throat.

Mitch and Ben were frozen, their faces filled with terror and exhaustion. But the captor wasn't giving up. With a grunt, he lunged at me again.

Fear twisted in my gut, a cold knot of dread. But something else stirred within me, something hot and fierce. A lifetime of football training had taught me to protect my teammates, to put their safety above my own. And right now, Mitch and Ben were my team.

He was stronger than I was, his rage fueling his every move. He swung a fist, connecting with my jaw, sending a shockwave of pain through my skull. I stumbled back, tasting blood, but refused to fall.

Adrenaline surged through my veins, blurring the edges of my vision. I lunged forward, tackling him to the ground. We rolled among the rocks and boulders, Randy trying to land a killing blow while I desperately tried to evade him.

Then, a suddenness took my breath away and we went over the edge of the cliff. There was a moment of heart-stopping silence, then the sickening thud of our bodies hitting the ground.

* * *

My head throbbed as I tried to regain consciousness, my heart pounding. I realized that I had fallen off the cliff, landing on top of Randy. His head had smashed against a rock. Blood pooled around him, staining the desert sand a dark, ominous red.

"Mitch? Ben?" I shouted, my voice bouncing off the rocks.

"We're here, Alex!" Ben called back. "Are you all right?"

I blinked, trying to focus. "I think so," I groaned, pushing myself off the man's limp body. "But I think he's ..." I couldn't bring myself to say it. A wave of nausea washed over me. I had taken a life. The weight of it pressed down on me, heavy and suffocating. "I ... I think he's dead ..."

But then I saw him move, pushing himself up on shaky arms. He looked at me, his face pale, his eyes wide with shock and anger.

I saw my chance when he stumbled on a rock, and I surged forward, ramming my shoulder into his chest. He slammed into a boulder, his head hitting the rock with a sickening thud. His body went limp, the fight draining from him like air from a popped balloon.

I stood over him, panting, my body trembling with exertion and adrenaline. A cold fear settled over me as I checked for a pulse. Nothing. *Had I killed him?*

* * *

Mitch and Ben were above me, shouting from the edge of the cliff, their faces filled with worry.

"Alex?" Mitch's voice cut through the fog. "Can you climb out? We have to get out of here!"

"Yes, I can make it," I replied.

I tried to climb the rocks, ignoring the pain in my head and the protesting muscles in my legs.

"Alex, the helicopter is coming," Mitched yelled. "We need to get to the clearing, so they see us."

With each foothold, the helicopter grew closer, its roar a sound of hope. I tried to reach the top. Ben and Mitch reached down. Then, I fell to the ground, the Earth tilted, and my head spun.

"Are you okay?" Ben asked.

"Yep, but I killed him," I said. I looked up at his eyes with a long-overdue apology. "I'm so sorry."

"You did what you had to do, Alex. You saved us. He told me he tried to kill her. He wanted her money for his real estate deals."

Anger surged through me, a hot, burning rage. "Bastard. He tried to kill her for money?"

Mitch interrupted. "I got through to 9-1-1. Help is on the way. But we need to get to higher ground to signal our position."

Hope. We'd survived.

The distant thrum of a helicopter cut through the tense silence. A speck in the sky grew larger, the silhouette of a rescue chopper. As the helicopter approached, its powerful searchlight cut through the desert. We'd survived, but at what cost? Had I become the monster I was fighting?.

I looked at Mitch and Ben, their faces filled with relief and gratitude, hope pierced through the gloom. We had faced these dangers together and were stronger for it. Suddenly, the rescue chopper heading for us turned away, flying off into the distance.

Chapter 20

Ben

Saturday, December 21—Abandoned mine, Joshua Tree.
The helicopter's roar faded into the distance, leaving a profound silence that felt like a physical presence. The rescuers hadn't seen us. We weren't safe, not yet. We'd escaped the mine, the clutches of a madman, and the dangerous situation worse than any threat in the desert.

But Alex was still in danger.

"Alex!" I shouted. "Can you hear me?"

A moment of heart-stopping silence, then, "Yeah, down here."

I rushed to the edge of the boulder cliff. There he was, fifteen feet below, standing next to the crumpled form of our captor. Relief washed over me, so intense I dropped to the ground, my knees buckling.

"Are you hurt?" I called.

"I'm ... I'm all right. But he's ..."

I didn't need him to finish the sentence. I could see the man's body, unconscious, his head against a boulder, utterly still. "Hang on. I'll get you out of there."

I turned, scanning the area, searching for Mitch, but he was gone.

"Mitch, where are you?" Panic flared, hot and sharp.

Then, a minute later, Mitch emerged from the mine, his face pale, his breath ragged, and a climbing rope in his hand.

"Here," Mitch said, tossing one end of the rope to Alex. "Ben, tie this end around something solid. Alex, Quick!"

I scrambled to secure the rope. Alex wrapped it around his arms, his hands shaking. Within seconds, he was hauling himself up the makeshift lifeline, the muscles in his arms straining, his face determined.

Alex collapsed onto the ledge. He looked like hell—a cut above his eye was bleeding freely, and his clothes were torn from the struggle.

Mitch, his face pale and his glasses bent, leaned against a rock.

"We need to stop the bleeding," I said, my voice taking on a calm, authoritative tone that always seemed to kick in during emergencies. It was like a switch had flipped inside me, years of Scout training and first-aid courses taking over. "Mitch," I barked, pointing to my flannel shirt, "help me tear a strip of my shirt. We need to make a bandage."

Mitch grabbed the other end of my shirt, ripping the fabric. "Okay, what next?"

"Wrap it tight around Alex's head," I instructed, handing him the makeshift bandage. "Press firmly, apply direct pressure. We need to stop the bleeding."

"We ... we have to go," Alex said. "I ... I think I killed him."

Those words, stark and brutal, shocked me. I looked at my hand, my wrist throbbing, the pain sharp. It felt broken. But there was a heavier weight on my chest, more powerful than any injury. As the son of a police detective and an Eagle Scout, I was raised to uphold justice and protect lives. We couldn't leave him there. Dead or alive, he was a human being, and my moral compass wouldn't allow me to walk away. I knew what we had to do—return and save his life, no matter the cost.

I looked at Mitch and Alex huddled together, their bodies shivering, not just from the cold but from the trauma we'd endured. Mitch was still pressing the makeshift bandage to Alex's head, the bleeding thankfully stopped. I could see the fear and exhaustion in their faces. They needed rest, care, and time to heal.

And so does he, a voice whispering in my head sounded suspiciously like my dad, who'd always taught me to help those in need, no matter the cost.

Let the authorities handle it. I remembered the lesson well after being grounded the last week of summer. But would they find us in time?

The man, his body crumpled against the jagged rocks, perhaps dead or his life slipping away with each passing minute. The man who had terrorized us, who had threatened our lives—he was still lying on the ground below.

"Alex ... Mitch ... we can't just leave him ..."

"Ben, are you crazy?" Alex said, his voice edged with panic and disbelief. "He would have killed us! We were lucky to get out of there!"

"We can't just leave him," I said, my mind wrestling with the thought of abandoning the man, even after everything he'd done. It felt wrong, and no matter how much I tried to rationalize it, my conscience wouldn't let it go.

Mitch placed a hand on Alex's shoulder. "Ben's right. We can't just leave him." He paused, his eyes sweeping the cliff face, already calculating angles and distances. "Look, we've got a responsibility here. Leaving him injured and exposed in this weather ... it's a death sentence."

"But if he's still alive and attacks us?" Alex said.

"We'll be careful," Mitch reassured him. "We'll approach cautiously and assess the situation. But we can't just leave him to die."

"Okay," Alex said. "I'll go back and get him."

"Not exactly," Mitch said. "*We* need to get him. Make sure he's stable, then get him to safety. But I need to be the one to climb down, especially with Ben's wrist." Mitch pointed toward the man lying crumpled below. "It's too risky for both of us to climb down. One person needs to act as an anchor." He turned to Alex. "You're the strongest, Alex. You stay up here, secure the rope, and haul him up. I'll go down."

"I ... okay," Alex said with hesitant acceptance.

"Ben, you'll be our eyes and ears from up here," Mitch continued, his voice taking on a focused, analytical tone that always meant he was already ten steps ahead. "Talk me through the first-aid stuff."

"Got it," I said, holding my throbbing wrist, as I pictured the man lying broken and bleeding.

Mitch nodded, already coiling a length of rope. "Let's do this."

The decision was made, and a sense of purpose replaced the fear. My mind raced through the wilderness first-aid protocols.

Mitch took a deep breath, his gloved fingers tightening around the rope. "Okay, I'm going down," he said. Mitch looked up at us as he backed off the step and the treacherous cliff, the earthquake having loosened rocks and debris, then moved cautiously, one step at a time.

"Easy, Mitch," I said as he lowered himself over the edge. "One step at a time. Feel for those footholds. Alex, keep the rope taut."

"Got it," Alex replied, his voice strained with the effort of holding Mitch's weight.

"Okay, Mitch," I said, "you're almost there. Just a few more feet. Watch out for those loose rocks."

"I'm down," Mitch said.

"Good," I said. "Now, scene safety first. Approach cautiously."

"Wrap his wrists tight," Alex commanded.

"Now, check his vitals, stabilize his neck, and keep him warm. Hypothermia is a real risk out here," I added.

Mitch knelt beside the unconscious man, working through the primary assessment. "Airway, breathing, circulation," Mitch murmured, checking his vitals. "He's alive!" Mitch shouted.

"Talk to him. Even if he's unconscious, your voice might help him," I said.

I listened, holding my breath, as Mitch described the injuries—a nasty gash on his head, a possible concussion, signs of hypothermia. His lips were pale, his skin icy and blotchy, and his breathing shallow.

"We need to get him out of here fast," I said. "Alex, do most of the pulling. Mitch, push and guide him, make sure he doesn't hit any rocks."

Mitch tried to lift the large man but found him too heavy. "I need more rope," he said, his voice strained. He wound the rope around his waist, securing it tightly.

"Ready when you are," Alex replied.

"On my count. One ... two ... three ... pull!" With Alex pulling and Mitch shoving, they dragged the man inch by inch, driven by grit and desperation.

Alex grunted. I could hear the scrape of boots against rock and the man's muffled groans. Alex, his muscles bulging, pulled with all his might, the rope straining with the tension. It was slow, agonizing work. The man's weight, heavy as the boulder he fell from, seemed to double with every inch. But inch by agonizing inch, they pushed and pulled him up, the sweat dripping from Alex's face, despite the cold.

Mitch was standing on his toes, all six feet of him straining against the man's weight, pushing as high as he could. But it wasn't enough. The man's body, limp and heavy, hung just a few feet below the edge of the cliff, the rope taut, a lifeline stretched to its limit.

"Push a little higher, Mitch! I almost got him!" Alex yelled.

"I'm on my tiptoes, man! This is all I've got!" Mitch shouted back.

I watched, my heart hammering. We were so close.

"I've got one good arm," I said, realizing I could help. "Alex, give me a little slack."

He eased up on the rope just enough for me to get a grip. Bracing myself, ignoring the throbbing pain in my wrist, I pulled with every ounce of strength I had, adding my effort to Alex's.

"One more time, guys!" I yelled. "Heave!"

With a final grunt, we pulled. And then, with a scraping thud, the man's body cleared the edge, tumbling beside us.

"Damn," Alex gasped, wiping the sweat from his forehead, "that was intense." He quickly moved to secure the captor, tying the man's hands and feet with additional rope to ensure he wouldn't escape. He took a deep breath, then tossed the end of the rope back down toward Mitch. "Your turn, buddy. This time, it'll be a piece of cake."

Mitch, looking exhausted but relieved, grabbed the rope and secured it around his waist. Alex, with a grunt, hauled him up with surprising ease.

"Thanks," Mitch said, his voice shaky but grateful. "We make a great team."

* * *

I carefully assessed Randy's condition. "He's alive. But he likely has a concussion and is at serious risk of hypothermia. His breathing is shallow, and his skin's already cold to the touch. We need to get him out of here, but he's too heavy to carry down to the van."

I glanced between Alex and Mitch, weighing our options. "We'll need to stabilize him here first. Let's use whatever we've got—jackets, blankets—anything to keep his body temperature up.

"My backpack," Mitch said. "It's got a sturdy frame. We could use it as a base for a sled." Mitch headed back to the mine for his pack.

"It's worth a shot," I said. "First, let's wrap him." I looked at Alex. "Can you find some sturdy branches? We need to stabilize his head and neck."

Mitch returned and rummaged through his pack. "We can reinforce it with these branches and use the rest of the rope as a harness."

As Alex and Mitch moved to follow my instructions, I focused on Randy. I checked him for other injuries, noting the shallow cuts and bruises marring his skin. The head wound was the most concerning; a gash on his temple had already begun to crust over with dried blood.

Alex bound his hands and feet, making sure they were secure and wrapped Randy with the blanket, hoping to trap some of his fading body heat.

"Hold on," Mitch said, his eyes widening as he looked at the man's pale face. "Are you sure he's secure? What if he comes to and causes more trouble?"

Alex smiled, a determined look in his eyes, as he tightened the rope around the man. "There," he said, dusting off his hands, "not even a 300-pound middle linebacker would escape this knot."

With the man secured and our makeshift sled ready, we started the treacherous descent. The icy surface made it easier to drag him. Still, the weight of the sled and the heavy man, even with Alex and Mitch helping, was a challenge.

Slow is smooth, and smooth is fast, I thought, remembering Dad's words, a reminder against the urge to rush, a mistake could cost us all.

The man groaned, his body shifting on the makeshift sled. I glanced back at him, his face pale and gaunt. It felt strange, reversing the roles of captor and captive. We were doing this for him, even after everything he had put us through. It was a strange and unsettling thought, but it fueled my determination.

"Easy does it," I said. "We don't want to make his injuries worse."

The trek was brutal, grueling, every step a battle between gravity and the unforgiving terrain. But we were driven by a shared determination to save a life, even the life of a man who'd tried to take ours.

* * *

The descent was agonizingly slow, the makeshift sled catching on rocks and brush, the icy ground treacherous beneath our feet. My wrist, throbbing with pain, was a constant reminder of our struggle in the mine.

"Take it slow, smooth, not too fast," I muttered. We couldn't afford to slip, not when every second counted. Alex was breathing hard and labored as he pulled the sled. Mitch, brought up the rear, scanning ahead, looking for the safest path.

"Damn, this guy's heavy," Alex grunted, his breath fogging in the cold air. "How much farther to the van?"

My heart sank. The trailhead, where we'd left the van, seemed miles away. "Not far," I lied. "Just another bend or two." But even as I said the words, I worried. Would we make it in time?

Then, I saw it—a set of headlights cutting through dark clouds.

"Help!" I shouted, waving my good arm. "Over here!"

The vehicle, a park ranger's jeep, skidded to a halt beside us, its headlights cutting through the swirling snow. A woman, her face strained with concern, jumped out, her eyes widening as she took in the scene—the makeshift sled, the unconscious man, our battered and exhausted forms.

"What happened here?" she asked, her voice precise with urgency.

"We need to get him to the ER," I said, my voice strained. "He's injured, hypothermic. It's life or death."

"He kidnapped us!" Alex blurted, his voice shaking with a mixture of anger and fear. "Tied us up in a mine! We barely escaped!"

Mitch stepped toward her. "We need a chopper, Ranger," he said. "I managed to get through to 911, but they couldn't pinpoint our location. We need to get him to a hospital."

"Okay. I'm Park Ranger Patel. I'll call it in." She grabbed her radio, her voice crisp and efficient as she pressed the button. "Ranger Twelve to Dispatch, come in."

Static crackled, then a voice. "Dispatch. Go ahead, Twelve."

"I'm off the Ryan Mountain trailhead. I have three hikers and an unconscious male subject with possible head trauma who appears to have been involved in a kidnapping. Requesting immediate medical evacuation and backup from local law enforcement. Suspect may be dangerous."

The dispatcher's voice filled the air. "Copy that, Twelve. Medical chopper ETA ten minutes. Sheriff's deputies en route. Stay safe, Ranger."

"Hang tight, guys. Help is on its way."

* * *

Within minutes, the whop-whop-whop of helicopter blades sliced through the air, its spotlight cutting through the dark sky. The chopper settled onto a nearby clearing, kicking up a whirlwind of desert dust and ice. Two emergency responders jumped out, their movements precise and practiced.

"He's dangerous," Ranger Patel said, her voice quick with urgency as she helped the responders secure the unconscious man to a stretcher. "Keep him restrained. And coordinate with the authorities, sheriff's department, and police—he's a suspect in a possible kidnapping."

As the chopper lifted off, its powerful rotors churning the air, she turned her attention to us. "Let's get you guys warmed up," she said, leading us toward her jeep. "Looks like you've all had a rough day." She examined Alex's head, cleaning the cut above his eye with antiseptic wipes. She then turned to me. "Can I take a look at your wrist?"

"Yes, please," I replied. "I'm Ben, and this is Alex and Mitch."

"Looks like a fracture, Ben" she said, pulling out a sling from her first-aid kit. "Now, tell me what happened. One at a time, slow and clear."

We took turns recounting the events of the past few days—the woman on the trail, the snowstorm, the abandoned mine, the kidnapping, the fight, the desperate rescue. At first, the stories were a confusing mess, our memories fragmented by the trauma and the cold. But as we talked, she listened patiently, asking clarifying questions, the pieces starting to fall into place.

By the time we reached the parking area and the campervan, we saw the flashing lights of the county sheriff's vehicle.

We told our stories again to a pair of deputies and managed to piece together a coherent story. The deputies, two grim-faced men with badges glinting in the fading afternoon light, took over the questioning, their voices sharp and professional.

"We'll need you men to come down to the station and file a formal report," one of the deputies said. "First," he added, locking eyes with me, "you need to get your wrist checked out. The Hi-Desert Medical Center isn't too far from here."

"No problem, Officer," I said. My head was pounding, my wrist throbbed, and all I wanted was a hot shower and a real bed. But this, I knew, was just the beginning of another long night.

"I'll drive," Alex offered, his voice subdued, the usual swagger replaced by a quiet humility. He glanced at me, his eyes filled with a look of remorse made my chest ache.

"You know, Alex," I said, placing a hand on his shoulder, "what you did today ... it took real courage," digging the campervan keys out of my pocket and tossing them over.

Alex caught them, his fingers closing tightly around the familiar key fob. "Don't worry, Ben," he said, "I'll drive carefully."

* * *

The fluorescent lights of San Bernardino County Sheriff's Department buzzed overhead, a stark contrast to the star-dusted sky we'd watched just a few nights ago. My head throbbed, a dull ache amplified by exhaustion and the lingering scent of antiseptic. The ER doctor had confirmed a fracture in my wrist, encasing it in a plaster cast felt both comforting and constricting. Alex had gotten a couple stitches above his eye—"a badge of honor," he called it—and Mitch had grabbed us cheeseburgers and fries from the hospital cafeteria. Food, even hospital food, had never tasted so good.

Now, sitting across from a stern-faced deputy, a police detective, and the ranger, the events of the past few days felt both surreal and terrifyingly real.

"So," the deputy said, "let's go through this again." Start from the beginning. You said you saw this man, your captor, with a woman at the Palm Springs Aerial Tramway?"

Mitch answered, "Yes. He was with a woman who seemed scared, like she was trying to get away from him. They were arguing."

"And you said he confessed to hurting her?"

"Yes," Alex said, "but she's alive. We found her on the trail. Ben saved her life."

The deputy's eyebrows shot up. "Alive? But you said she was—"

"We thought she was dead," I interjected. "But the paramedic, the escaped suspect—Kai Nguyen—he saved her life, stabilized her until the chopper arrived. It was Randall Thorne, not Nguyen, who tried to kill her."

The deputy scribbled furiously on his notepad, his eyes shifting between us as we pieced together the story—the woman on the trail, the man's confession, the photos on Alex's camera, the escape from the mine, the desperate rescue.

"You boys have been through a lot," the deputy said, finally looking up, a hint of respect in his eyes. "You did good, getting the woman to safety. And saving the son of a bitch's life, even after what he did to you ... well, that's something else."

The detective stood up, closing his notepad. "We'll get this all sorted out. We have enough evidence to put the bastard away for a long time. And I'll make sure your statements about Kai Nguyen get to the right people. Sounds like this guy deserves a medal, not a jail cell."

I nodded, my eyelids heavy, my mind a jumble of relief and exhaustion.

Do you have a place to stay tonight?" Ranger Patel asked.

"Yep, it's our last night in Joshua Tree," I replied. "One more night under the stars at Hidden Valley.

"Let's get out of here," Alex said, pushing himself out of the chair. "I'm beat."

"Sounds good," I replied. "But first I need to make a couple of calls to Jenny and my dad."

Chapter 21

Mitch

Sunday, December 22—Day eight, Hidden Valley Campground, Joshua Tree.

I woke up in my sleeping bag, feeling rested and feeling surprisingly at peace. The dream was still fresh in my mind—a woman in a rainbow shirt was there with me at a campground. She was smiling, and so was I.

Then, the scene shifted. I was back in Joshua Tree. Ben's voice, warm and familiar, drifted through the thin nylon walls of my tent. He was talking to his wife and kids. His laughter ... it sounded so ... natural. So good.

Then, a sound jolted me awake. I blinked, taking in the familiar surroundings of my tent. The dream had felt so real, but it was just—a dream.

It wasn't the usual jolt of a nightmare, the terror of falling, of losing control. This time, it was a gentle awakening.

I could hear Ben's voice outside my tent. He was talking to his wife and kids, his words a mix of love and exhaustion, ready to go home.

Listening to him, I understood what he had and what I was missing. *A family.* A sense of belonging went beyond friendship, the shared adventures, and coding worlds I'd built to protect myself.

I sat up, rubbing the sleep from my eyes and pushing the sleeping bag aside. Maybe, just maybe, it was time. I stepped out of the tent and smelled coffee and bacon.

Alex looked rejuvenated, at the camp stove, whistling as he flipped pancakes.

"Morning, Mitch," he said, handing me a cup of coffee. "Hope you're hungry."

I took the mug, the warmth seeping into my hands. "Thanks, Alex. Smells great."

He grinned. "Nothing like a good Texas-style breakfast to start the day."

Ben joined us then, hanging up his phone with a sigh. "Family's good," he said. "They're relieved we're okay."

We sat together, plates piled high with pancakes. The food was delicious, but it was the company that made the meal.

Alex broke the silence. "We've had quite a week, haven't we?"

I nodded. "An understatement."

"The Hall of Horrors, Chasm of Doom, flash flood, an escaped person of interest, saved a life, blizzard, a kidnapping, earthquake, an escape, and an arrest. All in a week's work," Ben joked.

We all laughed, the tension of the past week finally breaking. We were relieved and grateful, but most of all, we were together.

As we finished breakfast, Ben started to outline the plan for the day. "All right, guys, we need to get everything packed up and ready to go. We have a bit of a drive ahead of us to Palm Springs."

Alex laughed dramatically. "Can't we just stay here forever? I mean, minus the escaped-criminal-and-murderer part."

Ben smiled. "As much as I'd love to stay, I've got a family waiting for me back in Oregon. And I'm sure Mitch is eager to see Aunt May and get back to his coding."

I rolled my eyes. "Oh yeah. Can't wait to stare at a screen again."

We laughed, the sound reaching beyond our campsite. Despite the close calls, fears, dangers, and uncertainty, our friendship had become stronger. We were more than friends again; we were brothers.

As we packed our gear, I was happy. Yes, we were leaving the desert and back to our respective lives. But we had memories of an adventure, of danger faced and overcome, and of a friendship had stood the test of time. A reminder of who we were and who we could be when we faced the dangers in the desert together.

* * *

The other campers gathered around us, with a mix of curiosity and concern. Word travels fast in the desert, even without cell service.

"We heard about what happened," Sarah said. "Must have been terrifying."

"It was," I said, not sure how to even begin to explain it all.

Ben took a deep breath, trying to find the words to explain the rollercoaster of emotions we'd been through. "It was ... intense. We were having a great time, you know? Exploring the

Cholla Cactus Garden, stargazing, and hiking up Ryan Mountain. Then a snowstorm hit, and we got caught out in the open. We barely made it to the abandoned mine ..."

"We're just lucky to be alive," I added.

"Yeah, a real adventure," Alex said. "But we're good now. Right, guys?" He clapped Ben on the back, a gesture seemed more for his benefit than Ben's.

Little Sofia tugged Ben's shirt. "Did you see a ghost in the mine?"

"Not a ghost," Ben said, kneeling to her level, his voice gentle. "Just a troubled man. Someone who got lost, made bad choices ... and needed help."

Her parents, Marco and Isabella, exchanged a knowing look. "We're just glad you're all okay," Laura said, her voice filled with warmth. "And you, Ben," she added, glancing at his sling, "take care of your wrist."

"Can I sign your cast?" Sofia begged.

"Sure, kiddo. But only if you promise to draw a Joshua tree. My wrist could use all the desert vibes it can get."

We made our rounds, saying our goodbyes. Some campers just nodded, their expressions showing a kind of awed respect, while others, eager for a good story, peppered us with questions. We shared snippets of the adventure—the incredible night sky. the breathtaking view from Ryan Mountain, the snowstorm, the capture, and the escape. We left out the details, the darkest parts, still felt too raw, too real.

* * *

As we were about to leave the Hidden Valley Campground, we saw Sam sitting on a weathered camp chair and

Rusty dozing at his feet. Beside Sam stood Ranger Whitecloud, swaying gently in the breeze.

"Ah, the adventurers," Sam said, handing Alex a folded newspaper. "I was hoping to run into you boys before you headed out." He gestured toward the empty chairs around the campstove. "Care to join an old man for a final cup of coffee before you head back to the world?"

We accepted his offer. I glanced at the front page of the newspaper. There we were, our faces grainy and distorted in the photo, the headline big and bold: HIKERS ESCAPE CAPTOR, SOLVE MYSTERY.

"So that's where they got all their information," Alex muttered, shaking his head in disbelief as he scanned the article, his face a mix of annoyance and grudging pride.

Sam chuckled. "Word travels fast in these parts, son." He turned to us, his face serious. "There's good news. The woman you helped, she's going to make it."

"Great news," I said.

"And the escapee, Kai?" Ben asked. "What about him?"

"He turned himself in, and he now has a second chance," Ranger Whitecloud said, stepping forward. His voice, as always, was measured and deliberate, each word carrying wisdom. "The legal system is complex, and it might take time, but he's doing the right thing. Thanks to your statements, the charges against him are being thoroughly investigated. He acted heroically by saving the woman's life. The desert has a way of revealing the truth, even when it's buried deep."

Sam nodded. "Sometimes, those truths are harder to swallow than others. The legal process can be slow and frustrating, but in the end, justice, and the truth, find a way to the surface."

Ranger Whitecloud took a step closer. "Those bones you found, Mitch, most likely animal bones after all. But, with the capture of Randall Thorne, we now have much more to investigate. Seems Mr. Thorne had a few more secrets buried out here in the desert."

"There are all kinds of heroes in this world, boys," Sam said. "Some wear badges, some wear Scout uniforms, and some ...," he glanced at Ben's wrist, "some wear casts."

"Thanks, Sam," Ben said, shaking the old man's hand with his good hand. "For everything. We wouldn't have made it without your help."

"Take care of yourselves, boys," Sam said. "And maybe lay low on the adventures for a while, eh?"

"We'll try, Sam," Alex replied. "And see you soon."

"Of course you will." Sam chuckled. "To testify at the court trial."

* * *

As we drove away from Joshua Tree, the weight of the past few days started to lift. It wasn't just the physical exhaustion, the aches, the bruises were already fading into reminders of our close call. It was something deeper—a letting go, a sense of release. The desert, with its harsh beauty and hidden dangers, had forced us to confront the mysteries around us and the ones within us.

Ben was driving awkwardly with the cast on his left hand holding the steering wheel and the right on the stick shift.

"Are you sure you don't want me to drive?" Alex asked.

"Thanks, but I better get some practice before my long drive home."

The drive to Palm Springs was a blur. We talked about everything—the incredible stargazing, the heart-stopping moments in the Chasm of Doom, the bone-chilling snowstorm, the terrifying encounter in the mine.

"Remember the first night?" Ben asked. "Those stars, man, they were something else."

"And then there was the Chasm of Doom." Alex chuckled. "I still can't believe I got stuck in those rocks."

"Don't forget Mitch, overcoming his fear of heights," Ben added, glancing at me in the rearview mirror.

"Hey, I just did what I had to do." But inside, I was grinning. Maybe, just maybe, I wasn't the same scared kid anymore.

"We survived flash floods, snow, an earthquake, a crazed kidnapper ...," Alex said, his voice turning serious. "It's been a hell of a week."

"You know, I talked to my dad last night ... wished him happy birthday," Ben said.

"Oh yeah? How's he doing?" Alex asked.

"He's good. I told him everything about this week, every crazy detail. He couldn't believe it." Ben paused. "You know what he said? He thinks I should give being a police detective another try. Said I had a knack for it."

We fell into a comfortable silence, each lost in our thoughts. The desert, with its harsh beauty and hidden dangers, had tested us in ways we hadn't expected. But we'd come through it, together, stronger than before.

"You know," Alex said, breaking the silence that had settled in the van, "we should do this more often. And not just camping. How about a Cowboys game? Or a Mavericks game?

My business has got a killer expense account, and I can snag us some sweet seats."

Ben and I exchanged a glance. "Sounds like a plan," Ben said, eyes on the road.

"Count me in," I added, already picturing myself inside the massive Texas stadium, surrounded by roaring fans, a different world than my quiet, isolated computer workstation.

Alex grinned. "I'm serious, guys. I'm working on a new venture, and we're about to launch something big ... real big. And I want you two to be a part of it." He paused. "I need you guys on my team, to keep me focused on what's most important."

We congratulated him, promising to consider his offer. The miles flew by as Alex shared stories of his entrepreneurial dreams and Ben expressed his excitement to get back to his family, despite awkwardly holding the steering wheel with his injured left hand.

Ben pulled the van into the airport drop-off lane.

"All right, Alex," Ben said. "This is your stop."

Alex unbuckled his seatbelt and turned to us. "Well, guys ...," he said, his voice a bit husky, "it's been real. Can't wait for our next adventure."

"We'll hold you to it," I replied, a lump forming in my throat.

"Wait, we need one last selfie. For us, for the memories."

We all leaned in as Ben held up his phone.

"One ... two ... three ..." *Click*. The camera captured our faces, a snapshot of a moment, a friendship, felt both fragile and unbreakable.

Alex grabbed his suitcases and waved before disappearing into the crowded airport. As I watched him go, I was sad and then hopeful. Maybe this wasn't the end of our story. Maybe it was just the beginning of a new chapter.

* * *

After we dropped Alex at the airport, the silence in the van was heavier than before, a mix of relief and a familiar sadness always seems to settle when saying goodbye.

"Coffee?" Ben asked.

"Yeah," I agreed, my voice a bit rough. "Coffee sounds great!"

We found a little diner a few blocks from the bus station that smelled of coffee, greasy bacon, and desert souvenirs. It was the kind of place where time seemed to slow down, where the weight of the world eased just a bit.

As we sat across from each other, steam curling from our mugs, Ben's phone rang. He answered, his voice softening as he talked to his wife and kids.

A few minutes later. "They're excited for you to be home," I said.

"You know, being away right before the holidays was tough," he admitted, his eyes looking far off. "My wife was worried sick. And the kids ... they missed their dad."

I nodded, understanding his struggle. "But you're safe now, and you're going home for the holidays. That's what matters."

Ben smiled. "Yeah, you're right. They're relieved, and honestly, so am I. But this trip ..." He looked at me, his eyes filled with a kind of understanding I hadn't seen before. "I needed this, Mitch. More than I realized."

There was a long pause, the only sound was the clinking of silverware and the conversations from the other booths.

"You know, I've been thinking about the girl I met on the bus."

Ben's eyebrows shot up. "Yeah? Tell me more."

I smiled, the memories of her brown eyes, her laugh, a sudden warmth in my chest. "She's cool. We just ... clicked. Talked about everything and nothing. I even dreamed about her last night."

Ben smiled. "Sounds like you've got it bad, buddy. But I'm happy for you."

His words struck a chord. This trip, this crazy adventure, had been a new beginning for me. I'd faced my fears and taken risks I'd never thought possible. Maybe I was ready for something more, for a connection that went beyond friendship, beyond those coded worlds I'd built to keep the loneliness at bay.

"How about you, Ben?" I asked, feeling bolder than usual. "How did you meet your wife? How did you find the courage ... you know ... to ask her for her phone number ...?"

Ben smiled as he thought back. "Well, it wasn't easy. I was scared and uncertain. But when you meet the right person, you just know. And you do whatever it takes to be with them. That's how it was with Jenny. We met the summer after high school. I just ... knew."

As Ben talked, the diner began to blur into the background. The comforting aroma of coffee and greasy bacon gave way to the vivid memory of the desert. My mind drifted to the Colorado Rockies, to the bus where I met Jamie. I pictured her face, her warm smile. For the first time in a long while, I felt a glimmer of hope—a sense of possibility as vast as the desert sky.

***

"Mitch, we're running late for your bus!" Ben yelled, his voice suddenly sharp, as he glanced at his watch.

We dropped cash on the table, racing out the door.

I jumped into the shotgun seat, normally reserved for Alex.

Ben slammed his foot on the accelerator. The van lurched forward, tires squealing against the asphalt as we careened through the streets, horns blaring around us.

Then, up ahead, a traffic light switched to red.

I braced myself for the slam of the brakes, but it never came. Ben, his jaw clenched, eyes fixed on the road, floored it, shooting through the intersection. A chorus of horns followed.

The bus station came into view, and my heart sank. The bus, its taillights glowing red in the twilight, was already pulling away from the curb.

"Ben! The bus is leaving!" I shouted, my voice a mixture of panic and desperation.

"I see it!" Ben yelled back, swerving the van into the bus station, the tires screeching as he slammed on the brakes.

I barely had time to shout, "Thank you!" before I was out of the van and sprinting toward the bus, the remains of my ripped backpack bouncing against my shoulders, my lungs burning.

As I ran, I could hear the bus engine, the hiss of the air brakes. I pushed myself harder, running like I'd never run before. The bus was moving, but I wasn't going to miss it. Not after everything I'd been through.

With one final burst of speed, I reached the bus. I heard Ben honking the horn as I pounded the door of the bus.

Panting, I climbed aboard, relief washing over me. I'd made it. I was on my way home. The bus driver, a gruff, no-nonsense woman with a gray bun pulled tight, glared at me as I stumbled up the steps. "You need to load in the back. And hurry up! I'm not waiting all day."

I nodded, mumbling an apology.

As I climbed aboard, my heart pounding, I took a moment to catch my breath, scanning the bus.

A young couple huddled up front. An older man in a worn cowboy hat, his eyes hidden behind mirrored sunglasses, sat alone, a guitar case resting on his lap. An older woman, her face filled with worry.

Each person had their own story and path. But was there another danger lurking? Another escaped person of interest? Another murderer? The thought triggered an adrenaline rush. But I pushed it away. I couldn't let fear rule me. Not after everything I'd been through.

The bust was packed, every seat taken except one.

I made my way to the empty seat. Whatever lay ahead, whatever dangers might lurk around the corner, I was ready. I was stronger, braver, and more resilient than ever before. And with the memories of the past week and anticipation of what was to come, I knew this was just the beginning of my journey. And I couldn't wait to see what the future held.

I made my way toward it, asking the woman sitting there, "Is this seat taken?"

She turned to look at me, her smile warm and familiar. It was a woman wearing a rainbow-colored shirt. "It's available, will you join me?"

Book Club Discussion Guide

1. **The power of the past:** *Do Not Die Today* explores how childhood experiences and shared history shape men's lives and their relationships as adults. How do Mitch, Ben, and Alex's pasts influence their present choices and actions? In what ways do their childhood bonds help them, and how do they hinder them during this trip?
2. **Fear and courage:** Each character struggles with different fears throughout the story—Mitch with his fear of heights and flying, Ben with the weight of responsibility, and Alex with his reckless impulsiveness. How do they confront their fears? How does this shape their personal growth?
3. **Joshua Tree as a character:** *Do Not Die Today* vividly portrays the beauty and danger of Joshua Tree National Park. How does the desert setting act as a catalyst for conflict and transformation? Discuss the symbolism of the desert as a place of both isolation and resilience.
4. **Trust and betrayal:** The theme of trust is central to the story, both within the friendships and in encountering strangers. How do the characters navigate trust and betrayal? Discuss the impact of the person of interest, Kai, on their perceptions of who to trust.

5. **Nature versus luxury:** Alex's vision of "glamping" in Joshua Tree clashes with Ben's respect for nature. What are the different perspectives on enjoying and respecting the environment? How does the book explore the tension between the human desire for comfort and the need to preserve natural spaces?
6. **The power of stories:** Sam's stories add a layer of mystery and intrigue to the novel, blurring the lines between truth and legend. How do these stories impact the characters' perceptions of the desert and its hidden dangers? Discuss the role of storytelling in shaping our understanding of place and history.
7. **Moments of kindness:** Despite the danger and tension, there are moments of kindness and connection—Mitch helping a stranger at the bus stop, Ben comforting Sofia, the shared meals, and laughter. How do these moments contribute to a more complex exploration of human nature and the balance between lightness and darkness.
8. **What's next?** The ending leaves the future open to possibilities, both for the characters' individual lives and their friendship. What do you think will happen to Mitch, Ben and Alex? Will their friendship endure, and what adventures might they take in the future?

Conversation with the Author

This is the first book in the National Park Mystery-Thriller series. What inspired you to write the first book in Joshua Tree?

The idea for this book hit me like a bolt of lightning during a family trip to Joshua Tree. I spotted a sign that read, "Do Not Die Today," and the story popped into my head. I knew then that I had to write a story in this incredible setting. In a way, Joshua Tree itself became the fourth primary character.

***Do Not Die Today* is uniquely structured, told in the first-person narrative from the perspectives of Mitch, Ben, and Alex. What led you to this choice, and what challenges did you encounter?**

I wanted readers to feel a close and personal connection with each of the three main characters. I hoped they would experience the story through their unique voices, fears, hopes, and individual journeys. I felt the first-person narrative was the most intimate and powerful way to achieve that.

It wasn't easy. I faced challenges maintaining distinct voices and weaving the story together. But in the end, it was worth it. I hope that readers will find themselves drawn into each character's story, experiencing the adventure through their eyes, and ultimately feeling a deeper connection.

The novel explores the enduring strength of friendship between Mitch, Ben, and Alex. What inspired you to create these characters and examine their relationships?

I'm fascinated by the way our childhood friendships shape us, even as we grow into adulthood and our lives take different paths. I wanted to create characters who were both relatable and complex, who carried the baggage of their past but were still bound by childhood friendships. Mitch, with his anxieties and his need for control; Ben, the responsible one, burdened by expectations; and Alex, the charming risk-taker who often leaves a trail of chaos in his wake—they're all flawed individuals, but together, they form a kind of imperfect family.

You weave in thought-provoking themes about human nature and the delicate balance between enjoying and respecting the environment. Can you elaborate on what you hope readers take away from this aspect of the story?

I'm passionate about preserving our natural spaces, and I wanted to expose the tension between our human desire for comfort and the need to be responsible stewards of the environment. Alex's vision of glamping in Joshua Tree highlights the potential for overdevelopment and the dangers of turning our wild spaces into commercialized playgrounds. Ben's perspective, on the other hand, represents a deeper understanding of the interconnectedness of nature and the importance of preserving it. I hope the novel encourages readers to reflect on their own relationship with the environment and the impact of their choices.

The story takes an unexpected turn when a person of interest turns out to be a complex and sympathetic character. What was your intention in developing this character arc?

I love reading mystery-thrillers that challenge your expectations and deceive you; especially for characters that have the potential for good. I'm a positive optimist and wanted to create characters with redeeming life stories. Often, we're quick to judge based on appearances or preconceived notions. I wanted to challenge those assumptions with Kai's character. He's a man who has been forced to make desperate choices and ultimately chooses to save a life at the expense of his own freedom. His unexpected heroism and his complex motivations add a layer of moral ambiguity that I hope will prompt readers to question their own judgments.

Every author faces challenges when writing a novel, especially their first one. What was your biggest hurdle in bringing *Do Not Die Today* to life?

The biggest challenge, surprisingly, was bringing death into the story. My nature as a person and as a writer is towards optimism and positivity. I believe in the good in people, in the power of community, and in our ability to create positive change.

So, at first, it was difficult for me to bring in this element of evil, this act of violence that felt so contrary to my core beliefs. I struggled to imagine it, to write about it in a way that felt authentic without letting it overshadow the story's more hopeful elements. I learned to separate myself from the act, to approach it as a storyteller, as an observer.

You weave in realistic details about Joshua Tree's history, ecosystem, and potential dangers. How did your research inform the story?

Research is important, especially when writing about a real place like Joshua Tree. I wanted to create a sense of place that felt authentic, from the details of the landscape to the potential dangers that hikers might encounter.

I researched online, reading books and articles about the park's history, geology, and ecosystem. But nothing beats hands-on experience. I went on several hikes in Joshua Tree, immersing myself in the sights, sounds, and even the smells of the desert. I paid attention to the small details—the way the sunlight filtered through the branches of the Joshua trees, the crunch of gravel under my boots, the scent of creosote bushes after a rain shower.

You've created characters with a strong sense of empathy and a desire to help others, even those who might be considered "bad guys." Why was it important for you to imbue your characters with this quality, and how does this relate to your own worldview?

I believe in people's inherent goodness. I think most of us, deep down, want to help others make a positive impact on the world. My own experiences, both personal and professional, have taught me that even those who've made mistakes, who've stumbled down a dark path, are capable of redemption.

It was important for me to portray those complexities in my characters, even those who might seem like "bad guys."

I hope by showing their vulnerability, their moments of empathy, I can challenge readers to question their own judgments and to see the humanity in others, even in those who've done wrong.

***Do Not Die Today* is the first in a series set in different National Parks. What excites you most about continuing this series, and what themes or locations are you eager to explore in future books?**

I'm already working on stories in Maine and Oregon. The possibilities are endless! Our National Parks are more than just beautiful landscapes; they're repositories of history, culture, and natural wonders. I'm excited to take my characters—and my readers—on more adventures, exploring new settings and new challenges.

What advice would you give to aspiring writers, particularly those who, like yourself, might find it challenging to incorporate darker elements into their stories?

My advice is simple, just start writing. And don't be afraid to seek out support from other writers. Writing can be a lonely process, but there's a whole community of people who understand the challenges and the rewards. Find other writers, share your stories, and most importantly, trust your instincts.

Author's Note and Resources

Do Not Die Today isn't just a fictional mystery-thriller; it's a love letter to the beauty and enduring life of Joshua Tree National Park. While the story focuses on the fictional adventures of Mitch, Ben, and Alex, the park is a character in history, culture, and natural beauty that deserves respect.

Joshua Tree National Park has a rich history, predating its designation as a national park. The land was once home to indigenous peoples, including the Cahuilla, Serrano, and Chemehuevi tribes, who lived in harmony with the desert for centuries, leaving behind a legacy of stories, traditions, and rock art. I encourage readers and visitors to learn about these cultures and remember that we are guests on this land.

The desert can be a challenging and unforgiving environment. Be prepared to enjoy Joshua Tree safely and minimize your impact. Carry plenty of water, respect the trails, pack out everything you pack in and leave no trace, be aware of wildlife, check the weather, and plan ahead. Learn more.

- Joshua Tree National Park: www.nps.gov/jotr
- Joshua Tree National Park Association: joshuatree.org
- Leave No Trace: lnt.org

Acknowledgments

Do Not Die Today would not exist without the support and teamwork of an incredible community. I am deeply grateful to everyone who helped bring it to life.

Special thanks to Kathy Sharp, Margie Carpenter, Dr. Cass Carpenter, and Dawna Knapp. You tackled the rough first draft without complaint and helped bring Mitch, Ben, and Alex to life. Kudos to my editor, Jonathan Starke. Your edits and comments helped me clean up my manuscript and believe in my story. I appreciate all the early readers who shared helpful feedback and meaningful reviews. I am a huge fan of Kate Henke, whose breathtaking painting and book cover design captures the beauty of Joshua Tree and brings the dangers hidden in the desert to life.

This book is a lifetime dream. It brings together experiences, journeys, and relationships into a story that fuels my passion and purpose for enduring friendships, our national parks, and mystery thrillers.

About the Author

Kacey Carpenter was born in Colorado and grew up exploring the Rocky Mountains. His love for outdoor adventures created a deep appreciation for nature and its mysteries. After earning his undergraduate degree from UCLA and an MBA from the Wharton School at the University of Pennsylvania, he moved to Northern California. There, he raised his family while building a successful career in high tech.

His journey as an author began with non-fiction and his membership in the Berkeley branch of the California Writers Club. He served as the Chapter Digital Strategies leader for the Sierra Club, merging his love for nature with his technical expertise. Kacey now lives in Oregon, where he stays deeply connected to the outdoors as a Sierra Club local outings leader certified in wilderness first aid. He is active in the community volunteering, coaching, and leading the National Writers Union Writers Corner program.

His debut mystery-thriller novel, Do Not Die Today, is the first installment in A National Park Mystery-Thriller series. When he's not writing, Kacey enjoys spending time in nature with his family and volunteering in the community.

Stay connected at lifeisajourney.substack.com.

www.ingramcontent.com/pod-product-compliance
Lightning Source LLC
LaVergne TN
LVHW091719070526
838199LV00050B/2455